72 RAISINS

A NOVEL ABOUT FAME, DELUSION, AND INDECENT EXPOSURE

•

Nikki Nash

OVERHEAD BIN
PUBLISHING

72 Raisins

ISBN-13: 978-0-692-13946-2 (ebook)
ISBN-13: 978-0-692-14808-2 (paperback)

Jacket Design by Eric McGilloway
Formatting by Polgarus Studio

OVERHEAD BIN
PUBLISHING

www.nikkinash.com
www.instagram.com/nikkinash9

Contents

1

DROP THE BOTTLE!

Scott ran his hand over his scalp. His skin was warm. He'd left his baseball cap in the car, imagining this task before him would take less than a minute. But based on the thin film of sweat forming on his bare head, he must have been standing in front of his boss's fancy house for closer to ten minutes.

How could ten minutes have passed?

He felt the heat from his head transfer to his palm as he looked down at the pool of liquid at his feet.

"Do not move!" The baritone voice, filtered through a speaker, was forceful and severe.

Scott started to turn.

"FREEZE."

He froze, his left hand in midair above his head. His right hand, holding the bottle of water, remained at his side. He'd heard a siren earlier and wondered what crime had been committed. But he now made the connection—the siren had been headed to where he was.

He waited.

He heard a car door open and slam, followed by another open and slam. Footsteps up the driveway. He didn't want to move his head, partly out of a fear of getting shot, but mostly because he was good at taking direction and had been told to freeze, although his eyes were peripherally scanning his environment.

In front of him was the large hand-carved door. Flanking the door were matching manicured bushes in cobalt ceramic pots. Further to his right, by the side of the house, he caught sight of two men—gardeners based on their sweaty T-shirts, large-brimmed hats, and a leaf blower—peeking around and watching the action. They dipped back when he made eye contact with them. He scanned left and saw nothing but the white house and a large hydrangea bush that was blossoming blue. He'd read the color of the blossoms was based on the amount of aluminum in the soil. Useless information, as he doubted he was being taken down by a band of demanding horticulturists. He presumed the men behind him were cops, and this would be sorted out with a question or two.

One set of footsteps told him one person was approaching. Unless one cop was carrying the other cop. Scott almost laughed out loud at this image. The footsteps in the sand thing. "When you see only one set of footprints, it was then that I carried you." He felt both comforted and irreverent, imagining one cop carrying the other.

"Drop the bottle!" The voice was still loud but no longer distorted, as the guy was now standing a few feet behind him.

Scott dropped the bottle and stood perfectly still as thoughts of reaching for his ID came and went. He'd let this guy tell him what to do. Better for everyone.

"Turn around slowly."

Scott did. The cop was shorter than Scott, but then most people were, and in this instance, Scott tried to appear shorter by dropping his shoulders and softening his knees. The other cop walked up the drive and across the lawn to the side of the house where Scott had seen the gardeners.

"Name?" the cop said.

"Scott Mullan. Can I put my other hand down?"

"Yes. Slowly."

He did. He needed to get out of the sun. Standing under the big Los Angeles October sky, he felt the heat intensifying and knew he'd have a pink scalp before long.

"I can explain."

"Everyone thinks so. Do you have ID?"

"Yes."

"Where is it?"

"In my wallet." Scott tried to point with his eyes to his back pocket.

"Turn around."

"I just did."

"Now." Stern. Humor at this point didn't seem to be working. The guy was looking at Scott's torso rather than his face, as if to catch any furtive movements, ready to fire at the largest mass.

Scott turned back around to face the front door. He felt a hand reach into the back pocket of his Dockers. As the wallet was pulled from his pants, he stared at the step to the front door and the pool of liquid that was starting to evaporate at its edges. He should have been on his way home, not derailed by this whole *Adam-12* misunderstanding.

His mind raced forward while his shoes remained rooted to the driveway. This was going to be hard to explain. Cop Two walked across the lawn and, noticing the liquid on the steps, stepped around it and approached the front door. He knocked. Scott knew no one was home, but it still made him nervous. Cop Two knocked again. Waited. And then, as if again trying to leave a pristine crime scene, he stepped around the liquid and headed down the driveway.

"Turn back around," said Cop One, who was extracting Scott's license from his wallet. As Cop Two walked past them, he gave a little nod. Cop One nodded back without looking up and handed off the license to Cop Two, who took it, glancing at it as he continued down the driveway. They had this down.

"You can see my card in there," Scott said. "I work on *The Late Enough Show*. It's a TV show. This is my boss's house. Dylan Flynn." The mention of Dylan Flynn usually got a reaction from kids, housewives, plumbers, bankers. Most people said, "I love him," "He is so funny," "How tall *is* he?"

So far, this policeman did not seem impressed.

"You know—The Leprechaun?" Dylan was short and Irish and had reluctantly embraced the moniker early in his comedy career. Even if people didn't watch the show, they knew "The Leprechaun." But the invocation got no obvious sign of recognition from the cop who was questioning him.

"What are you doing here? Big party?"

Scott was encouraged by the sarcasm. He could have an exchange with this guy and be on his way. He exhaled for what felt like the first time since he'd been ordered to freeze.

"I work for him," Scott said.

"You work here?"

Scott tried hard to see this man. Not just see a cop. Find something special. "Look for the Messiah" as he'd read earlier. The cop had clear skin. Long eyelashes. Good posture. And a nice voice, despite the stern tone.

"You have a nice voice."

"Well, that's a new one."

"I stopped by to give him something."

"Right." The cop sighed. "And what was it you were going to give him?"

Scott heard the truth in his head and how crazy he'd sound if he said it out loud: "I was here to pour water on his doorstep and say a prayer for his family." Choosing to sound arrogant rather than crazy, he said, "An idea. For the show." Better to fib, although it made him uncomfortable, than say what he was actually doing, which could, if it got out, imply Dylan was having family troubles. There had been rumors on TMZ about a Down syndrome child, but this was never confirmed.

"You guys don't have email? On your fancy TV show?"

"Please. Call him. He'll vouch for me."

"What's his number?"

"I can't give you that."

"That's convenient."

"No, I don't have it. Sasha always connects me. His assistant. Call the main number on the card. They can either connect you to him or they can vouch for me." Scott realized it was Saturday and no one would be in the office. He could always give them Sasha's cell phone number, if it came to that.

"And what do you do there?" Cop One said, sounding bored. Ready to wrap this up.

"I'm the head writer." His face reddened as he realized he was not only lying but that this lie might get back to his boss. Maybe it was just wishful lying. "I mean, I'm *up* for head writer. I'm a writer. A comedy writer."

"Do you have a phone?"

"Don't you have a phone thing in your car?"

"Sir. Your phone please."

Scott moved his hand slowly to his other pocket and pulled out his phone.

"Password?"

"There isn't one. Try Sasha Kurganov. Or Trudy Polk. Their cell numbers are in there."

"Stay here."

Cop One took the phone and wallet and walked halfway down the driveway as Cop Two was walking back up. They spoke in low sibilant tones. Scott was unable to make out the words, but imagined something like, "This is nothing, but let's look like we're actually doing something. Then we'll get lunch. What are you in the mood for?" Then he figured the other guy was saying, "Mexican. But first, let's sweat this guy a little more." Scott would play along to keep the peace and be on his way.

Cop Two went back down the drive and Cop One remained where he was, writing things in his little flip book. Maybe things like "cheese burrito, nachos, horchata."

Cop One came back up and handed Scott his wallet.

"We cool?" Scott said, feeling the flush of blood to his face. He'd never used that phrase before in his life and wondered if, caught up in a police confrontation, he was now channeling some Elmore Leonard character. He felt a preliminary relief that he wasn't someone who actually ever got into trouble, and for a moment his heart raced with a strange gratitude for the simple and relatively unencumbered life he had been given. Or had chosen. Or was living. He said a silent thank you to God and imagined himself hugging his teenagers when he got home. Maybe he'd stop for flowers for his wife. But then thought—no. She wasn't the flowers type, plus flowers for no reason would just beg the obvious question.

The cop looked at him. "Are we cool? No. We are not cool." Cop One explained he was unable to verify identity and Scott would have to come down to the station until they could reach either Mr. Flynn or his assistant.

"Let me get my water." If nothing else, Scott wanted them to know he did not condone littering.

"Leave the bottle, sir. It is part of the crime scene." And as if on cue, Cop Two walked past them and started with the whole yellow tape routine.

Scott gave one fleeting glance over his shoulder to the gardeners, who were back watching from the side of the house, cell phones in hand.

"Should I follow you? I'll need my license." He laughed, trying to indicate he took the law very seriously. That he would never think of driving without his license. He wanted to reach for his keys, but knew this guy was jumpy about any furtive movements.

"Put out your hands, please." Cop One reached around to the back of his belt and pulled off the handcuffs.

"You're arresting me?"

"Until we can confirm what you say."

"You can't arrest me. I have to pick up a honey-baked ham."

"Oh, in that case we'll let you go."

"Really?"

"No."

"It's true, everyone is a comedian."

"Sir. I am not a comedian and until we are able to verify your employment, neither are you." There was something illogical about this supposition that he wanted to pursue, but he figured he should let it go. He was facing a more pressing problem. An actual problem. He had never even seen handcuffs in real life and was having a hard time processing the fact that they were being closed around his own wrists.

"What am I being arrested for?"

"Violation of Penal Code 602. Trespassing and trespassing with intent to damage property."

"Damage? You're talking about the step? It's water."

"That's something for CSU to determine."

Cop One took Scott by the elbow and they walked down the driveway.

"I can't believe this. I'm getting into the patrol car?"

7

"That's how it works."

"Are you going to do that whole protecting my head thing?"

No response.

"Who did you try calling? I can give you more numbers. Please."

"We can sort it out at the station."

Cop One maneuvered Scott into the patrol car, which included putting a hand on his head.

"Ow."

"Now you're crying police brutality?"

"No. Sorry. Sunburn."

2

NICE CHAIR.

The West LA Police Station was on Butler Avenue. It was a neutral beige building, and Scott wondered if the color might be called Desert Sunrise, or Sahara Stone or Dark White. He didn't really believe there was such a color as Dark White, but the idea amused him. His brain automatically put things into comedic lists, storing away present experiences for future mining.

The drive from his home in Studio City to Dylan Flynn's house, although maybe two miles as the crow flies, had taken almost an hour with all the lunchtime traffic on the boulevard and then the single lane up the canyon. The drive to the police station took another half hour, which increased the tension he was feeling. Rebecca was having a dinner party. Scott had been given the somewhat patronizing job of picking up the ham, and he had no idea how long it would take to straighten out this misunderstanding and get to the ham place on La Brea. The clock was ticking.

He was driven around to the back, escorted by Cop Two through steel doors and taken to an office that was more like a cubicle. It was cooler inside than he'd expected. Maybe he'd seen too many TV shows where people were sweaty and dirty and dressed in black.

There were no good-hearted prostitutes in spangly skirts. There were no drug addicts curled up in a cell, going through withdrawals. There were no greasy informants, furtively looking around to ensure their anonymity. He was pretty much the only action that day.

After one of his hands was freed, Scott was directed to sit and watched as the cuff was closed around a thick loop on the wall. He went to rub his now-free wrist, but instead yanked the other hand before he realized he obviously did not have freedom of movement. The chair, however, was nicely cushioned, probably to avoid lawsuits of abuse. He pictured a potential felon taking a seat on a hard chair, leading to inflammation and ultimately infection of pre-existing hemorrhoids—which would be ignored in a lengthy court process, exacerbated by poor prison conditions and multiple anal penetrations by a guy named Tweety—and ultimately a lawsuit against the West LA Police Station for its life-ruining hard chairs.

"You want water?"

"What?" He forgot he wasn't alone. Or where he was.

"Water? Or coffee?"

"No, I'm fine. Thanks."

Scott had never been to a police station. Although anxious about the time, he was also oddly excited by the new surroundings, the different smells. He'd often taken his own job for granted, and although there was always a little adrenaline thrill right before the show—that moment around four-thirty in the afternoon, right before the curtains opened and Dylan went out to the cheering crowd—there was also so much that was familiar after over fifteen years at the studio that the only way he experienced a newness was when friends outside the business came to see how things worked. He'd see through their eyes, like seeing through the eyes of a child, how lively and fun it was backstage with the clichéd oversized props, the crew guys in overalls, the stage managers with their headsets coordinating all the human activity, the greenroom with its flattering lighting and gluten-free snacks, or even the irreverence of the offices, the walk on the soft hallway carpets where comedy was created, polished, and sometimes dumbed-down. Where the college interns made copies of things and restocked the refrigerators, while writers yelled things out their doors to one another.

There was often random yelling and profanity as well as the usual office sounds of typing on keyboards and phones being answered. Every six months there was a new batch of interns and there would be an uptick in the writers yelling "fuck you" out their doors and theoretically into the doors of other writers. It wasn't like college kids never heard or said "fuck you," but it was fun to see their eyes light up as this phrase was tossed around in what could be seen as an office setting. Political correctness was out the window on a late-night comedy show. Defenestrated.

Sitting on this cushioned chair in the cool space of the grey room, he settled into the various muted sounds around him. A machine hummed nearby, but it was almost a polite hum. A phone rang behind a closed door. His intrigue with the police station was waning as he waited. As the adrenaline ebbed, he was left with an awareness of his still-quickened heartbeat and eventually his focus was more cerebral as he began running through the possibilities of how the afternoon might unfold. As he did when he was starting any new train of thought, he ran his hand over his scalp, but this time he flinched from the sting of sunburn.

He could stick to the story about having an idea for the show, but no one would buy that. He was bringing Dylan a gift? In a way that was true, although he wasn't facile enough with new-agey stuff to actually explain with any certainty or fluency why he was doing what he was doing. "This book, *Seven Mythic Doorways to Freedom*, told me to go pour water on his doorstep." Yeah, that didn't sound crazy at all. He could say he misunderstood an email and thought he had been asked to come by. But the police had ways of checking emails. By . . . checking emails. And now he was feeling thirsty and a little panicky as he was a slave to his own character, which for the most part was incapable of overt lying. With no immediate solution to the problem, he surrendered to the chair. To the room. To the moment, as Ben Doss would say. He could no longer imagine where this was all going, and so he settled into his only apparent option: to be where he was.

Despite the cool air, there was a hint of the scent of food somewhere, and he closed his eyes to determine not only what it was, but where it was coming from. He could smell onions, meat. Maybe tacos? Carne asada? Not Indian. Wrong spices. He could feel his stomach grumble. Maybe they really had been discussing lunch, standing out there in the sun on Dylan's driveway, and for a moment he had the illogical thought this was some elaborate joke Dylan was pulling on him.

Cop One came out of an actual office. He was carrying a file and walked past where Scott was sitting. Scott caught his eye.

"Nice chair."

"I'm sorry?"

"It's a nice chair. I read that restaurants make a point of having chairs that look nice but are uncomfortable to ensure customer turnover."

"I'm glad you're comfortable, sir."

"Not that I want to stay for any length of time. Although you've been very nice."

"And I have a nice voice." Cop One smiled.

"That too."

Scott was left alone and felt embarrassed by his instinctual need to be nice in all uncomfortable situations. His boss had once accused him of using "nice" as a way to survive, just as a whore uses sex. Which led to a discussion about prostitution and ass-kissing in general. That morning, he'd seen Barry go into Dylan's office early and it triggered the competition. Scott's goal, so many years before, had been to just get a chance to be a comedy writer on Dylan's show. Now that he'd been doing it for years, he was frustrated it hadn't turned into more. The previous head writer had left a month before to work on a web series, and Scott and Barry joked it would come down to a coin toss who would fill those clown shoes, a job that would involve giving more direction to the other writers, compiling and editing jokes, and bringing in new topics to ridicule.

Scott wondered if Barry's showing up early was a ploy to get the lead in the race. As he went to get coffee, he kept his head down as he passed Dylan's office. Not that Dylan could see anyone outside his office, but he did have both a talent for sensing people when they were nearby, and for yelling.

"JOKE MONKEY!"

That was Scott's cue to come in and provide outside comic relief when Dylan was bored. Or wanted to appear bored. Or needed a third person to change the dynamic in the room. When Dylan wanted something, Dylan wanted something. It didn't really matter what it was.

Scott walked into his boss's office and assumed the position, which was to stand with his arms bent at the elbows and mime clanging together two cymbals.

"See, Barry?" Dylan said. "That's a whore. He clearly wants to be my head writer more than you do and he's willing to mimic a child's annoying toy to get there. Even if it embarrasses him to do so."

"What makes you think this embarrasses me?" Scott said. He mimed one more clang, his face very Buster Keaton.

Barry said, "Yeah, he often comes back into the conference room and says, 'I love doing that Joke Monkey thing, debasing myself for the sake of a cheap laugh and guaranteed employment.'"

Barry turned to Scott. "Am I right?"

Scott made the mental leap that Dylan, in fact, debased himself on every show for the sake of a cheap laugh and guaranteed employment, but he knew to block that obvious leap by bringing the focus back to his own failings.

"There's a talent to ass-kissing that you have clearly not mastered."

Dylan jumped on board. "See, Barry. There's a distinction. Scott is a sycophant but more Thomas Cromwell than Eddie Haskell."

Scott turned to Barry. Despite their competition, they were friends, and picked up on each other's references with little explanation. "Remember that movie? With Steve McQueen and Faye Dunaway?"

"That was great. *The Thomas Cromwell Affair.*"

"Sexy."

"When I think Thomas Cromwell, I think sexy."

"That chess scene with Henry the Eighth?"

"Hot."

Dylan ignored them and summed it up. "It's subtle. How we get what we need. 'Only a whore isn't a whore.' I think the Buddha said that."

Scott said, "I don't think the Buddha said that."

"Prove he didn't."

"That's yellow journalism. You can't believe everything you read."

"*You* do." Dylan turned his head toward the door and yelled to his assistant, "SASHA! Google Buddha and the whores," knowing that any passing intern would be delighted by this.

Scott turned to Barry. "Lovely children's book: *Buddha and the Whores.*"

"My wife reads it to the kids every night."

"They're like in their twenties now?"

Dylan turned back to Scott. "Your beloved Jesus was big with the whores."

"He's your Jesus, too. I'm not the only Catholic in the room."

"Yeah but you're the one we're making fun of at the moment."

Barry said, "Don't look at me. I'm Jewish."

"No shit, Shylock."

3

MAY I TAKE YOUR MUFF?

Scott had been sitting in the station for over an hour and whatever delight he'd found by the newness of his surroundings was waning, and he wanted nothing more than to be back at work talking about ridiculous things.

"Yep. Only whores aren't whores."

"Excuse me?"

"What?"

Cop One was standing in front of him. "Calling me a whore isn't going to get you out of here any sooner."

"No, not you." Scott started to stand, but didn't know if it was allowed and sat back down. "I was thinking about something from work. My wife says I'm a blurter."

"We may have to call her."

"Because I blurted?" Scott felt panic flutter up his chest.

"We haven't been able to reach Mr. Flynn."

"Please don't call my wife."

Scott was surprised that his seemingly benign actions had escalated to the point where he was sitting in a police station, but he wasn't yet ready to explain to his wife the method to his madness. He needed to sort this out on his own. Or come out on the other side with the success he was anticipating. But no matter how much he tried to justify his reluctance to involve her in this, he couldn't deny that he had started keeping secrets. Secrets about his new focus, his involvement—albeit passive—with a guru who was laying before him a new kind of path. He decided that if this got any worse, or better, he'd come clean. But not yet.

* * *

Scott first met Rebecca in 1987 at a club in Boston called The Laugh Bin. He'd started out doing stand-up with open mic nights at smaller clubs and eventually became part of the Wednesday night lineup at the Laugh Bin, where he worked on routines about the plight of the privileged, in which he mocked his own lack of street smarts and feigned a lack of knowledge about hockey that always drew laughter in his hockey-centric hometown. He was not in fact "privileged," coming from a working class family, but he used his extensive reading to construct a persona of the befuddled elitist. He wasn't the guy that comic groupies hit on. He was tall and thin and bald and spoke quietly and didn't exactly exude a wild sexuality. Or even that dormant sexuality that can be an attractive challenge to some women. His buddy and roommate Dan tried to give him tips on being "smooth with the ladies," but Scott told him he'd never be "smooth with the ladies." Not only this, but he usually was in his head right after a set, and even though Dan had said, "Get out of your head and into your cock," Scott couldn't change who he was.

And so coming off stage and walking down the hall to the bar, he was not on the lookout "for the ladies." He didn't even notice the woman with dark curly hair who was standing at the bar.

Scott slipped in between two seats and handed the bartender his drink ticket.

"Hey, Jason. Scotch."

"Yep." Jason the bartender was already reaching for a mug. "Sounded good from out here."

Jason said that every time Scott got off stage. He said it to all the comics, and Scott knew now it was Jason's way of avoiding a long discussion with some needy guy about what worked and what didn't work. But the first time Jason said this to him, nearly a year ago, Scott had taken it as a sign of his potential and possible future success. He usually kept his hopes private, but had blurted out to Dan that Jason thought it sounded good!

"He says that to everyone. Sorry buddy."

"I'm the idiot then."

It became a running joke between them.

Scott's dad had died the month before, and after the service, Scott was shaking hands with people he hardly remembered when Dan had come up.

"You okay, buddy?"

"Yeah." He went for the joke. "This year I lost my hair and I lost my dad. Not sure which is the bigger loss."

"Hey, in twenty years the bald thing will be very popular."

"And being short will make a comeback."

"You're an asshole."

Their banter having run its course, they were both silent as they left a space for the obligatory respect for the dead. After a sad and thoughtful moment, Scott finally said, "How was the service?"

"Sounded good from out here." Which made Scott laugh.

Scott's father had owned a hardware store in Quincy and always said, "Real men work with their hands." Scott had always been a reader and knew this was an unintentional slam of sorts. But in God's infinite irony, Scott's father had slipped off a ladder when trying to clean out a heating vent in the store, and had been paralyzed. His mother prayed every day for some kind of healing, but eventually his father pushed them away. Whether he'd lost faith in God, or blamed God, or was overwhelmed with the shame of needing help, of having to be wheeled around, he stopped going to church and eventually rejected any help at all that was offered. He pushed away his family. His mother, however, with the help of the church, rented a small apartment above a musical instrument store and gave piano lessons in the afternoon and evenings, leaving Scott alone with his books and his homework. The time they spent together was primarily for Wednesday night Mass and the Sunday morning service. As time passed, Scott noticed a closeness growing between his mother and Father Delaney, and although he didn't believe it was anything out of the bounds of proper morality, he felt excluded. He spent more and more time at the school library, eventually securing a scholarship to Boston University. He'd called his father every Christmas and on his birthday, but those calls were short and his father's voice sounded slurred. And distant.

Eventually he stopped calling, and in early stand-up routines, he fashioned his father into a manly woodworker with Scott playing the brainiac challenged by tools—riffing on all the wrong ways to use a hammer and wondering why Mr. Phillips saw the need for another kind of screwdriver. He never mentioned his mother in his routines.

And now, standing at the bar after his set, he fell into his usual posture of staring at the bar as he replayed what worked or what didn't work in his routine, pondering if "mauve" was too specific a color in a bit he'd done about polo shirts. Pink? Mauve? Taupe? Did the audience lag behind because they were tripping through inner dictionaries to access "mauve" and therefore missing the punchline? Would "pink" be more universal? Would pink seem like he was making a stereotypical gay joke when he was actually tapping into the *Buffy and Troy* set? Does "mauve" sound like Maude? Would taupe get people wondering how it is spelled? Maybe lime green would have been better. Fuchsia. F words were always funny. Lime green might be good, as it subconsciously brings up the image of limes and cocktails on Long Island and…

"I thought you ordered a scotch." There was a girl with dark curly hair standing next to him.

"Huh?" Scott wished he could respond in a more clever way when taken by surprise.

"You ordered a scotch and Jason just gave you coffee."

"Yeah. That. It's an inside thing."

"Okay. I'll just stay here outside."

"No. It's not a secret. Just silly. You wanna hear this?"

"Yes." He noticed the fur from her hood framing her face. Her face was flushed from the cold that still emanated from her skin in a subtle way.

"I used to order coffee, and Jason said it was sexier to order scotch. Like I could get any sexier, right?"

She gave him a subtle once-over, like she was considering this.

"Jason's a knucklehead," she said.

"Right. So. He eventually relented, but said I'd have to order 'scotch' so it wouldn't seem like this was a coffee house. So I order scotch and he gives me coffee. And that is the really fun and boring story of my beverage situation."

"I see."

A little snow melted from the hood of her coat, leaving wetness on her shoulders.

"Snowing out?"

"Yes. Just started."

"May I take your coat?"

At this point his own fair skin heated up and he needed to pee.

"I'm not staying," she said. She pushed the hood back and shook her head a little, ruffling her fingers through her hair—restoring some flattened curls. How was it her dark hair looked sort of golden in the light of the bar? Scott looked up at the lights for some lighting trick. He looked back and saw her smiling at the bartender.

And there it was—the sense of relief that he would avoid any further stupidities by default. She was here for Jason. She'd called him a knucklehead. He thought back over his lack of being "smooth with the ladies." "May I take your coat?" Crap. The only way that could have been worse would have been if he'd said, "May I take your wrap?" *Who says that*, Scott thought. Could he sound any more out of it? Perhaps this woman with the magical golden-brown hair was warming her hands in one of those furry tubes from the trendy 1790s. A muff.

"May I take your muff?" he mumbled, shaking his head.

"My what?"

"I'm sorry. Sometimes my head gets ahead of me. And I blurt."

"My muff." She laughed but looked sort of smiley at the same time. It seemed a little sexual, but Scott just shrugged. Knowing, wisely, that anything further that came out of his mouth was sure to confirm his lack of ability in talking to women. But he loved words and couldn't help himself. Before he could explain, she said, "You do know what a muff is, don't you?"

"A woman's fur hand warmer popular in the seventeenth and eighteenth centuries, that had a renewed popularity in the 1940s."

She looked at him like she needed to put another coin in to get more information.

"And," he added, "it's slang for female genitalia." His hands went palms up and presentational as if he'd just performed a magic trick.

She laughed and shook her head, which appeared to be a cue to Jason who, keeping an eye on Scott, stepped over to her. She leaned over and whispered something to Jason, and handed him a key which he pocketed. He looked Scott's way and gave a little nod, as if to say: "See, that's how it's done."

Scott gave a lame thumbs up, sipped his coffee, and looked at his shoes.

"Your name's Scott, right?" And there she was standing next to him again. Looking at him. Not at Jason.

"Yes."

"I was here last week and saw your set."

"How fun for you."

"You were good."

"It's clearly hit or miss."

"Would you like to know my name?"

"Yes. Yes." He shot a look to Jason. Who seemed to be ignoring them.

"Rebecca."

Scott put out his hand. And she shook it. And she smiled.

And she left.

Scott was feeling a confusing sense of arousal, pulling him out of his head, but he also respected the man code and worried he'd been talking to Jason's girl too long. He finished his coffee. Jason cleared the mug and did a quick wipe of the bar.

"She's beautiful."

"She's a pain in the ass," Jason admitted. And there it was. Where love goes after a certain amount of time.

"How long have you been dating?"

Jason laughed and said, "I wouldn't date her."

"Not your type?"

"You could say that."

"What *is* your type?"

"Not my sister for one thing."

And with that Scott froze, and then inhaled and felt his heart rush up a bit. And with a few more questions, he'd learned that this woman had just moved back to Boston after college in New York and had been staying with Jason until she started an internship back in New York.

"Tell me more about her."

"Scott, she'll be in again. She likes you. She told me. Although I told her you were a perv."

"Thanks." Scott knew he came off about as unpervy as it comes, despite his muff reference.

Rebecca hadn't wanted to be picked up, so they arranged to meet at The Dugout, a pub on Commonwealth, which despite its name now had a hockey theme. Scott had asked for a table in the corner where it was warmer. He looked at his watch. Two minutes before seven.

He wondered if she'd show, and exactly two minutes later she walked in the door. Scott took this as a sign. He'd read being late was a sign of ambivalence. But here was Rebecca. She was on time. She looked around, found Scott, and started over. Her hands were snug in a brown fur muff. She pulled one small hand out and waved. And he fell in love.

At some point during a dinner of hoagies and beers, she leaned in.

"You know, I asked Jason about you."

"I asked him about you, too."

"I know. He told you I liked disco, right? He tells everyone that. He isn't very creative."

"He should just print up a flyer."

"Okay, I didn't mean 'everyone.' But, when guys have asked . . ."

"You can say 'everyone.' I'd believe it."

"You're kind."

"So I've been accused."

"Kind is good."

"Yeah, but not so sexy." He wasn't fishing.

"He told me you wanted to make it big in Hollywood."

"Whatever that means."

"What does it mean to *you?*" Her brown eyes looked innocent. She sounded interested.

"I want to say something jokey, but—I'll tell you the truth."

"Good."

Scott was quiet as he internally parsed an opening sentence, as if he had only this one chance to keep her attention. He was interrupted by Rebecca, who was actually saying words out loud.

"Scott, I'll sit here all night, but you said you blurt things out, so blurt away."

"I always wanted to be Rob Petrie. From *The Dick Van Dyke Show.* I want to be a head writer. I'm doing stand-up because I'm good at it and it helps me refine the words, but deep down—I want to be Rob Petrie." He looked down at the plastic basket with the greasy paper.

He looked back up. "Rob Petrie, but with less hair."

"Oh, Rob." She had done her best Mary Tyler Moore and he laughed.

She sipped her beer and said, "I think you'd be a great head writer. Or whatever you decided to do."

"Yeah. Well. Grab it while it's hot." Scott laughed as his face started to heat up.

"That wasn't a dick joke," he said, making it worse. "Crap."

"I didn't say anything," she said. "Although now you've got me thinking." And now she laughed and looked down. "I mean, it's a visual thing. I mean, I'm not thinking about that. Well, now I am. I mean, not sex. Dammit, you started this."

"Hey, I didn't walk in with a muff."

"Two muffs, if you want to be technical."

"Oh, I do."

Rebecca had returned to New York to work as an intern on the *Today* show, and Scott stayed in Boston writing jokes on spec and working at a comedy club at night, where he was an MC and had his own spot for doing stand-up. They found odd windows of time to talk on the phone, when he was just getting home to the apartment he shared with Dan, or as she was just getting up to go to work. In 1992, after three years of living apart, with many weekend visits and little vacations together, they were married. He moved to New York where he did stand-up, but started getting more income from the jokes he faxed to *The Tonight Show*, and after three years they moved to Los Angeles. Scott got a writing job on a comedy game show where Dan was writing questions, and Rebecca interviewed at a lot of daytime talk shows, eventually getting hired as an associate producer for a talk show panel that included Libby Trickett, who would go on to have her own show.

Four years later, the twins were born, and Rebecca took time off before returning to work when Libby's new show was launched. She and Scott eventually bought a house, which they slowly remodeled, and found a church nearby that they liked well enough.

Scott's big break came when one of the game show producers suggested he submit his jokes to Dylan Flynn, who was starting his own late-night show after a stint as a comedic correspondent on *The Late Show*. Scott had gotten the job writing monologue jokes and life was good. When the head writer left, he threw his hat into the ring.

He wanted this more than anything.

Except now he was sitting in a police station on the Westside.

4
I GOT A BOOK THING FOR YOU.

The week before he was arrested, Scott had finally heard back from his agent, Fred Kimelman. He'd gotten a little thrill when he saw the text on his phone, thinking maybe a decision had been made about the head writer position at the show. Scott had recently turned fifty, the kids were old enough to start looking at colleges, and he felt the pressure to secure the job he had coveted since moving to Los Angeles. A job that came with retroactive self-respect as well as an actual bump in pay. He and Rebecca talked about this, and he had stressed the importance of the money bump, steering clear of his feelings of shame for not having reached his goal sooner. But he was fifty. He was itchy. He'd never considered an affair and he wasn't really a car guy. But something was shifting, making him anxious. Would being head writer finally satisfy him? Give him room to settle in and breathe? Maybe this would be the good news.

Before pulling out of the lot, he put in the earbud and tapped the contact for Fred.

"Fred Kimelman's office."

"Hi, Jenny, it's Scott."

"Scott Mullan?" Jenny always used his first and last name despite their having had contact for several years. This was always mildly disconcerting.

"Yes, it's Scott. How are you?" There was the usual pause, maybe she was writing Fred a note, or closing up an email. Scott always took the time during the pause to amuse himself with things she may be doing that were more important than being on the phone with him. This time he'd pictured her knitting a nightcap, already four feet long, like on a Christmas card.

"I'm fine. I'll put you through." In his mind, she put down her knitting while she connected him to Fred.

"Can you come in?"

"Now?"

"That's why I called."

"Is it good news?"

"What?"

"Just give me the news, Fred. Did I get it? Head writer?"

"No decision yet. But, it doesn't mean I don't have news. Swing by."

Swinging by probably meant an hour and a half of traffic, but he said yes. He pulled over and texted Rebecca he'd be late, that he was meeting Fred.

He drove to the International Talent building in Beverly Hills and took the elevator up ten floors to the snazzy suite of offices.

Jenny sat at her desk in front of Fred's office. She was working on her big, clunky computer. Scott wondered how she drew such perfect black lines on her eyelids. He waited for her to look up.

"Oh, hello. You can go in." She looked directly into his face, but there wasn't a lot going on. "Would you like something to drink?"

"I'm fine. Thanks, Jenny." She smiled and watched him as he walked past her and into Fred's office.

Fred sat at his massive desk and stood to shake Scott's hand.

"Hey, buddy." And as he sat, he reached for the Newton's Cradle on the corner of his desk. He took the first silver ball that was hanging on a bar, pulled it to the side, and let it go, which transferred energy to the ball at the other end, setting up a back and forth. Scott thought it was Fred's way of getting his clients to accept whatever deal was on the table; they'd rather run screaming than sit through another cycle of silver ball clicking.

"You have next week off, right?" *Click. Click. Click.*

"Yes."

"I got a book thing for you."

Scott didn't know what this meant. Maybe this would in fact be good news. Maybe it would be the shakeup he was hoping for. "A book thing." He even forgot the balls for a moment. He'd talked to Fred a few times about writing a book, but Fred had always pointed out that short-form was harder than long-form, and Scott should stick with what he was good at. But, maybe he'd paid his dues and Fred was indeed looking out for him. It wouldn't be a far jump into the literary department of the agency, and if he wasn't going to be the head writer, maybe he'd be a book writer. Scott had thought of writing his own book at some point—he was interested in Henry Ford and the impact of the car on New York City—but wasn't sure there was a market for this. In truth, he was thinking this was maybe something for down the line, for retirement, when he'd wear a sweater with elbow patches and smoke a pipe.

"What kind of book are you thinking?" asked Scott.

"It's a spiritual self-help book."

"Excuse me?"

"I know. But read it and you can tell me what you think."

"Wait. You want me to *read* something?"

"What else would I be talking about?"

"For a second, I thought you wanted me to *write* a self-help book."

"Fuck no. What could you help with? How to steer clear of people? How to clam up in social situations?"

"I don't steer clear of people."

"Take a look at the pages. This guy could be the next Deepak Chopra. The next Eckhart Tolle."

"Who?"

"Jenny told me to say that. If there's anything there, maybe there's a job there. Edited by? I don't know. Just throwing it out there."

"I'm a comedy writer." And Scott was now hearing the silver balls. They were starting to annoy him.

"You're also a person. A smart person."

"Who knows about 'spiritual self-help' books? And isn't that a misnomer? It isn't self-help, it's other-help. The self didn't write the book, right? Some other did."

"Oh, shut up. Just read these pages and tell me what you think. If I should bother with it."

"Fred. If I'm going to write a book, it's gonna be—"

"Scott. You haven't written a book in the fifteen years I've known you. Plus, I gotta be honest. *Late Enough* isn't going to last forever, and if you don't have the head writer credit when it folds, I can help you better with an editor credit."

"So I'm not getting head writer?"

"I'm not saying that. Jesus. Dog with a fucking bone. I'm just looking out for you. And you'll be doing me a favor. I have a feeling about this."

"You have a feeling?"

"Yeah, don't tell my wife."

At which point Fred pulled out a box and set it on the desk. The box was old and had a logo of a white bear and the word "Sorel." On the side was a picture of work boots.

"Looks very professional." Scott stood up and pulled up the

cardboard lid. A few pages fluttered up in the vacuum created, and then floated back down. Scott looked at the first page. *Seven Mythic Doorways to Freedom*. Crap. Mythic doorways? Freedom? Didn't people have better things to do? Real things? This couldn't be more *not* in his wheelhouse than if Fred had asked him to edit a book called *Estrogen and Astrology*. He wondered why Fred would think he was the guy to edit this, or even read it. He had never expressed interest in New Age stuff, let alone the self-help genre or even mythology. He was Catholic, for Christ's sake. In addition, he found any book that contained the word "seven" in the title as suspect. Deepak Chopra had been on the show many times and it seemed he was always hawking some book with "seven" in the title.

"Scott. You have a week off. Have fun. This could be the start of something great." The balls were slowing down, and Scott knew he was being dismissed.

5

SELENA GOMEZ WANTS TO COOK SOMETHING.

Scott pushed the button on the visor and the garage door opened. He pulled in next to Rebecca's SUV, turned off the engine and, in what he'd later view as the point he started lying, he left the box in the trunk of his car. There was nothing to keep secret about this request from his agent, except for the fact he'd have to explain to his wife why he was working on someone else's book and not his own. Deeper down, he didn't want to explain he was feeling an ennui, a need to shake things up, a need to look outside his usual interests. He was, in fact, curious about what these mythic doorways were all about. He'd never had much interest in mythology—but maybe there was something to it. Mythology had always sounded like nothing more than ancient origin stories, something Marvel Comics would have come up with if they wanted to go earlier than the twentieth century.

He had to wonder at his own prejudices, his own elitist area of interest. And thought that at fifty, it was time to expand his interests. But these were unformed ideas, and he wasn't ready to talk about them with Rebecca. He didn't want to rock the boat. She had her hands full with the kids and looking at colleges and the application process, not to mention her own job at *Libby!* Maybe he still wanted to impress her, and if it wasn't going to happen at the show, maybe he'd find some unexpected success in this entirely new area.

So he left the box in the car.

He went into the kitchen. The room was empty, but he could hear the kids talking in another room.

"We're in the den," came Rebecca's voice.

Rebecca was tapping on her phone, and the kids were on the floor at the coffee table, reading forms.

"The TBAGs are narrowing it down." Rebecca loved acronyms, and she'd used this one for sixteen years. When the kids were born, she had called them the Twin Boy and Girl, which she shortened to TBAGs.

"Great."

"Let me send this." Rebecca kept tapping, and Scott figured it was something for her show. Libby was a large blonde woman who had worked a cable cooking show into an afternoon network talk show. She still cooked, but now there were celebrities and gossip segments and a "good works" segment where they either spotlighted a do-gooder or went into the field to do "good works." Rebecca was not only the supervising producer, but unspoken best friend to Libby. The *Libby!* show was also a source for ideas and games and hacks Rebecca dragged home and tried out on the family. "Libby Things." She usually sprung them on the family once a month, the most recent being last week's "Eat With Your Non-Dominant Hand Dinner."

"Okay. Sent." She looked up at Scott. "Selena Gomez wants to cook something."

"Good to know."

"So, what's up? What did Fred have to say?"

And he could have said, "I'm uncertain about the future, I feel like I have to kiss Fred's ass in case Dylan decides on Barry, or if the show is canceled, I don't know what I'm doing, I feel stuck and a little bored, and maybe scared and so I'm going to edit this dumb book." But instead he said, "Not much. Trying to get a timeline about the head writer announcement." Which was true enough. It wasn't really a lie. Plus, any further discussion would be better alone with Rebecca and not with the kids present.

"And?"

"Still waiting."

"You needed to go in for him to tell you that?"

"I guess," he lied.

And the separation had begun.

6

WE SHOULD TALK
ABOUT COSTUMES.

Scott had an office at home. He didn't do much in his home office, but if inspiration struck, he'd be ready. The door was open as usual, but he appreciated that Rebecca always gave a polite knock before asking him a question or reminding him of something he should be doing. And as his mind was, in fact, wandering, when he heard the little *knock knock*, he had to readjust to where he was. The *Seven Mythic Doorways* box was still in the back of his car, and although there was no physical evidence of his new project here in his office, he still wanted to protect his work space, even if for now it was only filled with his thoughts.

"What are you working on?"

"Jokes."

"Aren't you off this week?"

"Old habits and all . . . What's up?"

"We should talk about costumes."

"Halloween's a month away."

"More like three weeks. Plus, Libby has her party on the twenty-eighth. It's on the calendar, by the way. And next Saturday is the dinner party, and next week we're taking the TBAGs to look at San Diego and Irvine." She reached for her wrist, took hold of a rubber band, and snapped it.

"And . . . the rubber band?"

"The kids told me they don't want to be called TBAGs anymore and I keep forgetting."

"Sounds fair," he said, having already forgotten the previous calendar update. "And what *are* their real names?"

"Haha. You want a rubber band? You know, to retrain yourself?"

"I think I can remember."

"You just don't want to look silly."

"Well, true."

"A goal of mine is to see you look silly."

"Not all goals are attainable."

"Sad face. Okay. We have limited time with the school tour, so if you want to wear something different for Halloween, we'll have to think about it now."

Scott furrowed his brow, put his hand on his chin, and assumed the pose of Rodin's *The Thinker*. As if pondering the fate of the world.

"Fine," she said. "Just do the old Mr. Clean."

He smiled at her. "I thought you liked Mr. Clean."

It was a simple enough costume. Tight white jumpsuit and a gold hoop earring. Last year she'd dragged him to a costume party where a couple of her co-workers, maybe a little drunk, put their hands on his bicep and had then turned to Rebecca and said something along the lines of "ooh," giving Rebecca a lascivious grin. It was fun to be seen in a different way. Not the nerdy Joke Monkey husband, but the tall, hot guy with a flat abdomen and strong shoulders.

"A big hit with the ladies." He wondered if there was time before church to investigate this further.

"Mr. Clean is fine with me. But not the creepy one from that commercial last year. The old one."

He would be neither the old nor the new Mr. Clean. He'd hired the wardrobe person at work to make him a new costume. Rebecca didn't think he could look silly? Well, he'd look silly. The anticipation of her surprise made him smile. She smiled back, but seemed too busy to connect in some flirty way. It was Sunday morning. She had things to do. Schedules to finesse. Work emails. Calendars. She had makeup on. They wouldn't be going back to bed.

"Come on. The TBAGs are in the car. Crap." She snapped the rubber band.

"Sure you don't want one?" she asked.

"Did Mr. Clean use a rubber band on his wrist? Not very manly."

"Sweetie, you're always manly."

"Is that sexy talk?" One last try.

"Maybe." Which by the tone of her voice, meant probably not.

She was off, leaving a little trail of perfume. Late for Rebecca was anything less than twenty minutes early. But transportation scheduling was her department and he found it worked more smoothly that way.

Their son Marcus was sitting in the driver's seat. His hair was up in a bun. Rebecca was in the passenger seat, and his daughter Chloe was in the back seat. Scott opened the car door and waited for Marcus to get out.

"Dad, I've got my license. What better day to practice than on God's Happy Day? He wouldn't let me crash on the way to church, right?"

"Not everyone is as careful as you are."

"Yes, there could be heathens and pagans out there driving," he said.

"Exactly."

After Marcus got in the back with Chloe, Scott started up the SUV, feeling a surge of power he never experienced in the Prius. He backed out of the garage and when the car was clear, he pressed the button and the garage door closed.

They liked to go to the 10:00 a.m. service, as the choir was featured and Rebecca loved the singing. They found this church when they'd moved out to Los Angeles. On a little welcome tour, their new pastor told them the church had been built by Bob Hope's wife, Dolores. When he was out of earshot, Scott had whispered in Rebecca's ear, "I don't know. Is Bob Hope even relevant? I was hoping for something built by Jon Lovitz and his lovely wife, Donna."

Rebecca laughed. "How do you even know his wife's name?"

"I have no idea what her name is. I just make everything up. You know that."

Scott looked in the rearview mirror and found his son. "So, a man bun."

"Yep."

"I read that can lead to hair loss."

"Is that what happened to you?"

Rebecca laughed. "Oh, your dad was a real man-bun wearer back in the day."

Chloe the Innocent said, "Really?"

Marcus said, "Yes. And Mom has a big tattoo on her back."

"Maybe I would have had a man bun," he said, more to Chloe than to Marcus. He loved Chloe's innocence and wanted to protect her from a household of snappy retorts.

"How old were you?" Marcus asked. "I mean, do you think I'll lose my hair?"

"I was in my twenties. But, they say you'll follow your maternal grandfather."

Rebecca turned a bit in her seat to look over at Marcus. "My father was a real Fabio."

"Who?"

"He had tons of hair. You'll be fine." She turned back.

Scott said, "Thanks. No offense taken."

"Plus, you're a Leo and they have lots of hair."

Scott looked at his wife. "Oh really? You're dragging astrology into this?"

"I know. It's silly but it's fun."

His daughter spoke for the first time. "Astrology isn't real. It's not science."

"That's my girl." He glanced in the mirror to catch her eye, but she was looking out the window. Rebecca gave him a little hit on the arm.

"Fine, gang up on me. If you don't watch out, there won't be any more Libby Things."

Marcus said, "Yeah, we don't want to miss 'Blind Leading the Blind' night."

"Hey, they aren't all gems, but it's important to try new things."

Scott said, "They're fun."

"Dad," Marcus said. "Blind Leading the Blind?"

"It was trust-building."

"Chloe led me into the coffee table."

Rebecca turned back around. "Guys, when Terry Bradshaw was on the show, he swore by it."

Chloe said, "Eating with chopsticks for a week? To see what other people are like?"

Marcus added, "No electronics in the bedroom an hour before sleep?"

Scott came to her defense. "I read the screens mess with your brain and interrupt REM sleep. Sleep, perchance to dream."

Chloe said, "What about the baking soda toothpaste?"

"That sucked," Marcus said.

"No minty freshness?" Scott said. "You know, they add that minty taste to make you feel something is happening. But it does nothing."

"It was a mouthful of powder." Marcus had mastered the whiny voice.

Rebecca sighed. "Fine."

Marcus piled on. "Dinnertime word of the day? 'Penultimate'?"

"Hey, I got 'zeitgeist,'" Rebecca said. "I keep waiting to use it."

Scott said, "'Defenestrate'? I'd take 'zeitgeist' any day." ·

Rebecca was laughing as she said, "Defenestrate is from the French, you know. Fenestre is French for window, so 'defenestrate' would be—"

"Mom, now you're sounding like Dad."

"You suggest something then."

"'Do Nothing Hour.' You just sit on the couch for an hour without doing anything."

"I'm boring. You wouldn't want me to sit on the couch for an hour doing nothing."

Scott put his hand on her thigh. "Where is this couch you speak of, Marcus? Is that the thing covered with plastic in that room we never use?"

"It's not covered with plastic! Okay guys, when we get home, I'm going to sit on the couch and be boring. Look out."

She thought for a moment. "What about the 'Festival of Colors'?"

"That was cool."

"Yay. One for Mommy," she said.

The kids went back to their phones, knowing the timing of the drive left them only a few minutes before it would be "phones off and in the glove box."

In the relative silence, Scott thought again of the book and wondered if he should tell Rebecca. But he wanted to keep it private. Like he wanted something that was just his. For now. That could lead to something greater. He wanted to prove to her he could be more than a Joke Monkey. And he didn't want to jinx it by talking about it. He glanced in the rearview mirror and saw Marcus had pulled his hair out of the bun and it now fell limply at his shoulders as he tapped away on his phone.

When they'd first moved to California, he had hoped his stand-up career would take off, but the reality was he had gotten the job on Dylan's show and his dream of head writer—his Rob Petrie dream—wasn't far off. He still enjoyed the longer form of stand-up, crafting a story, adding or eliminating words to support a vision. He'd gotten into the stand-up scene in Hollywood, using his connection to Dylan Flynn as an entree, and had worked on new material in his head, usually when driving. Scott was never particularly wild, despite the articles about comics being screwed up and/or demonic and/or alcoholic and/or whatever. His routine had evolved from fish-out-of-water geek in a hip world to the more standard topics culled from his life—teenage kids, life in suburbia, dogs, slowing urinary issues, confusion about electronics, waning sex drive. Early on, he had fabricated the persona of his wife, as he had always been careful to protect any actual intimacies he shared with her. He was honorable. And loyal. And he loved her.

And now, sitting in a familiar pew in the North Hollywood church, he fell into his usual habit of refining a new bit about the difference between going to church in Boston and going to church in Hollywood. He had started by comparing the smells. That the smells in Boston churches were the smells of 500 years of dead Yankee skin cells combined with the fresher odors of bourbon hangovers and hairspray. In Hollywood, it was suntan oil and . . . He struggled with the couplet, considering sushi, which was still weird to him and seemed very West Coast, but was a stumble for the listener. Sushi sounded funny and foreign but would invite the audience to consider and reject the idea of sushi for breakfast. And he'd lose the audience for the next sentence. He thought of other Hollywood clichés and came up with screenplays, Botox, pilates, but none of them had a distinctive smell. He'd played with words, and then figured he could be a bit more figurative if the image was right and had settled on claiming that West Coast churches smelled like suntan lotion and failed screenplay pitches. Too wordy. Suntan lotion and sitcom ideas. He wanted to say something like "Teen Spirit" because of its non-smell concept, but thought a Nirvana reference would be too dated, plus it didn't seem like a lot of teens were going to church here. He didn't mind that sitcoms didn't actually have an odor, as that somehow added to the silliness. He'd settled on "the smell of suntan oil and the sound of unsold screenplays." To balance the smell/sound thing, he'd gone back and adjusted the beginning of the joke to "the smell of dead Yankees and the sound of exhaling judgment." Which still wasn't quite right.

He'd continued with script jumps—like a sacred eucharist of gluten-free wafers and baptisms in coconut water—until his mind just stopped. What was the point? He'd been down this tired road before, and his stand-up career had never really taken off. Maybe time to think in a new way. His brain began filling with new possibilities, even if they were the result of a spiritual guru who had written a self-help book that needed some editing. A self-help book that needed a little "punching up." He jumped ahead to a big Hollywood agent hiring him to punch up the Bible. Stop. Back to new ideas.

"What would Ben Doss do?"

He felt Rebecca's hand on his thigh.

A reminder that he was in church. She was used to his strange exclamations and usually could quiet him with her soft touch.

"Sorry."

Maybe he should listen to the sermon.

He sighed.

7

YOU DIDN'T TELL ME I'D HAVE TO *DO* STUFF.

On Monday, the house was quiet. Scott was home alone as *The Late Enough Show* was on hiatus, one of the many weeks off he had during the year. Rebecca was at work where someone was no doubt laughing with Libby and cooking something, the TBAGs were at school, and Scott's phone wasn't ringing.

He'd showered, he'd made coffee. He'd retrieved the shoebox from his car and put it in a drawer in his desk. He looked out the window to the pretty much never-used backyard. The TBAGs were too old to "go outside and play," Rebecca only went out there seasonally to clean off the pillows with a special lint brush, and Scott couldn't even remember the last time he'd been out there.

He felt a vague and unexpected surge of adrenaline as he was about to start something new and uncertain. Maybe everything would change. This could, in fact, be the start of something big.

He pulled the remote from its velcroed place on the monitor, flipped on the TV, and up came the familiar sound of a CNN anchor droning on in the background like a boring friend who is easy enough to ignore and doesn't take it personally. When he worked on jokes, he found the changing colors in his peripheral vision engaged some part of his brain that allowed him to focus on the words on a computer screen.

He was used to being in a small room in front of a computer. During the week, his work life was spent in a small office with his office mate, Manny. Manny was a younger guy, at least younger than Scott, and was a slob. Food stuck to his T-shirts, even, seemingly, before he'd had anything to eat. He wore flip-flops to work. His thick brown hair was a mess, like the hair on a hamster. He wasn't a monologue writer like Scott, but wrote "bits and skits," as he liked to say. The wall above Manny's desk was painted with dark chalkboard paint, and written in blue chalk was a numbered list of comedy tropes. The wall was a gift from a Secret Santa prank several years before and included the well-worn comedy reminders: "Chris Christie is fat." "Steven Tyler looks like an old woman." "Chinese children make iPads." "Kim Kardashian has a rather large bottom." "Anthony Weiner has a big weiner." "Angelina Jolie has a lot of kids." Under this, in a different hand was added, "Manny is a dick."

Scott's interaction with people at work was limited, although there was the noon meeting with Dylan to go over the jokes, and then another meeting an hour before the show to polish and switch the order of jokes. Just before the show, Scott sat backstage in case he was needed, but this was mostly a fluffing up of Dylan to assure him he was funny and the jokes were good and life was good and the show was good and whatever else his ego needed. It was strange to do this cheerleading while sitting in a folding chair, but Dylan liked feeling taller than everyone just before he went through the curtains. Although Scott didn't say much right before the show, it took energy to keep his face looking delighted and entertained, and once the show started and Dylan had gone through the curtains to the exuberant cheering and applauding, Scott finally dropped his shoulders. There was still the huddle around the monitor with the other mono writers, but there wasn't much to worry about at this point. The jokes were on cue cards and it was now up to Dylan to perform them.

Occasionally, he was summoned to the weekly "Trendy" meeting, where Dylan was made aware of words he was using incorrectly or awkwardly, or words he should be using to make him seem hip or with-it, (although "hip" and "with-it" would have been on a trendy list in the 1960s) as well as current events that were trending and worthy of jokes in the monologue. Those meetings were short and usually limited to one or two concepts that might be relevant that week, depending on the news. Scott remembered one meeting where Dylan defied anyone to make him say with a straight face that a CD "dropped." Although in a few weeks, CDs were dropping all over the place without the air quote inflection. So it wasn't odd for Scott to get a text that said "Trendy in 5." And off he'd go to Dylan's office.

Scott's other interactions, other than with his family, were limited to his morning workouts. After the obligatory nods and hellos at the gym, on went the Bose headset and out came the iPad for the latest David McCullough or Erik Larson audio book. Not a self-help book in sight.

Sitting at his desk, knowing there was a box of pages in the drawer, was daunting. At the show, he wrote jokes that were maybe two sentences. Three at most. A setup and a joke. Granted, getting the joke perfect took a lot of time and finesse, but it was second nature to him how to format the script jump that led to a laugh.

He looked into the drawer and re-read the title page: "Seven Mythic Doorways to Freedom." This potential masterpiece was written by a guy named Benjamin Doss. Ph.D., MFCC. A doctor. He'd Googled the name and found nothing, but then realized this was typed and not printed out on a computer, so maybe it was written by some luddite who lived in North Dakota. Or "Ben Doss" was a nom de plume. Or maybe this was a first effort, in which case Scott wanted to be generous. Give the guy a break.

He pulled the title page from the box, noticing the crunchy feel of the old-fashioned onionskin paper, and setting it aside on his desk, he glanced down at the next page in the box:

By the same author:

NON-FICTION

Synaptic Misfirings in the Age of Reason
Venus Flytrap—The Transition from Aphrodite to Xena: Warrior Princess
Mythic Doorways in Criminal Profiling

FICTION

The Prairie Land

CHILDREN'S BOOKS

Little Benny Has a Fever
Sleeping under the Wings of the Winter Woman

Okay, maybe Ben Doss knew what he was doing. He'd written six other books. Scott had written some jokes. He bypassed the foreword and acknowledgements, figuring he could always go back and read them later. He'd read enough books to know those preambles offered a lot of gratitude and background stuff that didn't really affect the meat of the work. And at this point, he just wanted to get to it.

He pulled out a half inch of pages, sharpened a pencil in a little green plastic thing he'd found in the drawer, and straightened the lined pad on his desk. He wasn't planning on making notes on this first pass, but liked the ritual of sharpening a pencil and having his pad nearby. Maybe he'd be inspired to finally start something of his own. He took a sip of coffee and began.

CHAPTER ONE
The Sin of Pride and the Power of Work

"The courage to face the trials and to bring a whole new body of possibility into the field of interpreted experience for other people to experience - that is the hero's deed."

- Joseph Campbell

INTRODUCTION

I did not set out to become a therapist. I was convinced for many of my adolescent years that I would have become an athlete, had it not been for the fact that I couldn't even throw a ball. My cousins, with whom I lived for several of my teen years, said that I "threw like a girl."

In the past, before my own personal work and before my studies took me deep into working with myth, it would have been an easy leap for the sensitive young man that I was to continue to blame my father for not taking me into the yard and playing catch with me. As if that alone would have somehow given me talent.

However, had I not spent many hours alone in my room—believing that had my father been more sports oriented, I would have been the next Don Drysdale—I would have missed the metaphoric boat that took me along the river of my true calling. It is in looking at it in this new way that we can approach pain as a gift. In my case, my father's obsession with his work indirectly watered part of my soul I hadn't known existed. And without this reflection, perhaps I would never have learned to help others put words to their dark feelings.

It wasn't until my third year of undergraduate school that I discovered the power of myth, and began to develop the tools of action that I employed to reinterpret my own life and would eventually use in my work with my patients.

The word mysticism comes from the Greek mystikos, which means to "shut one's senses," and I have found for me there are simple steps one can take to shut out one's senses and enter the mystical world of myth.

As I begin this chapter on Pride and Work, I find it synchronistic and mildly humorous that they've moved me into another office. This temporary disruption is the perfect opportunity for me to use some of the mythic tools that I've perfected in my practice. It is an opportunity to reflect on the nature of work, and the power of the creative and healing force that can't be contained, even if the vessel is now a smaller, grayer room with muted, muddy windows. Gray windows that are hard to open.

But I do have a choice. A choice in perspective. And I can turn to the internal windows that open onto an even more vast and enchanting panorama: the window to the soul.

To quote Robert Bly: "The brighter the light, the darker the shadow," and I believe, in my case, the inverse to be true. I am in a fairly dark room and it is by contrast, by necessity, by natural balance, that my inner light is, at the moment, very bright.

My earliest memory, not surprisingly, was in watching the intensity and magic of work. My father, being a scientist and professor at Stanford, had several of his afternoons at home, and I remember one fall day, when I was five, coming into his study and watching him work. His back to me, he looked focused, transported to a mysterious place where nothing existed except what was before him on his desk. A pad of paper. He would be still, he would scribble and then be still again. I held my breath so as not to disturb him and in that moment I knew that I did not exist. Or shouldn't exist.

And it was in running from his office that I was led to witness my mother's absorption in her own work as she sat quietly, candles burning around her in a circle, her eyes closed. Lavender powder on her eyelids. Perhaps she was dreaming of the Goddess or perhaps she was simply remembering her first encounter with my father. They met when he was a speaker at a workshop at Esalen, and he was captivated by her captivation.

We all know that the New Testament tells us "the truth shall make you free," but it is not always easy to carry the message, nor is it always easy to hear the message. Christopher Morley, in his Dogs Don't Bark at the Milkman, offers: "Truth, like milk, arrives in the dark, but even so, wise dogs don't bark. Only mongrels make it hard for the milkman to come up the yard." I've often felt like the milkman, carrying the milk of truth, and find I am met with so many barking dogs.

I get letters from people who have enjoyed my earlier books but have begged me for more tangible applications of the wisdom to be found in myth. One letter simply stated what would become the seed of this book: "It is fine to have my head in heaven, but what do I do with my hands?"

In this era of gray cubicles and clean white sheets, where bodily fluids are immediately cleaned up, STAT, where there is no room for the soul's flailings, where things must be tidy and manageable, I see no better time than now to revisit the Myth of Sicarius and the Magic Scythe.

I'm reminded of the joke: "How do you get a nun pregnant? Dress her as an altar boy." This joke, although crude and perhaps offensive, represents the often extreme results when we suppress, when we try to contain, all our natural instincts and desires. In fear that Dionysian energy will rage out of control into some distorted Bacchanalia, the pendulum has swung to the suppression of all those wilder feelings and we are left strapped down to a bed, our hands locked at our sides, our mouths open to scream, but sedated with the opiates of television, online chat rooms, pornography, and pills.

We find ourselves in the gray cubicles of a sterilized, air-conditioned, office prison, with no one to see our smiles, our tears. Only to be heard through our writing.

Scott set the pages down and thought, "Only to be heard through our writing." He could relate to that, but otherwise he was having a hard time digesting all the facts coming at him. Not that he wasn't used to dense reading. He liked dense historical non-fiction. He liked word play. He just wasn't sure he'd be able to contribute anything to this seemingly metaphysical realm.

He got up and walked into the kitchen. He got some water and went back into his office. He was hungry, but decided to read another section before making a decision whether he'd continue or abandon this little project. If abandoned, he could share this folly with Rebecca. If he continued, then it would be his secret until he had something of substance to share with her.

THE MYTH
Sicarius and the Magic Scythe

Sicarius, one of the many secondary Greek gods who colored the land of Olympus, was initially earthborn. His mother, a black-haired young woman named Absentia, masked her magical powers with a quiet and subservient demeanor and a luminous beauty. She was left alone much of the time, as her husband, Promascus, spent his days tilling the earth, raising barley and corn. Although she had not lain with her husband in many months, Absentia became pregnant. Her husband did not notice that she was with child, as he would rise early in darkness and return late in darkness.

One day, Promascus cut himself badly and was forced to return to the stone house in the daylight. He had chastised his wife for her use of magic, but at this time he set aside his condemnation as he needed the magic salves she would be able to apply to his wounds. It was then that he noticed that she was full with child. He did not believe the child to be his, and when he asked how this could have happened, he was met with silence.

He slapped her mouth to jar the words out, as was the custom when dealing with silent women, and Absentia admitted that she had been impregnated by the Black Crow.

Promascus allowed his wife to dress his wounds, and he went back to tilling the land. He did not believe in the village's myth of the Black Crow, but merely believed that his wife was crazy and had lain with another. Not wanting to move and build another stone house, he stayed while the child was born, and continued to live with Absentia as the boy grew, but spent more and more time at his work.

When word spread that Absentia had given birth to the son of the Black Crow, whom she named Sicarius, the villagers began to show up at the stone house for a glimpse of the powerful child, but Promascus, being a non-believer, left the village in the dark of night, leaving the mother and child to fend for themselves.

A dark cloud descended upon the village, and a blight took over the land that had been abandoned.

The people of the land feared the Black Crow and began to blame Absentia for the darkness, for giving birth to the dark side. She believed that Sicarius was a holy child, but feared the wrath of the villagers, so she kept him in a magic box in the tool shed until he was too big for the box. He was then free to walk around the tool shed. Or sit quietly.

Promascus traveled far and wide, tilling the soil of distant lands, until one night, the Black Crow came to him in a dream and told him to return to his homeland and pass the Magic Scythe on to his son. Never having been visited by night messengers, he took this as a sign and returned to find that the boy had grown into a young man. Promascus, now old and tired, gave Sicarius the big knife and wondered if this young man was indeed strong enough to clear the land of the gray clouds that had descended.

Sicarius took the scythe in his hand.

"But first you must slay me," said the father.

Sicarius did not know the man who stood before him. He felt his feet on the ground, he felt the knife in his hand, but he couldn't look into the eyes of the man who stood before him. He was frightened. So he closed his eyes and listened to the voice, knowing that the answers had always come to him in voice, not in vision.

"You must slay me first," he heard the voice of the man say.

Sicarius drew back his hand and brought his arm down, hard and strong, splitting the skull of his father. He collected the blood in a bucket and set out to begin clearing the land. He spread the blood of his father on the soil, making it rich and fertile. The bucket was never empty, and the clouds parted and the people came out of their homes. His scythe became mighty, and he became infused with the wonder and awe of the villagers. As he became stronger, he climbed a big hill and began hacking away at the clouds. Bringing sunshine to the darkened land. Each day he grew more powerful and more revered.

The gods knew that Sicarius was not the son of the Black Crow, but that he had become godlike in his strengths. So one day, as Sicarius descended with his magic scythe and his bucket of blood, they sent him the Winged Woman, a beautiful woman of the shadows, wearing white, who came out of the mist and promised to sharpen his sword. He had never touched a woman and he was mesmerized. He took her hand and followed her to the wishing well, where she first held his scythe under the water until it burnished a gleaming gold. Transfixed by the power she had with his sword, which she now held in her own hand, he heard her say, "In you I see the Messiah."

He allowed her to push his head under the water. His belief in her power to turn his thoughts to gold provided him with the faith to grow gills and he breathed water and swam down into the well and came up in a small square room. His head glowed gold with wisdom. But the energy was contained by the four walls as the gods knew his wisdom was too much for the world.

With the patience of a saint, he lay down on the straw and remained very still, listening for the door to creak open, hoping for the return of the Winged Woman in White to lift him to the heavens. And it was in his seclusion and stillness and containment that the land was made fertile and the people flourished.

Scott turned the page over and looked out the window. He believed he was a man who was open to new ideas, but had to admit it was more likely he was open to facts, not ideas. He realized by his current discomfort that his brain was not wired for the ethereal parables of mythology. The next chapter was titled "Exploration," which provided some relief as he didn't need to interpret anything at this point, but merely read. He could read. He knew how to do that.

EXPLORATION

"Sicarius and the Magic Scythe" is a beautiful cautionary tale for boys and men who have inherited much darkness from their fathers. Not surprisingly, it is female energy that is the strongest element in this myth, an energy that is lacking or suppressed in this time of feigned machismo, three-piece suits and power cappuccinos. (More on female energy in "Lust and Woman.")

Matthew Fox emphatically states that men need to claim their own phallic energies, and only then "will men recover active respect and reverence for their own amazing powers and thereby cease envying women theirs." Even Jung observes that "our civilization enormously underestimated the importance of sexuality."

What is beautiful, in a prodigal father sort of way, is that it is Promascus who must return and offer the tools of his own destruction to his son, for his own sin of abandonment has been so great that there are no amends except to invite Sicarius to slay him. Sicarius may indeed have been the son of the Black Crow, but just as we often do not see our own Christ images, Promascus denied the Black Crow that lived within him. The Black Crow was the dark holiness we all carry within us, and which we have learned to deny. And the seed of the Black Crow is carried in every man's seed.

When the dark wisdom of Black Crow is denied, transferred, suppressed, or ignored, it can lead to a fracturing of the family. What more tragic example do we need than the harrowing images of these boys in their black trench coats, bringing our unmanifested energy into Columbine High School, and screaming for us our pain with the sound of their bullets. Unleashing too late the screams of the other children. Perhaps we need more mythology taught in our schools.

Football is mythic in its own sense; it is but a slight, fractured, tiny, weak, pathetic example of the male energy that is sublimated and squeezed into uniforms with numbers and the names of our fathers. Acting out the pain and territorial violence that our weakened fathers can no longer express. Or never could express. (I fucking hate football.)

What if these fathers had been strong and wise enough to hand their sons the knives and had said, metaphorically, "You must slay me first."

Any unacknowledged parts of ourselves must be brought into the light, for if not, we run the risk of passing our darkness onto our sons, who will end up slaying us. Which only perpetuates the cycle of splitting off, as can be seen in the act of Sicarius literally splitting the skull of his father. The two parts are no longer integrated and the dementia continues. The splitting of skulls will continue unless a softening woman intervenes.

The Woman in White.

Sicarius inherits his father's need for pride and work, as seen in the bucket of blood that he carries and, in this early incarnation of Christ's basket of fishes, the bucket is never empty of blood.

It is at this juncture that Sicarius can choose to continue with the superficial pride of his work, or finally embrace the female spirit that his father was only able to accept superficially, when Absentia had dressed his wounds.

And this trust begins with the Woman in White with her words: "In you I see the Messiah." No one had until now.

Sometimes the freak is the Messiah. (BD - insert Valentine Michael Smith)

Scott Peck recounts the story of the four priests. They are in a quandary about the coming of a new messiah, and they send one priest to go to a holy source and ask, "who is the Messiah?". And the holy source says, "I cannot tell you anything more than this: One of you is the Messiah." The man returned and told this to his fellow priests, and from that day forward, they all held one another in the highest regard. Each one treated himself and his brother with a little more reverence, for perhaps he was the Messiah.

Look around you now, or if you are alone, think of someone you consider beneath you—in his station, in his color—and elevate him in your mind to the position of possible Messiah. With reverence. With respect. You will be amazed at how you treat this person after you've tried on the notion, even for a moment, that he is holy.

Scott flipped this last page over onto the pile of pages on his left and thought about his father. How things could have been different. His father had never handed him a knife and said, "You must slay me first." He'd handed him a hammer and said "Don't fuck this up," but Scott had to remember this was mythology. He wasn't used to looking at things poetically, metaphorically. He'd made some notes but decided to leave them alone for now. He would finish the book and then go back and look for value, for flaws, cuts, inconsistencies. He was reading as an editor, not as the converted.

He stretched and thought about getting another cup of coffee, but figured he should eat and then read another chapter. He glanced at the next page and saw the word: application. He scanned ahead and saw the layout of numbered actions. Okay, he didn't mind reading some wonky book, but he drew the line at actually doing anything. He remembered when one of Rebecca's bosses demanded that the interns burn sage in the new suite of offices to clean out the negative energy. He wasn't a sage-burner. He picked up his cell, tapped Fred's contact, and waited to have his awkward exchange with Jenny.

"Hi, Jenny, Scott Mullan." Wait. Wait. He looked ahead at the applications and figured the first two weren't that weird. But still. Slippery slope. He'd stop now before he started wearing tie-dye.

"Hi, Scott. He's at lunch. May I have him call you when he returns?"

"That would be great. Thanks." He heard a click as she ended the call.

He looked at the clock on the wall. It was after 1:00 p.m. How could that be? No wonder he was hungry. He picked up his cup, went into the kitchen, and put the cup in the sink. He made a turkey sandwich, pulled a fresh mug from the cabinet, and poured another cup of coffee. With an unfocused gaze, he looked out the window just for something to do with his eyes. He ate his sandwich.

He screwed the lids back on the condiments, returned them to the fridge, wiped off the countertop, picked up the coffee cup, and went back in to the office. He figured there was no harm in just reading ahead; he didn't have to actually do anything. In fact, he'd have some possible ammunition when Fred called back, reasons he could give to back up his inability to continue with the book. He was not the incense and prayer bead kind of guy that this book might need. He didn't even like to walk around barefoot.

Nevertheless, he straightened the edges of this next little pile.

APPLICATION

Using the power of the tools of myth, there are numerous tangible actions we may employ when feeling powerless. I run the risk of appearing simplistic as I list them, but I want to stress that it is in the simplicity of the action that the most power is afforded. For that reason, I shall not offer an in-depth explanation as to the "whys." But offer, instead, an elegant list of actions that will be all the more powerful when taken without over-analysis. Let the myth bubble up through the blood in your veins, the sweat on your palms, the wind on your face. And trust.

1) SHARPEN YOUR KNIVES

A sharp knife is not only a gift from our fathers, connecting us to our heredity and the strength of the generations, but it is a source of power from the gods, and the act of sharpening is an explicit action of acceptance and trust that we have put ourselves in the position to use our knives, if needed. That we will be empowered and the right time will become obvious to those who wait.

2) IF GREEDY FOR ATTENTION, STOP BATHING

Cleanliness is a fabricated quality elevated for the purpose of commerce, to sell soap, cologne, hair-removing products, creams, lotions. Not only to mask what is wild and natural and therefore seemingly untamable, but also to make money. Buy these things and you will have women, be successful, work in a tall glass building, and wear clean white shirts. We must eschew the marketing campaigns which are based on the greed of the advertisers and take actions that will diffuse this buying into this type of greed. The greed of cleanliness.

Sicarius was dirty from neglect. Let yourself get dirty. Feel water, wind. Smell something real. Feel yourself in your own body. All the products are masking God and feeding the voracious devil of greed.

3) IF YOU FEEL CROWDED AND SMALL, USE THE SAME COFFEE CUP

Our world is crowded and we contribute to the crowding by disposing of paper and Styrofoam cups every day, sometimes every hour. Thirsty? New cup. Discard it. More. Another. Another cup. Discard it. Trash full, feeling crowded.

I hear Janice coming with my vitamins in a little cup. And coffee. She uses the same cup for me every day. It is a small gesture, but in that way I know that I am no longer contributing to the overcrowding, the abundance of waste that is building up on our planet on a daily basis. It is a small gesture, but a holy one, to choose to not contribute to waste. I trust Janice knows my feeling on this and I simply communicate to her in the silence what my wishes are. And I know she hears me.

Scott jumped when his phone trilled.

He had been picturing Ben and Janice, in their environment of academia, their working relationship like a marriage where kind actions have replaced words. Thinking he'd ask Rebecca to bring him his vitamins every morning in a little cup. Which was not going to happen.

He glanced at the screen. Tapped to take the call.

"Scott Mullan?"

"Hi, Jenny." There was the pause that always followed when he said something.

"I have Fred for you."

"Great." He was put on hold. He wasn't even sure what he was going to say and thought about hanging up.

"Scott. What's up? I don't have any news."

Scott could hear in the background the clicking of the Newton balls starting up.

"I'm not calling about that. It's about *Mythic Doorways*."

"What?"

"The book. Why'd you give it to me?"

"A favor to someone at the agency. And a favor to you. I thought you wanted to write. You get antsy during hiatus."

"I don't want to write a self-help book. You couldn't have given me a cooking book or something?"

"Hey if it's too hard, I can get someone else to read it."

"Reading isn't the problem. Did you see? The applications chapter?"

"Scott, I'm not reading the book—you are."

"You didn't tell me I'd have to *do* stuff."

"Scott. You'd have to do stuff if it was a cookbook."

"Good point."

"Come on. All writers at some point start sniffing around here for a book deal or whatever. Why not start now?"

"Have I ever 'sniffed around'?"

There was no response.

"Fred."

"No. But you're a comedy writer. You do stand-up. At some point all writers like you want a bit more of the spotlight. You just disguise it better. With all your 'outside interests.'"

"Did you just put air quotes around 'outside interests'? I read historical novels. Not that exciting."

"What? Are you a baby? Like I'm asking you to make your bed? I was trying to do you a favor. But hey—do whatever the fuck you want."

"No, I appreciate it. It's just that I haven't read much mythology."

Fred made a fake cry like a newborn. Then in a normal voice said, "We done here?"

"Yep."

"I'll call when I hear more about the head writer thing."

Scott set his phone down. He was angry. He wanted to defend himself, but to whom and about what? He looked back over the first three applications.

Pissed, he went back into the kitchen to sharpen the knives. True, it was not a cloudy day, but if he waited for a cloudy day in "Sunny Southern California," he'd never get on with it. If nothing magical came of this, at least the knives would be sharp. He pulled out a few drawers until he found the electric sharpener. He plugged it in under the cabinet near the sink, and one by one, pulled the knives from the magnetic bar on the wall and sharpened them.

Check.

He'd showered in the morning but would stop until he'd finished with the book.

Check. Well, a check that would be retroactive once a few days had passed.

And as for the coffee cup, he'd keep using the same one from this point forward.

Until he finished the book.

Check.

And now to the next application. He'd have these done in a day.

4) WHEN SOMEONE ANGERS YOU, CLOSE YOUR EYES AND DECIDE THAT WHEN YOU OPEN THEM, THE PERSON YOU ARE LOOKING AT COULD BE THE MESSIAH

Most anger comes from fear. Fear that you won't get what you need, or that getting it will be threatened by someone else. Don't look in the eyes of the person who angers you, but simply close your eyes and ask for another way of seeing. Closing one's eyes is a good way to connect to other senses, and the choice to see someone in a different way is a powerful and effective tool at turning the arrows of greed into the openheartedness of generous spirit.

In the absence of other people, I suggest you stand before a mirror and close your eyes. And know that when you open your eyes and look at those reflected back to you in the mirror, you are indeed looking into the eyes of the Messiah.

Fuck.

Scott went into the bathroom and stood in front of the black-framed mirror over the sink. He thought of flossing. He looked at his face. And then closed his eyes. He found it hard to keep them closed without feeling he was doing some sort of closed-eye blinking, but eventually his body calmed down and when it did, he waited a couple of more seconds and opened his eyes. And he looked for the Messiah. But it was just his face. It was a nice enough face, but still, there were no metaphysical fireworks. He smiled at himself and then felt like an idiot and left the bathroom.

Check.

8

WHAT COLOR IS 'NOMAD'?

A new day. Scott was unshowered, had fresh coffee in yesterday's mug, and had said hello to the Messiah in the mirror when he brushed his teeth. No one said he couldn't brush his teeth.

He glanced at the next application in the little stack before him, and wondered if he was indeed feeling alone. He *was* alone. That's how you feel.

5) WHEN FEELING ALONE, LOCK THE DOORS, PUT TAPE OVER YOUR EYES AND YOUR MOUTH AND LIE ON THE FLOOR UNTIL THE LONELINESS PASSES

The obvious homeopathic element is powerful, in that the solution is often found in the problem, and we must embrace what we fear. If you are feeling alone, abandoned, or lost, embrace this by blocking the usual paths of sensation—the eyes, the mouth—and lie on the floor close to the beating of the earth. And listen. You'll feel the answers in your belly. If possible, remain in this position until someone from the outside comes. Or the phone rings, or a siren screams outside the window. In this way, you are not the only decider and will be able to increase the feeling of involvement in the world around you. It is a beautiful form of surrender.

Scott thought this sounded like meditation and was tempted to put on his magical Bose headphones which would easily block out the world. It worked when he was at the gym, and if it wouldn't look completely douchey, he'd wear his headphones all the time. But glancing back at this application, he saw the words: 'and listen.' So he would listen. To the empty house. Whatever. He went back into the bathroom and found a couple of cotton balls in Rebecca's drawer. There were a lot of mysterious ointments and brushes and lady devices and he was tempted to investigate further, but that was her drawer. He was as protective of her privacy as she was of his. He loved that in their marriage. That trust. He closed the drawer, feeling vaguely superior. He went back to his office, got the tape from the drawer, put the tape and the cotton balls on the floor in the middle of the room, and crossed to the door, which he closed. And locked. He'd never locked the door, so it took a moment or two to find the little lever under the knob. He sat down on the carpet and looked behind him to make sure there was enough room to lie down. He didn't need to hit his head and bleed out behind a locked door. He put a piece of tape on his mouth and lay down on the beige Berber carpet, which felt scratchy on his back, even though he was wearing one of his regular polo shirts. It was too warm for a sweatshirt, so he pulled off the tape, brushed little pieces of Berber fibers from his fingers, got up, and went into the guest bathroom. He'd been trained to stay out of the guest bathroom, had been told there was a color and placement combination of the guest towels that was apparently above his design skills. Not to mention that these towels were to be used by guests only, "hence their name," as Rebecca had once pointed out. He looked at the beige towel. Rebecca called it "Winter Wheat," which he remembered because there was endless discussion about whether he'd preferred "Winter Wheat" or "Sand."

"I like those," he'd said, pointing to a different page in the Company Store catalog she was holding out to him. Although the towels looked the same, he wanted to play along and see just how many options he'd be asked to consider.

"That's 'Autumn Grey.' You like that better than 'Winter Wheat?' It's a little cooler than the tile in the bathroom."

"Oh," he said.

"I think we need to narrow it down to either 'Winter Wheat' or 'Khaki.' Although if you really did like the grey tones, I could go more 'Storm Cloud' or 'Fog.' But I like the 'Winter Wheat.'"

He seemed to consider it. "I like the wheat," he said.

"And the hand towels and face cloth? I think a contrasting color would work. Maybe we could use the 'Summer Stone.'"

"Okay, come on."

"What?"

Scott was entertaining himself in the conversation gaps by thumbing through a Pottery Barn catalog she'd had in the pile, settling on a page with paint cans and colors.

"There is a paint color here called 'Software.' Did they really run out of names? 'Software?'"

"I'm not looking for paint. So 'Winter Wheat?'"

"That would look great."

"Are you writing a bit in your head?"

"No." He looked up at her. "Well, a tiny bit."

"A bit about towels? Or about your control-freak wife."

"Umm. Towels?"

"Good answer."

"I mean, 'Simply Taupe.' Wouldn't calling it 'Taupe' imply the 'Simply'? Doesn't the act of adding an adverb make it less simple?"

She folded down the corner of a page in the catalog, gathered up the others, and put out her hand for the Pottery Barn catalog he was looking at.

"'Barley,' 'Toasted Almond,' 'Pecan,' 'Wheat.' You know what we have here?"

"I'm sure you'll tell me."

"What we have here is granola."

She did her best version of a rim shot that always fell short. She was waiting for the catalog.

"Can you leave this one?" he asked.

"Sure. Write away, Joke Monkey."

As she left to order towels, he called out to her, "'Nomad'? What color is 'Nomad'? Is there a 'Summer Wheat'?"

"Ever clever," she said. Which he'd learned could either be a compliment or a dig.

Standing before the towels, he had a moment of genius. He went back into his office, grabbed his phone, pulled it from the charger, returned to the guest bathroom, and took a photo of the towel tableau. Confident he could now recreate its placement, he pulled out the big beige towel, went back to the office, laid the towel on the floor, and got back to the business of Ben Doss. Okay. Ten minutes of this and he'd call it a day.

He sat back down, set and activated the timer on his watch for ten minutes, put the tape on his mouth, laid back, and taped the cotton balls over his eyes. At first, he just noticed his spine loosening up. Having nothing ahead for ten minutes, his mind wandered, and he thought about the myth, then about his father. There was an unfamiliar stinging behind his eyelids. He thought about his kids. When they were a year old, he'd asked Rebecca if they were doing it right and she had logically said, "Hey, I'm doing this for the first time as well." He thought about work. About the news. Jokes he could be writing about Melania Trump. Did she consult her husband about towels? He began listing towels names in his head.

And fell asleep.

The alarm on his wrist jerked him awake and he briefly panicked, thinking he was blind, but then he got his bearings and remembered what he was doing. He removed all the Ben Doss paraphernalia, got up, pulled the towel off the floor, gave it a shake and held it under his chin to do that special fold Rebecca seemed to be able to do in her sleep. That's when he saw hundreds of tiny Berber fibers clinging to the towel. Shaking didn't help. Furiously brushing with his hand only embedded the fibers further. Carrying the towel over his arm, he hurried into the kitchen, pulled out the junk drawer, grabbed one of the lint rollers, pulled off the Post-it Rebecca had written, and after laying the towel on the counter, he pulled off a sheet and rolled the newly-exposed sticky surface over the towel. That was when he learned why Rebecca loved Post-it notes. He'd teased her once, only to be told, "Fine, but you'll be sorry when the trains stop running on time." He'd said, "We're not in Switzerland, we're in Studio City. I drive a Prius." But now he understood her organizational skills. He now realized that in the junk drawer had been two lint rollers. The Post-its indicated that one was for "Indoor Furniture" and the other for "Outdoor Furniture." The one marked "Outdoor Furniture," he realized too late, clearly had adhesive super-powers and was not to be used on anything found inside the house. This clearly included towels. Crap.

9

I'VE HAD A TOWEL ACCIDENT.

Bed Bath and Beyond was HUGE. The customer service counter was just inside the sliding glass doors and Scott got in line. He was holding the lint roller by the handle. And still wrapped around the roller was the Winter Wheat towel. He had tried to unroll the towel, but the adhesive pulled out random threads along with the Berber fibers. Rolling in the other direction had made things worse. And now he was standing in the customer service line at Bed Bath & Beyond, holding what looked like a gun wrapped in a beige towel. He looked around, trying to appear as non-threatening as possible, until he remembered Rebecca said Bed Bath & Beyond was great for everything *except* towels.

Crap.

But here he was. Next in line. Too late to turn around and leave.

The young woman behind the counter glanced up at him.

"Next." She moved some hangers to the counter behind her. "How can I help you?"

She was in her twenties or thirties; Scott was never sure with younger, pierced and tattooed women. She stood about four feet ten and wore her black hair in some kind of 'do from another era.

"Hi. I've had a towel accident," he said, holding up the rumpled mass. Realizing that might sound like an older man with an incontinence issue, he quickly set his bundle down on the counter and tried to unroll the towel, again pulling out more fine threads.

"Your wife mad?"

"She hasn't seen it."

"Aha."

She gave him a quick look and then whipped the mess over and checked the label on the towel.

"We don't carry this brand."

"Do you have something similar?"

"We do. But I can't refund you for this."

"Oh no. I wasn't expecting you to."

There was a lot of typing on her computer. Then—more typing. Scott was a little panicky, which turned to anger. More at himself. But still. He thought of Ben Doss and what he'd written about anger and the Messiah. He wasn't exactly sure the girl before him was the Messiah, but he could at least say something nice. See something good in her.

"I like your hair."

"Thanks." She didn't look up and kept typing.

Scott decided to see her as the Messiah. The Messiah of Towels. Which was maybe too specific, but it was a start. He was seeing her. He was still in a bit of a panic, but he paused long enough to see who it was who was helping him. She stopped typing, inhaled and exhaled.

"Okay. This is a Company Store towel. You can either go to the Company Store website or I can point you in the direction of towels we have that are similar."

She was looking at Scott, waiting for direction. Rebecca had mentioned something about a party in three days and he wasn't sure how quick deliveries were from online towel websites. Plus, he didn't want to explain an unplanned delivery to the house. He was here and they had towels and he'd do his best.

"I'll look at the towels here."

"Great. I'll print out the names of the ones that are most similar in color and texture. If you get lost, just find someone and they'll show you."

She tapped a few more keys, her eyes focused on the screen. Scott watched her work, impressed with her ability to help him. To know her job. To know how to help.

"You are the Messiah of Towels," he told her.

She laughed. This girl who looked dark and tough and confined. She laughed like little bells, like little kittens, and her eyes crinkled up, bending the black eyeliner. Pulling the printout from the machine, she looked at him and shook her head. She was smiling.

"Let me know how it goes."

"Oh, I will. You'll be the second to know."

Scott turned, almost bumping into a woman behind him.

"Sir." The Messiah of Towels was calling him back.

He turned. "Yes."

"The lint rollers are halfway down on the right."

10

WE HAD TO PUT
A PATIENT IN COLD PACK.

Back home, Scott took the new towel out of the white plastic bag (he'd ended up with something called "latte"), snipped off the price tag, and then balled up the bag and took it to the trash container in the garage. He buried it under some other trash, which seemed foolish. He thought about other men who kept secrets from their wives, and was sure theirs were more egregious than buying a towel. And yet he felt guilty. He found the picture on his phone and, using it as a reference, he placed the new beige towel in the guest bathroom. He took his dirty cup into the kitchen and planned to reuse it as directed. While the coffee was brewing, he noticed the sun from the window was coming in at a different angle. Glancing at the clock, he saw it was late afternoon. He'd have time to read chapter two before everyone got home. He was experiencing an odd kinship with Ben. He wanted to tell him how it had gone with the whole "see the Messiah" thing.

Sitting at his desk, he put the pages he'd read in a different drawer and from the box he pulled more of the onionskin pages, although he could feel that the pages further down the box were no longer onionskin. Curious, he looked deeper and found regular printing paper with words now written in orange crayon. His mind jumped to further applications and imagined being directed to write some thoughts in crayon. He wondered if the TBAGs still had crayons in their rooms, but a few years ago they had made him swear to never enter their rooms without knocking. He had wanted to question their logic, saying that he could knock and enter regardless of whether they were actually in there or not, but had decided to solemnly respect their developing needs for privacy.

Now he was wondering if there was some way he could sidestep his promise, but decided no. He would not go into their rooms. Maybe he could bow out of the crayon application for lack of a crayon. Maybe there wasn't even going to be a crayon-related application. Maybe his head was getting ahead of him and the exercise was for him to just take the pages as they came. He knew he tended to consider all possibilities, but this was also the nature of his job. To run through all the options and find the most comedic jump. But in terms of this book, he'd need to stay with what he was reading. He'd read and do. And try to not anticipate.

He exhaled, picked up his pencil for no reason, and continued reading.

CHAPTER TWO
The Sin of Greed and The Power of Money

"If my devils are to leave me, I am afraid my angels will take flight as well."

- Rainer Maria Rilke

INTRODUCTION

Many of us have used the Myth of Sisyphus as an example of the pointlessness of this journey that we all share. Why push the stone up the hill each day if it is to roll to the bottom again, leaving us with the same task the next day? It was Rollo May, however, who opened my eyes to a new perspective in terms of the interpretation of myth. And to extrapolate, how we see and judge others. May tells us: "One thing Sisyphus can do: he can be aware of each moment in this drama between himself and Zeus, between himself and his fate." He goes on to point out that we "do not know Sisyphus's reveries, his ruminations . . ."

"A Course in Miracles" offers us a direct and simple prayer that contains an abundance of presupposed humility and inherent faith, which leads to wisdom: "Dear God, please help me see this in a different way."

Without really knowing why, the Rilke quote about devils and angels came to me, as if in a dream, and I realize that behind all greed is fear. Who will I be if not my defects? Who will I be without my devils?

To be starkly honest, even in writing this, I see that I hold on to my own greedy need to be accepted. I am greedy to be the good boy, always the good boy, don't make waves, don't make mommy mad. Don't say a bad word. Fuck Fuck Fuck. I say it here, because "fuck" is the word of the fool, cutting through our Victorian need to be docile and subdued.

And playing the fool is the antidote to greed.

I shall play the fool. I shall play with my sanity for the sake of my readers. And I ask: If you were stripped of your sanity, would you still have God? Or is God a manifestation of your insanity?

Dr. Schemion just stopped by and mentioned that Janice had called and will not be in today. I find my reaction curious in terms of this chapter on greed. I feel hurt that she didn't tell me directly (although she knows not to bother me when I'm working, so this is a subjective and unrealistic hurt), but I feel a slight greed in terms of time, that although we spend only minutes together during the day, I find my mind trying to wrap itself around where she is, and who is getting her time now. I know Love/God is not a finite quality, but this subtle tinge of my own greediness, even for the indirect attention and support of my assistant, is something I want to understand. As Rilke said, "Love brings up everything unlike itself for the purpose of healing and release." And if I love her, even if it is as her mentor, then it follows that anything that is not love is going to surface.

I had a patient recently—Tom—who became enraged when our time was up. My job as a therapist is to provide boundaries, a framework within which the patient can work, and it is painful at times to see these men squirm with anguish as the minutes tick by. They want more. Even if they sit for fifty minutes in a nearly catatonic silence, they want more.

Tom spent many sessions in complete silence, jerking his head around the room, to the mesh on the windows, to the big clock in the room. Jerk, turn, shift, jerk, turn, shift. It was a breakthrough the first time he became enraged, stood like a giant, walked past me, and ripped the clock off the wall. He threw it at the window, and at that point the floor assistants came in and took him back to his room.

We seem to swing in this society from shame about needs, to misdirected needs, and finally to needs that are so blown out of proportion that twelve-year-olds are pulling knives on their classmates for Pokémon cards.

As we shall see in the following myth, there is always a knife. First representing the absentee father, then the misdirected phallic energy, and eventually manifesting in rage against the mother. A boy is left alone with his empty, lonely rage. The rage that raises a knife into the air, the rage at a mother who is vaguely sexual with her son, trotting around the house in high heels for her little man, when all he wants is help with his homework. Or maybe breakfast. Breakfast would be nice. I like breakfast.

Alone with a mother who has an even more extreme delusional need for attention, manifesting in her hours of chanting and incense and feigned holiness, her extreme fears and misunderstood sexuality resulting in the taping down of her own son's genitals. Leaving him the only phallic expression left for him: a sharp knife.

In this myth we see that the mother's greed for more, more sexual attention, more spiritual succor—it doesn't matter what she's grabbing for—it leaves our sons with nothing but rage. Or even more misdirected greed.

Another siren just went off in an adjacent wing of the hospital and I am brought out of my head and must put down my writing things and see what I can do.

I am back.

We had to put a patient in cold pack.

My hands are cold.

Usually the techs administer the cold pack, but we're short-handed today and I pitch in where I can.

I need something warm.

Where is Janice?

I don't remember what I was writing.

I am cold and must lie down.

Okay. Feeling better. New day. Where was I. Rebirth.

I am in a simple room, much like that of a monk, with a world in my head, a world of love and God and service.

What is interesting to note in this myth are the independent references to the holy trinity. In this case, the trinity of mother-father-son. We have come to be influenced by a trinity of father-son-holy ghost, a patriarchal trinity, the result of Mary being replaced by frightened, sexually abused Catholic bishops and popes who had their own misplaced sexuality and rage, and which went underground in denial. Making the trinity a little boys' club that could stay neat and nice and controllable and secret without the icky influences of a female. But nature is male and female.

I have no doubt that my assistant Janice is my equal: intelligent, capable, responsible, honorable. But she also brings an intuition, a softening. And it is her skill at discerning my needs during my silences that makes her so valuable.

When she comes in tomorrow, I shall tell her how much she means to me. And I shall tell Henry the night janitor how much he means to me as well.

Scott sighed and worried he hadn't told the people who mattered to him that they mattered to him. He thought about making a note to himself, in case this didn't come up in future applications; he didn't need Ben to remind him to do nice things. He was curious about the next myth, but also oddly excited about the next applications. There was an unknown ahead that sent a surge of adrenaline into his body. He sat up, inhaled, and kept reading.

THE MYTH
Boy of Dirt and the Grand Canyon

God, who was able to shapeshift, took the form of a wild dog and ran with the wild dogs across the plains. One day he came across the pale thin body of a boy, who had been discarded by New England travelers. The boy, naked and bruised, had a misshapen penis, and God the dog wrapped the boy's loins in bark and then dragged the boy by his foot, during the dark of night, to the land of the Lahoyas. God wept to see the damage to the boy, and cried dog tears every step of his journey. Where the tears fell, a tree grew. These became the aspens of Colorado. God cried many tears for this boy and his abuse.

God, however, was running out of time and dropped the boy off beside a tree at the nearest teepee, just as the sun was rising. God knew this boy to be a holy child, and trusted the Lahoyas to take care of him until he reached manhood and could carry out his higher purpose.

At first light, the squaws came out to gather wood and discovered the boy, and named him Boy of Dirt, as he was covered with blood and dirt from his travels with God. They took him into the teepee and dressed his wounds, eventually unraveling the bark on his mangled and misshapen genitals. They took this to be a sign of power and, fearing his power, they ran from the tent. When they returned, they had a vessel filled with water and proceeded to hold Boy of Dirt's head in the water, in an attempt to cleanse him. They sensed he was holy and knew that the water would connect him more quickly to the gods.

Boy of Dirt was taken in by the father of the tribe, Neck Like Log, who tried to teach him to hunt as he had taught his own strapping sons. But Boy of Dirt was quiet and thoughtful, and as he grew into his manhood, he was left alone much of the time to look at the sky, while his adoptive cousins were out gathering the white horses that were so valuable to the tribe. In exchange for these white horses, the young men were invited to share in the medicine of the magic pipe.

The tribe often gathered in a big field for the competitions of the young warriors, and Boy of Dirt was left behind to watch the fire. He was able to listen to God in the fire, just as he listened to the distant cries of the tribesmen. He could hear everything everywhere. He was this special.

One day, Swift As Lightning, the firstborn son of Neck Like Log, took the squaw Slow Hyena into the woods and was mating with her when he discovered Boy of Dirt standing nearby. Watching. Boy of Dirt was aroused, and Swift As Lightning offered him Slow Hyena, but when he approached, Swift As Lightning laughed. And when Slow Hyena saw his misshapen genitals, she also laughed. When she became heavy with child, the wrong child, Boy of Dirt knew that he had to act.

He went to Neck Like Log and, using the skin of a buffalo and a knife, drew him a picture of the pregnant squaw and the sign of bad weather to come, and began stabbing at the buffalo skin.

But Neck Like Log had other concerns and forgot to share his magic pipe with Boy of Dirt. Instead, he went off to the Big Field to officiate the warriors' game.

Boy of Dirt closed his eyes and listened to the wind for the voice of God, and began to rock back and forth. Slowly at first. Then more quickly. He went into the woods and found a wild dog. He tied the dog to a tree. He put twigs in his own hair, knowing they would provide a conduit to the heavens, and went to find Slow Hyena.

She laughed at him as he approached, but he had a sweet look in his eyes and she followed him into the woods. He tied her to a tree near the tree that held the wild dog. Her screams were loud enough for Swift As Lightning to no doubt hear. The dog told Boy of Dirt to end the life of the demon child growing in the belly of Slow Hyena, but Boy of Dirt was weak and slow to move. Water poured from between the legs of Slow Hyena, and as Swift As Lightning ran to Boy of Dirt, Boy of Dirt turned the knife on himself. The blood flowed from his belly into the earth.

The water from Slow Hyena poured and poured into the earth, causing a grand canyon, and the blood from Boy of Dirt colored the walls of the canyon bloodred. And in this way, they were finally united.

EXPLORATION

Here we have yet another permutation of the original Holy Trinity, as represented in the Father-Mother-Son triangle. The Holy Father being of course the wild dog, the squaw being the Holy Mother, and Boy of Dirt the son.

Godliness that can be found in nature.

Land creation is not, of course, solely the mythic landscape of the Native Americans. Norse myth tells us of the giant Ymir, whose bones formed the continents, whose hair was the vegetation, and whose blood became the rivers and the seas. An Aboriginal myth believes that the Milky Way is the smoke from a celestial campfire. And again we see the myth of slicing and splitting, as Marduk, an early Babylonian sun god, split Tiamat—his female counterpart—in two. Her top half became the heavens and her bottom half became the earth.

Looking further, we find Cronus, youngest of the seven Titans in Greek mythology. Urged on by his mother, Gaea, and fashioning a scythe made from flint, he castrated his father Uranus. The blood of Uranus formed the oceans and his testicles rose again from the sea in the form of Aphrodite. The goddess of love.

Scott thought this must be a mistake, and although he wanted to keep to his plan of reading and doing—to get a general feel for the book—he had to stop and Google this. He'd heard of Aphrodite, but this whole rising testicle thing seemed a little far-fetched. He typed in "Aphrodite testicles" and there it was. Hmmm. Then he cleared the search history as this would look like some pretty strange fetish he wasn't ready to explain.

He needed a break from the dense outlaying of information and scanned ahead to some of the more personal parts as he wanted to get a feel for Ben Doss the man. He hoped that when they met, Scott could impress him with his own reading list, his own experiences, and he was embarrassed that he was already planning ahead to impress someone. Jeez, Scott. Just shut up your head and read.

As a teenager, I myself traveled with my aunt and uncle and my cousins to the Grand Canyon, and although I had not yet discovered its mythic origins, I was profoundly struck by its inexplicable power. I stood at the edge, rocking back and forth, as if hypnotized by the music of nature that it seemed only I could hear. Back and forth. Eventually I could hear through God's music and depth the sounds of my aunt, screaming for me to step back from the ledge, screaming for my Uncle Frank who was off with his sons, gassing up the station wagon. She didn't dare come near me. I imagine her fear of the cliff was stronger than her perception of God, and I continued to rock and commune with God and the power of nature until I heard behind me the voice of my uncle, Uncle Frank. I could hear everything at that point, my hearing so refined, and I heard him say, "Fine, leave him." And I heard the car door open. I heard my aunt get into the car. The door slammed and the car started to drive away. I stood perfectly still, hearing only the wind. The car stopped. The door opened. My uncle came back to me. I was hoping to commune with him about the wonder of God.

"What the fuck is the matter with you?"

I said nothing. And in that moment I knew I could step

into the physical abyss of the Grand Canyon, or I could turn and step into the seeming spiritual abyss that was my young life. But I will talk more of spiritual journeys in Chapter Six: God and Envy.

Scott skipped through more analysis and found more personal revelations. He paused and rubbed his armpit. It felt moist. He smelled his hand, and something was ripe. Something was coming alive here, and maybe it was starting with his body. Other than working out, he didn't really have much of a relationship with his body. Was that a thread he could connect here, in editing this book? The two narratives. The head and the heart. The head and the body. Maybe there was indeed an editor in him that was already looking for cohesion, for connection, for story. He'd go back and read over the rough notes Ben Doss (BD) had made about antlers, ("antium is Latin for receiving,") turbans, crowns, and the high hats of cardinals and bishops. It was fun to see the icons of his own religion referenced here, even if in an indirect, nature-related fashion. He laughed at his own subjective "yay team" pride about cardinal hats.

In early Celtic times, the pagans believed that God came through the hair and so these people fashioned tall manipulations of bark and sticks to pull their hair upward, closer to God. This is also seen in early Chinese cultures, in the elaborate hair constructs that start at the top of the head, all the hair woven together with colored string, creating a filament to the heavens. But there must be a lightning rod, a receiver, an uptake center for any energy to pass from one source to another. This is what is meant in today's New Age term as "being grounded." One must be grounded to be a strong channel for the electricity of the spirit. A lightning rod does not float freely in space, but must be connected to the ground.'

And so we must return to the Boy of Dirt myth to be reminded of the gifts that come from nature. So often, the child of God is wrapped in what we now see as an uncommon manner. But if we see that nature is God, then we can understand that it is perhaps uncommon, but actually stronger than your fine Armani suits. Or your football jersey. Jesus had his swaddling clothes. He didn't need a cashmere cardigan to tell him he was the anointed. Eskimos believed their gods to be impervious to the cold, and so any man found wearing shoes of paper was thought to be holy.

Sometimes I wear little shoes of paper to connect with the Eskimo myth. Sometimes I put twigs in my hair. Sometimes I just sit looking up.

My work environment is the perfect place to look around and see the elements and create an arena of nature where others see nothing. There is the water in Henry's bucket. Janice wears a lighter around her neck, as she is often assisting in the smoking area of the more damaged patients who are not allowed fire. A small plant at the nurse's station brings us the earth. Rather than try to gather up all the elements and horde them in one's room, look around and see if you can expand your vision of nature's forces, nature's elements, in the seemingly small world around you. This expanding of one's vision is an antidote to greed.

Water.

Water is always a source of wisdom, and just as the river is a metaphor for our soul's journey along the waterway of wisdom, the well, or any bucket or vessel of water used for the immersion of the head or for baptism, is a powerful metaphor for immediate wisdom.

I witness this thirst for wisdom and holiness everywhere. You can see it in the obsession we have with water, that seems to have sprung up (no pun intended) wherever you look. Everyone carries some form of bottled water, as if this is a sacred amulet that must travel and bless our journey. Everywhere, this obsession with water. One's own water.

I am reminded of my own mother. Who with her own holy visions, fashioned a baptism when she held my head under the water. Granted it took place in the bathroom, my head in the toilet, but it was baptism just the same.

I have a tendency to feel grief every afternoon at dusk. What do you do with your own sadness? Rather than feel a little fucking sadness, you leap up and demand that someone go to Starbucks and get you a cranberry muffin and double half-caf venti latte. Dry or Wet? Wet. Wet. If you want to have wet, then get in the fucking water. That is where you'll find wet. If you can't handle the sadness, maybe it is time to put your head in the bucket of water. Enforced wisdom. Where is Henry. And his bucket.

Where the fuck is Janice? (BD - take this out)

The particulars of my story may not be yours, but the feelings are similar. When my father left, I thought that was pain. But I was then left to witness the pain in my mother as she dealt with this abandonment. Pregnant and alone. She tried to commit suicide, and it was I who found her bleeding on the floor after she had apparently made an attempt at stabbing her own pregnant belly. People thought I'd stabbed her, but they were stupid. She was hospitalized, and I went to live with my Uncle Frank in San Diego.

It was a different world for me. After a quiet, thoughtful childhood with my parents, I was thrown into a world of sports and uniforms and drinking. Uncle Frank was a football coach, and my cousin Larry was on the football team. It was fascinating to watch this world of loud, crashing, sweating territorialism, and I viewed this new world with the keen eye of a researcher, which would lead to my early writing about the ritual of sport and testosterone. It was here that I first witnessed a certain type of greed that is a combination of hormones and societal pressure. Larry, as with many team-oriented athletes, had the mindset of more: more points, more yardage, more territory. Is it any wonder that this translated to the unregistered sexual conquest point system that existed for him? Which can be seen at its most extreme in the case of the point system and eventual rape charges against the Lakewood Spur Posse. The accumulation of more points, all kinds of points, whether it be in sports, sexual conquest, SAT scores, or even the accumulation of punches in a coffee card, we are trained to get more. To want more. More is better.

I was wondering about Janice, and Dr. Schemion told me that she will be in tomorrow. Maybe he already told me this? Did he tell me this yesterday? I could survive alone, we all could, but it takes a certain strength to depend on others and I depend on her. She has started me on better vitamins and brings them to me every day. It is one less thing I need to worry about as I focus on the writing of this book. So, eccentric that I am, I did not take my vitamins yesterday. I want to see if they are helping. And someone else brought me lunch today, but I find I miss Janice's quiet support and beautiful smile. She could talk me into the vitamins, but she is not here. I need her to be here tomorrow!

You see, she often looks over my writing and leaves me articles she finds that are germane to the work that I am doing. It is a special communication that we have that is not necessarily verbal, but quite personal and important to me.

My proposal of more freedom will no doubt frighten some people. If we were to give the wild horses their freedom, they might lead us somewhere beautiful. Somewhere real. We see this in Swift As Lightning's need to control all the horses. Control all that wild energy. However, energy cannot be contained, and if suppressed in one place, it manifests in another. And so in a way, Swift is responsible for the actions of Boy of Dirt, as Boy of Dirt is simply acting out all of the repression in which the others are participating. If you require everyone to walk the straight and narrow, the energy must manifest in someone to the extreme. Whether it be the fool, the crazy person, the trickster, the pedophile priest, or the psychopath.

We witness this subtlety in relationships. Have you ever walked into a room where someone is standing, and you have felt strangely and immediately enraged?

Angry for no reason. Whether you blame it on the position of the toilet seat or the status of the trash, what is really most often happening is that you are expressing that other person's unexpressed rage.

Barbara De Angelis likens this to a tube between the bellies of people, and as the plunger pushes the feelings down in one, they push through the tube and erupt in the other person. There is a paradoxical and beautiful selflessness in expressing one's self honestly and cleanly. Express your own rage so someone else doesn't have to do it. Sometimes these expressions are violent.

I had so much more to write and I wanted to finish it today. But I am getting sleepy. I want to blame Janice because she was not here and I spent a lot of my time analyzing my own reactions, but rather than . . . I must return to this tomorrow.

Groggy.

New day.

Janice just came in. Explained to me her absence yesterday. None of my business. I didn't ask, she doesn't have to explain it to me, like I'm a baby. It's her life. If she wants to get pregnant by some asshole who doesn't know a thing about her, that's her fucking business. See, that's where I get to learn detachment and love, by loving her and at the same time letting her be free with her own life, free to make her own mistakes, follow her own journey. I can say a little prayer for her well-being. I can just shut the fuck up about it and go back to my own work. And I can write anything I want at this stage and if I need to go back and edit, I can do that. I've never met

Janice's husband, but Dr. Schemion met him at a hospital Christmas party. I was unable to attend as I was working on a lecture series for one of my books.

I need some water.

Janice will bring me water even if she doesn't know that I'm not feeling good about this.

She will bring my vitamins but I won't take them.

Need to walk. Need to walk.

Can't leave my office. Need to move. Need to let the ball of yarn unravel, but who will roll it back up? Can you roll up your own ball of yarn, and if so, what would be the purpose of other people? What's that Twilight Zone episode?

Pacing is nothing more than a moving meditation. Need to move. Maybe I'll go for a walk. A circular walk. A mandala. Walking. Walking.

I'm better.

I'm fine.

11

PUT TWIGS IN YOUR HAIR.

Scott felt stimulated by the new ideas and the rawness of the writing. There were more typos and cross outs, and he could see that one of the keys on Ben's typewriter must be sticking at this point. But he was able to get the idea of the freedoms that were being presented. He was able to access gratitude for the book and for the project, which gave him a sense of purpose during this hiatus week from work. He noticed his uncertainty about the head writer position had receded, and although it was still his primary concern, he had room to open up to other ideas. Other ways of being. And there was something freeing about the style of Ben's writing. Granted, the book clearly needed a strong editor as the ideas seemed to flow, from time to time, from an unfocused mind, but Scott was envious of Ben's ability to access and expose personal experiences, pains, feelings.

Scott looked back on his own work and had to admit he'd never once written down anything personal. Of course he wrote jokes for a late-night comic, where not only were the jokes structured specifically for Dylan's delivery and point of view, but there wasn't a lot of room for personal expression. He wasn't sure why, but he was feeling agitated. Maybe from reading about agitation, or maybe it was simply the implied frustration of a funky typewriter. But whatever the cause, he, too, needed to move before jumping into the applications and take a break to go to the gym. He needed a break from reading and thinking.

When he got back, he turned on the shower out of habit but remembered he had stopped showering—at least as long as he worked on the book. He turned off the water, took off his gym clothes, balled them up and put them in the hamper, and got back into his sweats.

More coffee and he was back at his desk.

Despite having decided to read the book one time through before going back and making notes, he'd started a list of thoughts on his pad. Some were new ideas, some were questions he'd ask Ben himself, and some were factual things he'd Google later. He looked over the list of applications from chapter one. He was proud of himself for having accomplished them but then laughed at the irony, as they had been in the chapter on pride. Was he really this needy that he tried to find value in any small action he accomplished? He'd stopped showering. How much pride was there in that? He set aside these self-judgments and decided to just shut up his head and push forward. He was ready to continue.

APPLICATION

1) WHEN BEREFT OF GOD, LOOK FOR HIM IN NATURE

We look to everyone around us for what we think we need. And forget to look to nature. Boy of Dirt heard the voice of God while looking in the fire. Light a candle and stare at it until you hear the voices. We see this strong need for spiritual connection in our lost children, the fire starters, who have little hope of love and protection, and have an inherent sense that God is in the fire. If you are particularly closed off from feeling, from hope, from vulnerability, it may be necessary to hold one's hand over the flame until feeling returns. This is a very quick way to re-enter one's body.

2) IF CONFUSED ABOUT WHAT TO DO, ROCK BACK AND FORTH

This is a simple active meditation and, just as rocking massage has become popular in Europe, the motion of rocking is quite healing. Think of rocking a baby to sleep. It is also a good solution if you aren't able to take a walk, or to recreate the Sisyphistic journey on a StairMaster or a treadmill. Simply rock back and forth. Our heads are clogged, and sometimes it takes simple rocking to dislodge the crusty thoughts we've inherited, genetically as well as socially.

This is a simple and subtle action that can be utilized almost anywhere: on a crowded subway, in an alley, or in the stall of a public restroom. So often in today's grasping all-or-nothing world, we think that it will require something very large, very fast, very expensive to match the lack we are feeling inside, and it is at just such times that the paradox of small action must be employed. I can never take actions as big as my head thinks I need. I have found that the only solution at these times when I feel so disconnected is to slow down and create the vortex of energy, a funnel if you will, to God, by stirring a molecular cone above my head, creating my own spirit chakra—a mini-hurricane of energy, a black hole, in which a vacuum is created where there is no other outcome except for the intake of God. And this hurricane, this vortex, this swirling invitation is created most effectively by standing in place and rocking back and forth.

3) THE NEXT TIME YOU FEEL INTERRUPTED BY SOMEONE, STOP WHAT YOU'RE DOING AND SAY HELLO

Henry, coming in with his mop, is my signal to see that his work is just as powerful as mine and that I should say hello to him. And I do.

Even though the people here have gotten used to me not speaking, there are times I say hello, even if in my own way. I don't want to fall into the trap of my own father, thinking that the work is more important than those around me. Work is the vehicle, not the destination.

Janice just came in and sat in the metal chair. I stopped and looked at her. Really looked. She looked sad. She was wearing her pastels. She was a sweet sad smiling Necco wafer, and I didn't say anything. I wonder in these times who is yearning for the companionship. She didn't say it in so many words, but what I understood was that she wanted to end her pregnancy. (BD - take this out? Too personal?) Should I have said something? I too fail.

I read an article about a comedy troupe, and I will always remember one key point about training in improvisation: "The answer is in your partner's eyes. If you don't know what to say next, stop talking and look in your partner's eyes. There you will find the answer." Start by saying hello.

4) WHEN YOU FEEL GREEDY AND DISCONNECTED FROM GOD, PUT TWIGS IN YOUR HAIR AND GO OUTSIDE

Until you realize that greed is not the path to God, you will be unable to risk letting go of your tight-fisted little grabby-handed hold on money. Begin by tightly grasping a dollar bill. Hold it tightly until your hand aches. Then set it down and pick up the twigs and place them in your hair. Stand under the sky and feel the connection, like the high hats, like the antlers, like a lightning rod. This is an active indication of the willingness to connect to a higher source rather than a lower source—greed. I would suggest doing this in privacy, as this visual could be misinterpreted by those on the street who have not yet read this book.

Scott was beginning to get a sense that Ben Doss was in love with his assistant, Janice. Scott liked facts, he liked dates and time frames and names. He was not good with innuendo, but he was getting a sense that there was something more going on in the self-help book. Maybe it could be reframed in that way, although that would make it a very different kind of book. He set these thoughts aside and went back to the applications. "When bereft of God, look for him in nature." Was he bereft of God? God was God. He was there. Like Jesus. Scott was tempted to check this off the list, because God wasn't a problem for him. He felt lucky that this wasn't a problem for him. At work, Dylan rode the comic train of being a sexually inept, guilt-ridden, self-loathing Catholic, so there was a lot of joking about faith and guilt and Jesus, but it was tacitly understood that deep down, he and Dylan shared a certain knowing. That he and Scott didn't really doubt their faith. Scott didn't doubt his faith now. Not really. Maybe just considering other perspectives? No harm in that.

He looked at the time and his notes, and although there was a final application for this chapter, he figured he could knock it out before Rebecca came home: 1) light a candle; 2) rock back and forth; 3) say hello (he'd say hello to Rebecca later); 4) put twigs in hair. Or lack of hair. He'd figure it out.

So first, the candle. Rebecca had various candles of varying fragrances around the house, and he knew they were primarily for when they had company. There was a candle in their bedroom, for the times she felt romantic and closed the blinds, sometimes even in the daytime. But that was happening less and less, particularly with the final push to get the TBAG's school choices and applications sorted out. He had this thought that in less than a year they'd be away at school and he and Rebecca would fall on the bed and not really move for a few weeks. An accumulation and manifestation of all the rest they'd missed raising their kids. He imagined that at some point they'd have sex again. Okay, he wasn't going to use the bedroom candle, especially in his office as Rebecca (like a bloodhound) would wonder what was going on. He imagined himself saying, "I thought we'd have sex on the Berber carper. Let me just grab a guest towel." The scenario made him laugh.

He mentally scanned the house to locate any benign, i.e. scent-free candles, and remembered there was a scent-free candle in a glass container on the table in the backyard. That would do. He went through the living room to the sliding glass door. He unlocked the door and when he slid it open, there was resistance as the door got hung up on the metal slider, and as he pushed, it created a loud and squeaky wail. He slid it back and forth, but it was hiccupping and squeaking. Rebecca teased him for not being very handy around the house, but he knew enough to realize that what was needed was WD-40. Here was a tangible problem, one that he could solve. He opened the cabinet over the refrigerator but there were more cleaning things than squeaky-fix things. He knew he'd seen WD-40 at some point in the last twenty years and remembered Rebecca had relegated the man tools to the garage. That was to be his domain, although the time he spent in the garage was the time it took for him to get out of his car and press the button to close the garage door.

He went into the garage, opened a few cabinets, and looked around a few shelves. Not only was he not finding what he needed, but the day was getting away from him. It was time to act.

He went back inside for his phone, wallet, and keys. The pockets of his sweat pants were loose and unstructured. He thought he should change into his "going out" clothes—Dockers and a polo shirt—but this would be good practice in just "going with the flow."

He pressed the button to open the garage door. He got in the car, tapped in the address for the nearest Home Depot and began his drive to Van Nuys. With the windows closed, he became aware of an odor and, after glancing around peripherally, he finally determined it was coming from himself. He smelled an armpit. It was strong, but really not unpleasant.

12

AND YOU, SIR, ARE THE MESSIAH OF LUBRICANTS.

Home Depot was porn to some guys, but not to Scott. Although he was tall and muscular and looked like the kind of guy who should know his way around a hardware store, he had no idea where to look for WD-40. He thought Bed Bath & Beyond was massive, but this was a small city. His mind started on a little trip of public space Russian nesting dolls, Matrytoshka dolls, starting with someone in a bathroom stall, which was in a bathroom, which was in a Starbucks, which was in a Bed Bath & Beyond, which was in a Home Depot. This was getting him nowhere.

He started walking. He spotted an occasional guy with a Home Depot vest, but they were usually helping women with light bulbs or paint. There were other male customers pushing carts of large, manly things, and Scott figured if they could sort out their needs, surely he could, but he was feeling lost. His father would be turning in his grave, if he hadn't been paralyzed.

He found an aisle with lubricants, sprays, caulk and caulking guns, and scanned the shelves for what he needed. He first looked up and down, but then abandoned this method for a more left to right scan. He was mesmerized by the items on the shelves, and he allowed his body to follow the rhythm of his vision and began rocking from side to side. He felt entirely alone standing on the cement floor with a fifteen-foot wall of unfamiliar items. Time seemed to stop as he gave up his search and just took in the beauty of all the labels, the cool of the air, and the smell of sawdust. The rocking was hypnotic.

"Sir. Are you okay?"

Scott was brought immediately to the reality of where he was and what he was doing. He was standing in an aisle at Home Depot, rocking back and forth. He could check *that* off the list. He wanted to say, "I'm fine!" and disappear, but he remembered the next application after rocking, and in an exuberant and welcoming voice he said, "Hello!" Which to his own ears sounded a little crazy.

"Hello. Can I help you find something?" The kid was as tall as Scott, but looked about fourteen and had a complexion that was acting up. He had a slight lisp. Scott remembered to see the Messiah.

"I *do* need help and I'll bet you're the guy! It would be great if you could help me!"

Scott looked into the kid's brown eyes, and then at the sheen of oil on his forehead, the pimples. He envisioned the next sixty years for this kid, the clearing of the skin, the marriage, the confusions, the losses, the joys, grandkids, old skin, loss of hair, foot pain, laughter, sad smiles, an old face, a slow and careful gait. He saw a lifetime in a moment and experienced an overwhelming love for the life before him.

"What're you looking for?" this beautiful boy asked him.

"What are we all looking for?"

"I don't know."

"I don't know, either." Scott smiled at him. "So, in the meantime, how about WD-40?"

"Kay." The kid turned and reached up and pulled a can from a row of similar cans. "Here you go." He handed the can to Scott. "Anything else?" And there was that subtle lisp.

"Nope. And you, sir, are the Messiah of Lubricants."

"No problem."

Scott loved this kid with the lisp and bad skin. He put the can in his left hand and reached out with his right to shake hands. The kid reached out to meet his hand and they shook.

"Really appreciate the help."

They disengaged, and the kid nodded and walked away.

Scott checked out and felt a bit lighter, the can and receipt in hand as he headed toward the exit, where he smiled at the heavyset man who striped his receipt with a yellow marker.

He walked out into the breezy, clear air.

He stopped and noticed the air was very fresh. Very hopeful. Hopeful fresh air. Could air be hopeful? "When did I start thinking about the air?" He said this out loud. And then he thought, "When did I start talking to myself out loud?" He inhaled. There was a breeze that smelled like roses. He looked for the source and saw bucket after bucket of orange roses. But then he noticed the sheds. He could use a shed. Rebecca would hate a shed. Plus, what would he put in a shed? His can of WD-40?

He got into his Prius. Looked at the bird shit on the windshield and felt a strange connection to the bird who got to fly through this hopeful, fresh air. He put his hands together. "Thank you, God, for this perfect day." He prayed regularly but never in gratitude for a day. He was happy to feel so connected. Had he been feeling a disconnect lately, from God, from church? He had to admit yes. This was his own dark challenge, his own secret. He didn't know how to mend this waning connection, and so he was greatly encouraged to be sitting in his car with a new way of seeing. A renewed connection to God.

He looked forward to talking to Fred, to thanking him for this project, and he looked forward to eventually talking to Ben himself about the changes he was experiencing. Changes that in such small and simple ways seemed somehow profound.

13
DID YOU JUST CALL ME JANICE?

Scott wasn't expecting to see his wife's car in the garage. It was Thursday. He looked at the time. It was 5:15 p.m. Had he really been in the Home Depot for two hours? He pulled in to his spot in the garage, grabbed the plastic bag that held the WD-40, and headed in.

Rebecca was on her knees wiping down the inside of the oven. Which reminded him they were having a dinner party Saturday night. Scott had once questioned Rebecca as to why she cleaned the oven *before* people came over when she was going to be cooking, but this was before he learned of her many quirks. He probably had his own idiosyncrasies he imagined she had either accepted or ignored.

"Hi, Janice," he said. He could check off application number three!

"Did you just call me Janice?"

Crap.

"Scott? Who's Janice?"

"It's something I'm reading."

"Oh. Good. I thought you were having an affair." She laughed, and he knew she didn't believe that.

"You're home early."

"We went early today and we're off tomorrow. Yay. Which is why I planned the party for this weekend."

"Right." He watched as she got up, went to the sink, and washed her hands.

"How's your week at home alone? Whatcha got there?" She indicated the bag.

The second question eliminated the need to answer the first. He pulled the can from the bag, as if it was some elaborate magic trick.

"WD-40. For the slider."

"You're fixing the slider?"

"You asked me to."

"Like four years ago."

"Good things come . . . blah blah."

He crossed through the living room to the glass door, unlocked it, and slid it open, almost reveling in the squeal of metal on metal. He looked at the can and wasn't sure what to do with the little straw taped to the side, but there was a nozzle to depress so he pressed it as he ran it along the metal on the floor. He stood and slid the door back and forth a few times and it now produced a very subtle and delightful whoosh. He turned to Rebecca, who was standing in the kitchen watching him. He raised his hands in victory, as if he he'd just scaled Mt. Everest.

"You are my hero." She went to him and kissed him on the cheek. He was glad she wasn't flinching at the odor of the oil, which he assumed would dissipate quickly. She went to the kitchen and lit a candle but still said nothing, and he loved her for that. She went back to her iPad on the counter where lists were being consulted, amended. Scott went back to the kitchen, drawn to the candle. He could cross another application off the list. He stood and looked at the flame and thought about fire. How it worked. No idea. The wonder of heat. He held his hand over the flame and pulled it away.

103

"I said, 'Scott'." Her voice came back into his consciousness.

"What?!"

"What are you doing?"

"Just looking at the candle."

"You're being a real weirdo."

"Sorry. I'm reveling in my newfound manhood," he said, indicating the sliding door. "What did you say?"

"I'm going to be prepping. Can you help the TBAGs—DAMMIT." She snapped the rubber band on her wrist. "Can you help Marcus and Chloe with the applications?"

"With the applications?" What? What was she asking? Had she been reading the book? Why would the kids do them? He could feel his eyes move left and right as he scanned his memory for a clue.

"Their applications? For school?"

Oh. "Have they decided?"

"No. We're looking at San Diego and Irvine next week." She pointed at the refrigerator. "It's on the calendar. You remember about the ham, right?"

"They need a ham for college?"

"Ha ha."

"Ever clever."

He glanced over to the refrigerator. "Yep, picking it up Saturday."

"I want them to start getting familiar with the process, the forms. The essay questions."

"I'm your man," he said, and walked back to the slider. He opened and closed it a few times. She glanced over at him. He gave her a little smile and raised his eyebrow, like *yeah, king of the world.*

14

WHAT THE FUCK
ARE YOU DOING?

Scott stayed in his office while Rebecca vacuumed. Right, party prep. Eventually the noise stopped, and after a while she yelled in his direction that she was going out to do errands. He heard the door to the garage open and close. He heard her car start up and felt oddly unfaithful that he had been waiting for her to leave so he could be alone with his book.

He'd gotten up early, made coffee, and while it was brewing, he'd gone out back and gathered up a few twigs from near the door. He'd put the twigs, the duct tape, and the dollar bill in the middle drawer of his desk. And now he sat, ready. Reveling in the quiet. He had two applications remaining before getting to chapter three and felt the pressure to accomplish all this before going back to work Monday. He wanted to consolidate his notes, maybe do a little research, meet with Fred, and map out the next steps in the editing process. But for now, the pages were tucked away in the bottom drawer and his desk was cleared, like a fresh start. He knew Rebecca would do a quick cleaning pass in the office. He didn't want her coming upon a pile of messy, onionskin, typewritten pages and have to explain to her what he was doing. What he had been doing all week. He would tell her next week after he'd sorted things out with Fred. Maybe he'd have a contract. Maybe he'd be head writer and would have *two* surprises for her.

He took a deep breath. It was time to put the twigs in his hair, which was going to be a challenge since he didn't have much hair. He pulled open the drawer, put the duct tape on his wrist like some manly bracelet, put the dollar bill in the pocket of his sweat pants, put the scotch tape in his left hand, and with his right hand, he picked up the napkin on which was stacked the little bundle of twigs.

He carried these things to the living room, and slipping his finger through the tape dispenser, he used his index finger to unlock the slider. He pulled it open with a smooth whoosh and looked outside. There were maple trees along the perimeter of the backyard near the fence. Beyond that, the land sloped up and there were more trees and eventually another home on the road above. The leaves were green. There was a hammock. And to the right, on the beige pavers, was the little setup for outside dining. A teak table, six teak chairs, blue cushions, and an orange umbrella. There had been much discussion before buying teak furniture: Teak lasted longer. But it was expensive. The show was doing well, and the future looked secure. No future is secure. It won't wear and cause splintering. When do we even eat outside? When do we have company? Eventually, they'd decided on the teak and Rebecca made a note to have people over for dinner. Or at least eat outside some night with the kids. Which hadn't happened. And now, eight years after the teak discussion, he stepped outside. Twigs, tape, and a dollar bill in hand.

The air felt like no temperature and he wondered if that meant it was 98.6 degrees or at what temperature do you not feel the air. He'd have to look it up. But probably not 98.6. He was guessing maybe seventy-seven degrees. Whatever it was, it felt perfect. The sky was blue. The air was still. He placed the twigs and tape on the table. He pulled the dollar bill out of his pocket and put it on the table next to the twigs.

He did a 180 visual of the yard. So many different greens if you really looked. And the orange umbrella vibrated a bit where the vivid color met the blue sky. A woodpecker tap-tap-tapped somewhere on a phone pole.

He pulled off his sweatshirt, gave it a sniff out of habit. It smelled familiar, like his own scent, but more intense. The no-showering suggestion in the book was taking hold. He folded the sweatshirt and set it on the bench. His chest was exposed. The air triggered a rippling response from the hairs on his belly. The pavers felt cool to the bottoms of his bare feet.

He pulled about four inches of duct tape and tore it off and placed it sticky side up on the table. He did this three more times. The ripping sound was harsh and sharp and had a beauty of its own for a brief moment, and then there was silence. And then the birds were back, as if they'd paused to discern the sound of the duct tape being ripped.

On one of the strips he placed the twigs and then held them in place by placing another strip on top. Like a twig and tape sandwich. He repeated this with the remaining twigs and tape. He took the dollar bill and crumpled it in his hand while he said an internal mantra about material things not mattering. He couldn't quite remember the words from Ben Doss, but it was something about not being run by material things. Or was it claiming one's own power? Not being greedy? Dammit. He should have brought out his notes. He opened his hand and the crumpled dollar bill fluttered to the table.

He remembered the twigs would be a way to attract nature, to submit to nature, to claim his place and connection. Using the scotch tape, he taped a twig sandwich over each ear, pleased with himself that he hadn't duct-taped the twigs directly to his scalp. He could only imagine the big red rectangles he'd have to explain when he pulled off the tape. This had been a good solution. His pride had found a tiny little crack and gurgled up, even if it was to confirm he was smart enough to avoid damaging his scalp.

He set this aside and refocused on the twigs that were reaching up into the air. He stepped out onto the grass. It tickled his bare feet. He liked the feeling. He put his hands out a little. A breeze touched his face. He became aware of the twigs and imagined God as nature coming into him. He closed his eyes. He heard the birds, he felt the air on his eyelids. He imagined energy coming from the sky and into the twigs and believed he could feel his head heating up. At the same time, he pictured his feet on the ground, the energy coming up. His heart was warm and open. He raised his arms, turned his palms upward to the sky, feeling the receptors simultaneously taking in energy and returning energy. He was a loop of sun and wind. Like liquid electricity in his body.

"What the fuck are you doing?"

Rebecca's voice cut into his reverie.

He would have heard the sliding door if he hadn't sprayed the damn thing with WD-40 the day before. And what just ten seconds ago was making perfect sense and actually feeling kind of amazing was quickly reduced to ridiculous as he saw himself through her eyes. Her husband, barefoot and shirtless, standing in the middle of the yard, twigs taped to his head, hands raised in some beseeching manner.

He turned around.

She was standing there wearing her errands outfit—a floral dress, a white jersey hoody, and sandals.

"Hi," he said. Yeah, as if that explained anything.

His wife, the woman who had verbal skills and opinions and solutions and directions and anecdotes, seemed to be rendered speechless. He could almost see synapses firing, see her accessing any memory pod that might explain what she was seeing. He could feel her search for any reference or past experience that might explain this, but she was clearly coming up blank.

He walked across the grass to the door where she was standing and took her by the shoulders. She felt stiff. He gave her a kiss on the cheek. She pulled back a bit.

"Have you even showered?"

"Okay. Let me explain. I wasn't expecting you so soon. Don't errands take at least an hour?"

"It's been like two. And this is what you do when I'm gone? Is this a thing? Are we completely ignoring what is on your head?"

"You want me to explain?"

"Kinda." Her eyes were wide.

"Come sit down." Scott took her hand and walked her outside to the table. He took a seat. Rebecca remained standing. He waited. She pulled out a chair and sat.

"Fred gave me a book."

"Fred?"

"My agent?" Like it was *her* fault.

"I know who Fred is!"

Scott quickly explained how Fred had given him this book. Had asked him to take a look at it with an editor's eye. It wasn't all that weird or scary; he was just trying some of the suggestions in the book.

"What kind of book is this?"

"You know, like Deepak Chopra but with practical applications."

"Like you even *read* Deepak Chopra."

"We had him on the show."

109

"And we had him on *our* show. So?"

"It's a book about—it's spiritual I guess, but about nature and ego. I'm trying to be more open-minded. Try new things."

"That's all fine, but how many 'new things' involve standing in our backyard half-naked with twigs taped to your head? I mean, for someone who never wants to look foolish—"

He had forgotten about the actual twigs. He reached up and found the edge of the tape. He pulled the tape off each side of his head and held them up to Rebecca.

"Like Jesus," he joked. "Crown of thorns."

"So—you're Jesus?" She looked horrified.

"Beck . . ." He put the twigs on the table next to the crumpled dollar bill and pulled on his sweatshirt.

"Is this a religion? Are you in a cult or something?"

"It's just a book. I'm just editing a book for Fred."

"You're editing a book. A self-help book?"

She seemed to be sorting through any number of questions and finally came up with, "Why didn't you tell me you were doing this?"

He exhaled.

"I don't know. I had the week off. Fred thought it would be a stepping stone of sorts. I wanted to surprise you."

"You've surprised me. What else is in this book? Walk on coals? I mean, are you ever going to shower?"

"Yes, I'm going to shower. And I'm taking the book a chapter at a time. So far, I'm actually noticing some positive changes. I'm not done with it, but there are some things—"

"Things you don't find at church?"

He looked around the yard, searching for a way to explain it. But noticed a strange separation as he downplayed what he was doing. He was torn between telling the truth and keeping the peace.

"That's not what I mean. Church is church. This book—it's just a different way of looking at things. I'm not even saying it will be *my* way. But it's worth reading. You know I like to read all kinds of things."

"Historical things. Real things."

"Like astrology?"

"That's just for fun. I know you don't believe in it, so I don't read it to you."

"And maybe this was just something I thought I should do alone until I sorted it out, or had more information. I'm still forming an opinion."

"Scott."

He looked back at her. "What?"

"Does this book end with seventy-two virgins or something?"

"Okay, you found me out. I'm now Muslim. Surprise." He smiled and noticed his wife was warming up to his subtle humor. But he still wanted to explain, wanted to be understood. "I'd say it's more . . . intellectual. It's not like some guy dug up tablets and that was the word."

"Was that Mohammed? I wasn't a religious history major."

"I was going for Mormon. I should have thrown in the polygamy part. But you know what?" He silenced himself. "Never mind."

She wiped her hands and noticed a layer of fine, dusty dirt on the table. She looked down at the cushions on the benches. She stood. Did a quick wipe of her behind to get rid of any dirt. "I'm going in."

"So we're done talking?" he asked.

Scott was torn. He wanted to be done talking, but there was something else he needed to say. That he was intrigued by this book. That he was searching for something but had no idea what that was.

"I don't know," she said. "I'm just getting the lint roller."

"You need the roller right now?" Scott pictured her opening the junk drawer and seeing that the "Outdoor Furniture" roller was new, and that the Post-it was written in Scott's recognizable hand and not her own. He didn't think this was the time to explain the whole towel debacle.

"Just sit," he said. His voice was stern.

"This book is making you bossy."

"Yeah, look out sister." He smiled at her. Tried to make it faux-sexy. She did a quick pointless wipe of the chair cushion and sat. She crossed her legs, and he saw her foot, the leather sandal, the bright pink toenails. Her foot started the up and down air-tapping. Which either meant she was bored or mad or had better things to do.

She sat and waited. She finally said, "What? You're scaring me."

"It's just a book. I'm just reading a book."

"Wait! Is Janice in the book?"

"Yes. She's his assistant."

"Ahh. Have you met her?"

"NO."

But for the first time he thought of Janice as a real person, someone he might soon meet. He was fascinated by her for tending so silently to Ben's needs, for her seeming reverence and support of his project. He realized maybe she was in fact the woman behind the man. "I haven't even met Ben. I've just started."

"Okay. I have stuff to do. And I have notes for next week. I have emails to return and I have to start cooking and it would be nice if I had time to tape sticks to my head and wander around the backyard. Or yip yap about mystics. Or talk about why you haven't showered. All the mysteries of the twenty-first century."

"I want to tell you something."

"Oh, God. What?" Her face had the look of someone who had the world's problems to solve and a child was tugging at her sleeve, wanting something small and pointless. There was a discounting in her voice that told him she didn't really want to hear more. But he wasn't ready to be dismissed.

"Just so you know, it wasn't seventy-two virgins, in the Koran. The word was mistranslated. It should have been seventy-two raisins. Like the land of milk and honey. Martyrs were promised seventy-two raisins!"

"Really? Stop it."

"No, really. CNN did a story on it. Look it up."

She thought about this. "Maybe it was really seventy-two raison d'etres."

"There you go, being all smart with your French and stuff." He smiled at his wife and was relieved to think she'd go inside and start sautéing onions and he'd hear the familiar hum of the washing machine and the voices of his kids laughing about something. He picked up the things on the table and followed her in, watching the fabric of her sundress sway back and forth. He always loved her walk. She turned back.

"I don't like it when you keep secrets," she said.

"When have I ever?"

"Well, I wouldn't know, would I?"

"I mostly wanted to do this, have it be a success and surprise you with my literary empire."

"You can surprise me by taking a shower."

"You don't want to go all Napoleon and Josephine?"

"Not really."

"You wanna take a shower with me?"

"And now you want to have sex?"

"Kinda."

She shook her head and walked toward the kitchen.

He closed the slider with a nice whoosh and headed for the shower.

15

MAY YOU NEVER THIRST.

Scott had one application left in chapter two and then he'd go to the gym, pick up the ham, and come home and keep out of Rebecca's way until guests arrived. He'd gotten up early, made coffee, and was in his office with the pages. He still needed to write up some kind of review before calling Fred on Monday, which left this morning for him to work. There was an agitation building up, and he dropped his shoulders and tried to remember it was just his pride and ego that was pushing him to achieve some kind of fame or success. To set a deadline that didn't really matter. He wanted to trust that if he put in the work, then the outcome would sort itself out.

He pulled out the next few pages and started reading.

5) POUR WATER ANONYMOUSLY IN FRONT OF THE DOOR OF SOMEONE WHO TROUBLES YOU.

As mentioned earlier, prayer is a powerful force. Its effect has been quantitatively measured.

However, prayer is not always comfortable for those of us who have grown up in spiritual vacuums, and so we must go back even further to the source of baptism, which is water. Rather than keeping our water (wisdom/healing) to ourselves, I suggest you pour water in front of the doors of the people you have judged, mistrusted, hated, or feared. I was going to add 'misunderstood,' but if you knew you'd misunderstood, you'd no longer misunderstand. I am reminded of Heinlein's seminal work "Stranger in a Strange Land" and the beautiful prayer: "May you never thirst." In offering water, it is implied that God is not finite, as we fear. That there is an infinite source and we can be a conduit. And by becoming a conduit, we become God.

And like the "X" painted on doorways in the Old Testament story of the Passover, those we love are protected by our ritualistic actions of prayer and love.

In Poland, on a day referred to as Easter Monday, celebrants splash each other with water in a tradition known as "watering." This is believed to bring good luck and good health to others.

According to a Serbian folk custom, it is believed that pouring water behind someone before he goes on a journey or takes an exam will bring good luck.

The ideal form of an effective prayer, of course, would be a formal baptism, even if the vessel is a bucket, but this can come as a shock to the unsuspecting. If you fear someone and put their head in a bucket of water, they may not understand you are doing this with love, which is why I have adapted the action to something more seemingly benign.

You can't get arrested for pouring water.

As I write this, I am not surprised to hear Henry come by with his rolling bucket of detergent. The rolling bucket of water reminds me that it is late, that it is time to immerse myself in the wonder of sleep. I see a little liquid come under my door and I see it is a prayer from Henry.

Go spread your prayers.

Scott told Rebecca he was going to the gym and then he'd pick up the ham.

He got in his car, plugged in his phone, and did a search for Dylan's address. He'd been to Dylan's once for a Christmas party when his own kids were young and Dylan and Pinky had just had a baby. Rebecca had been a little nervous to go as she hadn't yet gone back to work, having stayed home to take care of the kids, and worried she'd have nothing to talk about except formula and the lack of sleep. But she had an over-the-top love of Christmas and had gotten excited to see all the twinkly lights lining the drive up to the house, the valet parking attendants in Santa costumes waiting to take their car. Dylan's wife Pinky was petite, with short brown hair like a French pixie. Dylan had once said he'd found the perfect wife in Pinky. To which Barry had said, "Yes, she's shorter than you." But the joke had fallen flat.

There had been no parties since that Christmas party years ago.

Scott wondered if this was just the nature of lives getting busy, show pressure, age, but there had also been talk in the office that Dylan had had a second child with Down syndrome and hadn't wanted to make that public knowledge. But this could have simply been TMZ gossip.

This morning, when Scott had read the application, he thought immediately of Dylan, but didn't make the connection about the second child, or the possibility of a second child, until he was driving. He thought about the Christmas party and his own kids. He thought about work and if he could be happy continuing on as a mono writer if the head writer position was given to Barry. Driving up the canyon, he thought about Ben Doss and pride and wondered if it really mattered where words ended up. Whether they were read on paper or electronically or spoken by the author. And he thought of the odd fact that with this new world of electronic exposure, words were rendered even more ubiquitous, as well as ephemeral. And yet they also lasted forever somewhere on the internet. Did this make his work more important or less important? Maybe he was judging himself by the wrong standards.

After his week of exposure to new and unfamiliar ideas, he was looking forward to being back at work Monday, when he could exhale into the routine that was so familiar to him. He would sit at his familiar desk, scan the news, and write as many jokes as came to him. Refine, cull, and submit.

He was even looking forward to the Trendy meeting. He often cannibalized stories Rebecca told him from her work or from the kids, and he was excited he could offer up "bottle flipping," something he hadn't heard of until he'd heard the relentless slapping of the plastic in his own home.

"What is going on?" he'd asked Rebecca the night before.

"Marcus."

"And?"

"Bottle flipping."

"And?"

Scott knew she was distracted. Her back remained turned toward the stove as she stirred something, and the one-word answers all came with a little delay, which could mean she was truly distracted or still bugged about the twig episode. He wasn't sure, so he pressed on. He'd worked with the kids on their essay prep, and liked getting back to a normal routine at home after the departure into woo-woo land.

"Bottle flipping?" He waited. If she answered with one word after a delay one more time, that would be his clue to leave the kitchen. But she set the spatula down on a plate and turned to face him.

"We had some guy on the show, Michael Senatore. It's really pretty impressive. I mean not really, but it's hard to do."

"They throw bottles around? Like juggling?"

"Marcus can show you." She yelled out past the kitchen towards his room. Marcus came into the kitchen. He was carrying a fat plastic bottle that was partially filled with a colored liquid.

"Your mom says you have a new skill."

"Yeah. Lemme show you." He pulled out the bar stool by the kitchen counter. "Ready?" Scott nodded. His son flipped the bottle in the air in an arc that allowed for nearly one rotation, and it landed straight up on the bar stool.

"Mom. Check this one out." He took the bottle and flipped it across the room and although it wobbled a little, it landed upright on the fireplace mantel.

"You're getting good."

Scott went to get the bottle. "So what are we going to do with the money?"

"What money?" His son always unknowingly played the straight man for his dad.

"The money we're going to save not sending you to college. Oh my God, I am hilarious. Okay, let me try it." Scott stood by the counter and flipped the bottle, which bounced off the edge of the counter and onto the floor.

"Nailed it," he said.

Rebecca laughed, and he knew things would be okay.

Now as he drove up the canyon, he wondered if bottle flipping would no longer be cool by Monday's Trendy meeting, but his thoughts were interrupted by another directional order from his phone, telling him where to turn next. The reality of what could be a fool's errand came to the forefront of his thoughts. He knew Dylan wasn't home, as he and his family were in Iceland doing one of his comedy/travel specials, but he was still unsettled about going up to the front door, even if no one could see him. Which was when he realized the gate would probably be closed and locked. Relieved, he figured he could pour the water in front of the gate and be on his way. But the application said to pour water in front of the door of someone who troubles you. And he wondered why Dylan troubled him. And was there no troubling person who lived closer?

His phone told him to turn right in 200 feet. On Liebe Drive. He thought Liebe was possibly German for "love" and that was fitting, considering he was supposed to have love in his heart as he poured the water. He turned right and remembered the house was at the end of the cul-de-sac. He could feel his face flush as he noticed the gate was, in fact, open. Was Dylan back? Could Scott back down the street rather than turn around in front of Dylan's gate? But as he got closer, he saw that up the drive was a truck with gardening equipment and he could hear the leaf blower's low hum somewhere behind the house.

He parked on the street, took the bottle of water from the passenger seat, got out, beeped the car lock, and pocketed his keys. He flipped the bottle into the air, high enough to arc down onto the roof of the car, which it hit and then rolled off into the dirt. "Nailed it." He picked up the bottle and walked through the open gates.

He saw no one on the driveway, so he walked up towards the front door and stopped just before the first step. Terra-cotta tiles formed the walkway which led to the front door, an area which was large enough to not only wipe one's feet but to set up a small badminton court. On the risers were Malibu tiles in blue and gold hues. The front door was magnificent. A deep mahogany that looked like it was polished daily. On both sides of the door were frosted vertical windows in a pale blue, and on either side of the frosted windows were corkscrew plants in large, glazed pots. It looked almost like an altar, and Scott thought this was a perfect spot for his Ben Doss water-pouring-and-prayer assignment.

He thought of kneeling, but he was wearing his usual Dockers, and how would he explain the dirty knees? He hadn't given a lot of thought ahead of time to what prayer he would say, but he had trusted something would come to him, God would direct him. But now his mind was blank. Think one positive or generous thing. He experienced an unspoken, shared affinity with Dylan for words, for humor, for '60s game shows, for hard work, but that didn't necessarily mean there was a friendship. Nor was there animosity. There was a passing by of the days. Work done. Often a lot of clever banter that never really felt like anything. Scott side-stepped gossip at work, not for any moral reason, but he didn't think it was very clever. He deflected uninvited conversation when walking on the lot by wearing a hat and his headphones. He looked like he was thinking hard about a joke or a concept, but he was usually listening to books on tape. The latest being an eight-million-page book on Alexander Hamilton.

Standing on Dylan's front step, he felt nothing. He wanted to at least feel a degree of generosity, of kindness. He thought of Dylan having a son, all the decisions of raising a child, the back-burner unsettled feeling of worry that for Scott had included student driver lessons, the fear of sexting, and he thought of Dylan's possible guilt about spending so much time at the office. Even if the office was on TV, talking to millions of people five nights a week.

Scott wondered if there was indeed another child and if he should alter his prayer to accommodate this possibility. Knowing he wouldn't answer that question standing in front of the door alone, Scott uncapped the water bottle, took a step up towards the door and said, "May you find peace with your family." That would cover it. He poured the water out across the first step, some of it rolling down the tile grout to where Scott stood. He stepped back and watched the water puddle near his feet. He thought of his prayer, and although he could debate what peace looked like (that it may in fact mean different things to different people), it was the best he could come up with.

He stood up and ran his hand over his scalp.

His skin was warm and slightly damp.

Then he'd been arrested.

16

THAT ISN'T A DICK JOKE.

"Sir?"

Scott opened his eyes. Cop One unlocked the handcuffs on Scott's left hand and handed him his cell phone.

"Follow me, please, sir."

The tone of voice was more like a maître d' than a cop, and Scott immediately mashed the concepts, imagining a prison-theme restaurant with cement tables, where you had to eat with one hand lightly cuffed to the chair. No knives. The bill would look like a subpoena. Going further, he segregated the restaurant by race, and even had an area for first dates, where thick plexiglass separated the would-be lovers who were forced to communicate via the handsets—

"Mr. Mullan!"

"Yes?"

"We were in fact able to verify employment and determined that no one will be pressing charges at this time."

Scott stood and felt strangely bereft. For a few minutes he'd experienced a new kind of freedom, which he found ironic considering his circumstances. He had liked sitting in a nice chair with nothing to do but look around and feel the air conditioner blow crisp molecules his way. He didn't have to accomplish anything. Decisions had been taken away, which left his mind free to wander. The feeling of freedom passed quickly as he stood and followed Cop One. He saw another man in uniform, filing something, but clearly looking at him. Scott worried the man would be distracted and a file would end up in the wrong folder and an innocent man would end up on death row. He was amused by how quickly he could take a clerical error to death and that he himself was important enough to set this tragedy in motion. And also how quickly he had gone from the freedom of experience—from what Ben Doss had described as the eternity in the moment—to the familiar, extrapolating habits of his brain. He wondered why this guy was looking at him and figured he had probably heard some conversation about Scott and his connection to *Late Enough*.

As he and Cop One walked past another office, he heard something familiar, but couldn't place it until he closed his eyes and focused on the sound. It was his own voice. Someone was clearly on the internet, most likely YouTube, Googling Scott's name. He heard his own voice from an old stand-up routine he'd done; he heard a crowd lightly chuckling. He focused on the words and heard himself say, "I'm not saying my wife is a control freak, but the other night I got up at three in the morning to use the restroom and when I came back, the bed was made." Laughter.

He had pondered with that joke whether to "use the restroom" or "pee." He thought "pee" brought too much focus on the actual act. He didn't want the audience picturing him standing there with his dick in his hand. The focus was on his wife. And "restroom" would be the word she'd use. Or the fictional wife he had created, just as he had created for himself the persona of the put-upon husband with the wife who knew everything. Well, his real wife did seem to know everything. She was a bed-making, Post-it-using, schedule-keeping dynamo.

He listened to his own muted voice and remembered that night. Every year the show writers, both mono writers and sketch writers, organized a stand-up show at the Comedy Store and it was always fun to return to the familiar. Not only the familiar feel of telling jokes in front of a crowd—feeling the rises and lulls, both riding and creating the wave—but to share the night with friends and co-workers. Something shifted in his thinking. The galvanized thoughts of "Head Writer or Die" seemed to soften and crumble and there was a whoosh of freedom not for the actuality of his realization, but by his ability to try on a new idea. He thought of the Holy Grail he'd created in his pursuit of the head writer job. It had become not a goal, but an obsession, and for the first time, he felt a surrender. It was in God's hands now and he would accept whatever came his way. Everything that had come his way so far had been, he realized, beautiful and perfect.

He felt a hand on his elbow as they neared the back door of the station, the YouTube audio receding as they walked, the air conditioning chilling his sunburned scalp. Blood was returning to his hand, and there was a stinging around his wrist. There hadn't been massive struggling, but he had let his arm hang and saw that the pressure of the handcuff had in fact depressed the skin at his wrist, leaving a red indentation. Cop One gave the slightest nod to Cop Two, who walked over and opened the door, walking in front of Scott and Cop One. He thought maybe it was double protection in case this scary, middle-aged, bald monologue writer tried to wrestle the sidearm away from Cop One.

"Officer Gonzalez will return you to your car."

And with a panic, he thought of work Monday and who it was who would be looking at him with a secret smile. He wanted to know who at work had been called. He could try and put a lid on this before it became part of the rumor mill.

"Officer, may I ask who you talked to about this?"

"Have a good day, sir."

"If you ever want to come to a show, either of you or your—"

"I think you should leave now."

* * *

Scott pulled into the strip mall parking lot on La Brea and was grateful there was no line. But then again, Halloween wasn't known as a big honey-baked ham holiday. Even so, he'd have to explain to Rebecca why he was getting to the ham store so late. She'd be nervous, wanting all her culinary ducks in a row hours before guests started arriving. He went in and stepped up to the counter, where a woman with short white hair was writing in a binder. He pulled the order slip from his wallet. His wrist was red, his scalp was hot, and he had to pee.

"Hi, can I help you?" She had a tiny, high voice.

He smiled and handed her the order slip. She put on her reading glasses.

"Oh, yes," she said, reading the slip. "Mr. Mullan. Your wife usually comes in."

Scott didn't know what to say, so he said nothing. He tried for a smile.

She took the slip and went into the back and after a minute, returned with a large box. She set it on the counter and slid a piece of paper and a pen to Scott. As he signed, he caught sight of his left wrist.

"Can you see that?"

"What, Mr. Mullan?"

"My wrist. That red mark."

She adjusted her glasses to look more closely. "Why, yes."

"I thought so." He stood there for a few seconds, thinking.

"Do you need help with the ham?"

"No. It's not that. Do you have a rubber band?"

"I'm sure I can find one." She searched around on a shelf under the counter and came up with a few choices. Scott pointed to the thickest and she handed it to him.

"Thanks." He slid the rubber band onto his wrist and picked up the ham. He was tired and distracted, and his mind was elsewhere as he walked to the door. He turned back, and in a voice that didn't feel strong, he said, "You are the Messiah of Hams and Rubber Bands."

"You too." Maybe she hadn't quite heard him.

He put the box in the trunk, got in the car, pulled out his phone, and texted: "Home soon. Ham in hand. That isn't a dick joke."

He imagined she'd either be amused or annoyed. It was always hard to know how she'd respond when in pre-party prep mode, but a few seconds later he got the text back that said, "Too bad."

And he was relieved that things were back to normal, that things were going to be okay.

17

APHRODITE CAME FROM THE TESTICLES OF URANUS.

"Where are the TBAGs?" Libby asked. She was early, and after asking how she could help, she settled into the kitchen and leaned against the counter sipping white wine as Rebecca tossed the salad. Candles were burning in various rooms, ambient music was playing at a low level in the living room, lights were dimmed, and the table was set. Something carb-related was baking and smelled great and warm.

"We can't call them that anymore," Rebecca said. She held up her left wrist and showed the rubber band she used to remind herself. "Scott's better than I am at remembering."

"No, I'm not." Scott held up his wrist and snapped his rubber band.

Libby said, "Wow, you got him to do it."

"He does a lot of the 'Libby Things.'" Rebecca glanced at Scott and down at his wrist. She put down the utensils and stepped over to Scott and took hold of his forearm.

"Sweetie, you're snapping way too hard."

"I'm new to this." He smiled. "Everything smells great. So, Libby, how's the show going?" Which led to an animated monologue from Libby, distracting Rebecca from Scott's red wrist.

The guests arrived and eventually they were all seated, saying the usual "Everything looks beautiful, everything smells so good."

Scott was trying. He was tired from his day, from the panic, from the sun, from the driving. From the police station. Even the pre-party shower had done nothing but remind him of his stinging wrist and tender scalp. Although he was friendly with everyone at the table, the mere gathering of them together put pressure on him to be clever, although this was a phantom, self-imposed pressure. The fact was, most of the conversational heavy-lifting was effortlessly handled by Libby and his old buddy, Dan, who was now a game show host. He relaxed and let them run the show, as it was what they did for a living. Also at the table was Rebecca's brother Jason and his second wife Beth. After bartending in Boston, Jason had eventually landed at the Arizona Department of Transportation. He was still a wise-ass, but now deferred to the comedic professionals.

"There they are!" Libby jumped up and gave Chloe a big hug. Turning to Marcus, she seemed to sense he was already embarrassed.

"Maybe I should just shake your hand?" She approached him with her hand out. "BUT NO WAY." She wrapped her arms around him. She was big and wore flowy kimono things that had always seemed to consume Marcus and make him nearly invisible. But for the first time, Marcus held his own and looked like a young adult and not a boy.

Libby turned back to Chloe. "So, Chloe. What are you studying?"

"I like physics. I'd like to eventually do research to find a molecular isotope for neutralizing nuclear waste."

"Great. Marcus?"

"Check it out." And he flipped his half-filled bottle up into the air and it landed on the credenza with a thump and remained upright.

"Like the guy we had on the show! Impressive."

Rebecca added, "He's also in AP classes for biology."

"Fantastic. And the latest 'Libby Thing'?" She nodded in Scott's direction. "Aside from the rubber band thing."

"We had to eat left-handed," Marcus said.

"I was pretty good at it," Chloe said.

"That's because you have greater simultaneous access to both hemispheres of your brain," Marcus said.

"Yay for me."

"But that's why 'math is hard.'"

Chloe reached for her hair, just above her ear, and flipped the bulk of thick mane from one side to the other, and with perfect vocal fry said, "Math is hard."

Everyone at the table laughed at Chloe's party trick. Libby laughed the loudest.

Scott was zoning out and heard the rise and fall of the words and expected Libby to throw to commercial at any moment.

"Why didn't I have kids? Dammit!" she was saying.

There was some yip-yap about schools and why were they going so far away, and Marcus explained it wasn't that far, and Chloe was studying the lines on her palms.

"They hate this discussion," Rebecca said. "Okay, guys, go do your homework."

It sounded as if the kids were being dismissed, but Scott knew they were happy to escape to the privacy of their rooms. Scott was wishing he could do the same.

Jason said, "So what's a 'Libby Thing'?"

Rebecca explained the Sunday night monthly ritual and Jason said, "I didn't know you were so free-spirited."

Scott looked at him and said, "Don't be fooled. Her free-spiritedness is on a very rigid schedule."

Rebecca gave him a confused look and said, "Because we talk about it on the way to church? Is that too rigid?"

"I was just making a dumb joke."

Rebecca gave Scott a faux wide-eyed look. "But *you* enjoy doing new things, right Scott?"

Despite the jab, he could feel the grass under his feet and the crown of twigs on his head.

"Yes. I love Libby Things."

Dan said, "It must be weird to have these academics for children." He turned to Libby. "Scott dropped out. I didn't even go."

"They get their smarts from Rebecca," Scott said.

"Scott, you're the smartest guy I know. I may be way more attractive, but you're the smart one."

Rebecca said, "Well, he does read a lot." She gave Scott a look, which he took to be a reference to the Ben Doss book.

Scott thought about Ben Doss. He was a professor. He had a PhD. That was impressive. Maybe Scott's life would have been different if . . . But as Ben would say, "There are many paths up the mountain." Maybe playing the "what if" game was just an exercise in futility. His father hadn't spoken to him for months after he'd learned Scott had no intention of taking over his hardware store. What if . . . What if. What deadly sin had he fallen prey to? Envy? Envy of someone else's life, in this case Ben Doss's life? He liked reading about the working relationship Ben had with Janice. Chaste. Affectionate. Supportive. Romantic only in the old-school way of a woman subservient to a man. Scott smiled, as that was something he had never experienced, and in truth, wasn't a relationship he'd want to have. He loved Rebecca and their unspoken equality, but he couldn't help trying on what it would be like to have someone like Janice, someone who tended to him. He was looking forward to getting back to the book and reading the next myth. And seeing what more Ben had to say about Janice.

"Scott?"

"What?"

"Have you heard anything about the job?" Libby took a sip of wine.

"What?"

"Head writer?"

"Nope. Still waiting to hear. But what will be, will be."

"Well, thank you, Doris Day," she said.

Rebecca looked at Scott. "So now you don't care?"

"Janice, I care."

And there was a big hole in the room where all the energy seemed to whoosh through.

"Janice?" Libby asked.

Rebecca was looking at him with that sweet face. She turned to Libby and the others. "He keeps calling me 'Janice.' It's something he's reading."

She sounded like a wife who lied for her husband and no one seemed to know what to say. Libby finished her wine, turned to Jason, and asked him how things were going with the new job in Arizona. Everyone kept eating and saying things about how good everything was. Scott could feel his energy emptying and felt overwhelmingly fatigued. He zoned out and felt he'd either fall asleep or have to contribute something to the conversation.

"Did you know that Aphrodite came from the testicles of Uranus?"

Dan said, "And there's Mr. Non Sequitur Man. I wondered how long we'd have to wait."

Libby turned to Rebecca. "I thought you'd cured him of blurting."

"Hey, I'm not the boss of him." She stood. "I usually like his blurting. I know there's no deception."

Jason's wife Beth stood, ready to help clear the table.

Libby said, "Yes. It's hard to lie about the testicles of Uranus."

Dan said, "Why would you want to?"

Rebecca took Dan's plate. "I'll get dessert. Scott, tell them about the raisins." Her voice was pointed, referring back to his adventure in the backyard the day before. She and Beth gathered a few more empty plates.

Scott felt an overwhelming relief at the mention of dessert—the evening would soon end. But he was confused by Rebecca's tone.

Dan said, "Yes. Tell us about the raisins."

"I read the Arabic was mistranslated in the Koran, and that it wasn't seventy-two virgins that were promised to the martyrs, but seventy-two raisins."

Dan said, "That decides it. I'll take heaven or hell. Not a big fan of the raisin. Although where do I go for the testicles of Uranus?"

* * *

"Scott."

They were finally in bed. Air kisses with guests had been had all around, plans made for Rebecca and Jason to have lunch, front door finally closed, dishes into the dishwasher, a check on the kids. Faces washed. Teeth brushed.

"Great dinner."

"Thanks."

"What?"

"What's with your head?"

"I'm just tired. Tired of worrying about work. You know how my thoughts ramble." He turned toward her and put his hand on her waist. "But I'm not *too* tired. It's a post-party tradition."

"No, I mean your scalp. You're sunburned. Where were you all day? At the beach with Janice?"

"I don't even *know* Janice."

"So you've said." She exhaled. And waited.

"Okay—Janice. Yes, she's the woman I have a completely separate life with, including kids and a dog. And a parakeet. Janice." He nodded to himself as if it had slipped his mind to tell Rebecca about another family. "Oh, she's very nice. We have a house in the Inland Empire. Wherever that is. I need to clean out the gutters."

"Stop making jokes! Goddammit."

He was going to have to say something about the sunburn and he couldn't lie and say it was standing in line for the ham. "I was at Dylan's."

"Begging for the job? That is so not you."

"He wasn't there."

"So. What were you doing in the sun? And isn't he in Iceland? That's why you were off work, right?"

Scott was thinking ahead and figured he could tell the truth, but just stop shy of the whole police arresting him part.

"I was saying a prayer for his family."

Rebecca sat up, energized with some kind of panic.

"What is going on with you? Is it that stupid book again? The twigs. The distractions. And now you're praying at someone's house—your *boss's*—when he isn't even home? I mean, TELL ME. Are you like a Hare Krishna or something? What is happening? I feel left behind by wherever you're going. Wherever you are. Crap, I don't know how to say it, but there's something you're not telling me and I really wish you would because you're freaking me out."

Scott didn't know what to say.

Rebecca hit him, not hard, but enough to shake something up in him.

"And I don't want to hear about Aphrodite and testicles!"

"If I had a nickel."

Silence. Scott sat up.

"It's just a book," he said.

"Then stop reading it!"

"I'm trying to be open to new things."

"Since when?"

"What does that mean?"

"I like how you are. I like how we are. I'm not all yearning for more. But obviously you are. So what is it?"

"I don't know. It isn't anything. I guess I just want to *be* something more. And I thought maybe editing might be something I'd like."

"You've never had *any* interest in editing."

Scott thought about this. He took her hand. She didn't pull away, but she was waiting. His mind was a jumble of responses. He picked one.

"I just want you to be proud of me."

He looked over to her, she no longer seemed angry. She was softening, and her hand seemed like a small miracle in his. Like he'd never held this small hand in his life.

She leaned in. "I'm *so* proud of you. Do I not let you know that? Do you not know that? If so, I'm sorry."

Which nearly crushed him. He turned and took her face in his hands and said, "Please don't ever apologize for something that's on me. I'm sorry. It's just a rough time."

He didn't want to tell her about any of this. He wanted things to return to normal. He pulled his hands away from her face, sat up a little straighter, and said, "I'm done with the book. I'll stop."

And he meant it. There was a flood of relief this would fix things, that he could bury the police memory and he didn't have to open any more mythic doors in his mind that didn't need to be opened. Or even found. This would be the best and only solution for all that had been going on.

"I mean it. I'll call Fred on Monday. It's just paper. You mean more to me than words on paper. Well, I'm saying that in a really stupid way."

"I am not forcing you to do anything. I just need you to include me. Or explain to me or something. It's like being gaslit. Gaslighted?" And there was the start of a little smile. "Which is it? See, you're always smarter than I am."

"No. I'm just more annoying about it."

"You're done with the book? I don't want you to do this for me. Okay, I do."

"I'm done with the book. For many reasons. The most *important* one being you."

"Good." She leaned over and kissed him on the cheek, lingered near him. He turned and kissed her, then pulled her closer and they made love for the first time in a long time. It was like going home, and he felt the release and the relief and the rebirth all in one climactic moment. His love was renewed, and he was ready to settle back in to his sweet life. But mostly he felt reconnected. To God. To Rebecca.

Then he immediately fell asleep.

18

HOW WAS YOUR HIATUS?

Scott parked.

He was looking forward to hearing Manny say, "How was your hiatus?" It was a running joke with them. Neither liked yip-yap, as Dylan called it, and in a rare episode of post yip-yap conversation, they had actually admitted to one another they both dreaded the first walk down the hall after a hiatus. The smiles and the "Hey, how was your hiatus?" Manny and Scott had then started their own personal routine of finding unexpected or awkward times to ask one another, "How was your hiatus?" Sometimes Manny would wait until Scott got the rare call at 12:30 p.m. to go up to Dylan's office, which meant that the mono jokes weren't good enough. Just as he was out the door and the door was closing, he'd hear Manny call out, "Hey, how was your hiatus?" Which always made Scott smile.

A few weeks before, Scott had come in late, and Manny was rehearsing a bit with stand-ins on stage. Their lunches didn't coincide, and then there was the mono notes meeting, and then the show, and then an unexpected return to his office to make some notes for the next day. He'd opened the door just as Manny was turning out the lights, his *Late Enough* backpack slung over one arm. "Hey, how was your hiatus?"

But nothing could really top Manny from a few years ago. The Sandy Hook slayings had just happened, and people were back from lunch. Office monitors were tuned to news services, computer pages were being scrolled; many employees, producers, and crew had children and there were little pockets of people on the second floor, gathered around the screens. Some people were in tears. Some appeared angry.

Scott was standing next to Trudy and Nick, the office manager, as well as Jeannie and Flora, a couple of the talent bookers. News commentators were speculating and summing up and reporting and reviewing and rehashing, and clips were played over and over. There was a silence rarely experienced in the office. Jeannie was quietly crying. Flora had a supportive hand on her back, even though she herself was wiping her nose with a tissue. Manny slid in, standing as close to Scott as possible, and leaned in, his mouth very close to Scott's ear. "How was your hiatus?" Scott had to step away so as not to guffaw in the face of such tragedy. He shook his head and walked toward his office, hoping his co-workers would assume the pain was too great; he could watch no more.

After parking, he'd called Fred, who wasn't in. After getting Jenny's usual tone of disinterest, he laid it out very clearly, almost as much for himself as for Fred. "Just tell him I'm not doing the book." There was a pause. He didn't know if Jenny was listening or texting a boyfriend or shelling pistachio nuts or judging him. After what seemed like thirty seconds, she confirmed: "Scott Mullan is not doing the book."

"Yes. Thanks, Jenny."

In his head he counted to five, and then she said, "You're welcome."

He disconnected the call. He was done. It didn't even matter now if Fred called back. Sitting in his car on the top level of the parking structure, his hands on the steering wheel, he looked out at the big, open sky. He noticed his wrist was no longer red, removed the rubber band, and put it in the glove box.

Walking onto the lot, he passed a group of people who were in line for another show on a nearby stage. He said hello to the guard, put on his headphones and walked across the lot. His mind was forming jokes about the president, and as he neared the office, he wondered if he could be the first one to hit Manny with the hiatus question, how he could weave it into something completely unrelated and come in from the side.

So it wasn't a surprise that Manny's first words to Scott were "Hey, how was your hiatus?" Although Scott thought it was lazy for Manny to not frame the question in a more outlandish situation. But maybe this *was* the outlandish situation. Scott felt a momentary jolt as he tried to see if there was anything to read behind the question. Dylan wasn't usually in when Scott and Manny showed up, but he still wondered if Dylan had heard something about the weekend and Scott's trip to the police station. Did Dylan even know? He had to know, unless Sasha kept the secret. Did the office know? Who had been called? Maybe it wasn't Sasha. Maybe it was Trudy. Should he ask Manny what he meant? It could mean nothing other than the continuation of their dumb joke.

What would Ben Doss do? He was reminded of a Christmas several years ago when he'd gotten a metal bracelet from his mother, and at first he thought it was some kind of medical alert bracelet as it had an elongated oval painted red with some kind of symbol. Where he anticipated the possibility of words reading: Manic-Depressive Introvert, he made out the words inscribed, "What would Jesus do?" It was a mantra of his mother's when he was growing up.

He'd handed the bracelet over to his wife, who looked it over.

"At least it looks new?" she offered, as if to find the good in the gift. His mother was wildly inconsistent, and there had been years where gifts were oddly wrapped in newsprint and included used cookbooks and partially burned, scented candles. Some years, nothing. Other years, a Lalique bowl.

Scott had waited for more, as his wife always had an amusing take on his mother. But she had looked at him and scrunched up her face like she felt sorry for him. So he stepped in.

"Well, it's handy. If I had a heart attack or something, the EMTs could read this and, you know, think of Jesus. Consider what he'd do. Granted, Jesus probably didn't know about epinephrine, but whatever." He made this joke for her benefit as he knew her faith was well, not less strong, but less apparent than his, and he wanted to show he could indeed joke about Jesus. But deep down, he believed that if something happened, Jesus would somehow step in if Scott hadn't yet accomplished his work on the earth. He trusted Jesus to know when it would be Scott's time.

But now he wondered, "What would Ben Doss do?" There was a lot of wisdom in what he'd read, and although he may have felt a bit of a fool when Rebecca had discovered him in the backyard with twigs taped to his head, he *had* experienced a new strength. A connection. A Ben Franklin-type lightning rod, pulling in energy from nature.

But now he was done with all that.

"Scott?"

Manny pulled him back into the room. He tracked back to the last question and heard the "How was your hiatus?" and knew it didn't require a response, so he just smiled.

"I do have a real question."

Had Manny ever asked him a real question?

"I'm all ears." Scott had a newfound wisdom about things he was happy to share and hoped this would be some kind of philosophical question. Not that he was a spiritual master or even an expert, but he was taking some chances stepping into different ways of seeing. This could be fun.

"Is it one-size-fits-all?"

"Is what one-size-fits-all?"

"Your ankle bracelet. Or is it something the police custom made for you? Does it buzz when you get too close to Dylan? Are you here on a work furlough?"

Crap.

"So, really, how was your hiatus?" he repeated.

"Who told you? Was it Sasha? I had to give them a number to call. It was all just a big misunderstanding."

Manny tapped a few things into his computer and turned the screen for Scott to see. The TMZ website. Scott was familiar with the website, as were all the writers, as it was a source for news that could be turned into a skit or bit, or in Scott's case, a monologue joke. He was familiar with the layout, and scanned the busy page for a clue of what Manny was indicating. There was a big story about Miley Cyrus, and yet another about Rob Kardashian and Blac Chyna. Wasn't that done yet? He scanned around.

"Lower left," Manny said.

Scott zeroed in on the image, which wasn't more than a tall green hedge with a play button in the center, but when he scanned the sentence under the image, his stomach lurched.

"DYLAN WRITER ARRESTED FOR URINATING ON HIS HOUSE"

Scott ran his hand over his scalp. The sunburn was subsiding.

"They need a copy editor. It sounds like I was urinating on *my* house." But the overwhelming panic was too great to linger on the poorly constructed headline. He glanced at Manny to see if he should hit play. Manny nodded. He did, and the camera moved from the street to the hedges and up to the fence with the words plastered on top of this image: "Pee-pee-peeing on Dylan's Door." And then the story, which he scanned. "Sources say . . ." "It's been reported . . ." "*The Late Enough Show* has not returned calls from TMZ . . ."

"That's not what happened!"

"You wanna talk about it?" Manny was plainly concerned. Expressions of concern or support were rarely expressed, as most problems were turned into jokes and any commiseration was filtered through sarcasm or irony. So it was perhaps more jarring to hear the sincere concern in Manny's voice. What did he think happened? Did Manny believe this was even a possibility?

His phone chirped. They wanted him upstairs.

19

I WASN'T PEEING.

The Late Enough Show didn't have an actual Human Resources Department. Nor were the staff and crew subject to the sexual harassment meeting that was mandatory on network shows. Most cable comedy shows got a pass on having to watch the forty-five-minute video that explained how a banana should remain just a banana. Most of the language in writers' meetings, and in fact many of the jokes in the monologue, were dick jokes. This allowed for a broad range of conversation and gestures, so it was pretty much anything goes.

So when Scott was called upstairs, he had to report to what was as close to Human Resources as the show had: the line producer, Trudy Polk. Scott had gotten the text from Erica, Trudy's assistant, asking him to "pop up." He "popped up," poked his head into Trudy's office, and was waved in as she finished up with something on her phone. She gave him a quick smile, as if to say this would be cleared up with a brief conversation. She finished with her phone and set it down on her desk.

"Hey," he said, ever clever.

"Hi." Well, that didn't sound good.

Trudy, single and without children, occasionally brought her three-year-old nephew to work, and although there was no nephew in sight, her couch was clearly the repository for all things "nephew." Scott looked back to Trudy, who was making a note on her pad. Her usually tidy brown braid had a few loose ends. She pulled off her glasses and looked up at him. Her eyes were the same brown as her hair. Scott hadn't really noticed that before. Brown on brown. The Messiah of Brown.

"Can you close the door?"

He did.

There was a grey folding chair, flattened and leaning against the wall next to her desk, and Scott reached for it. Trudy waved him off with an "oh please" face, like this wasn't a formal sit-down anything, just a moment, a need to mention something.

Scott straightened, feeling a bit of relief, but wondered why he had been asked to close the door. The air was starting to feel closer.

"So." She put her glasses back on and typed a quick something on her computer, then took her glasses back off and looked at him, as if it was now his turn. Trudy was never very direct, and if he didn't want to stand there all day, he knew he'd have to figure out what she was getting at and get the conversation rolling.

Out of his mouth came, "How was your hiatus?"

"Well, speaking of the hiatus, I guess you know this story is kind of all over social media. Personally, I think it's between you and Dylan, but I'm supposed to take you upstairs so you can talk to him."

"I know the way."

"I'm supposed to walk you up there. Ready?"

"What would the definition of 'ready' be in this situation?"

They walked down the hall to the stairway, and he wondered if the interns were watching him or if he was imagining it. Maybe no one else had seen the news, which was unlikely, especially for the interns, who seemed to have endless avenues of information. He followed Trudy up the stairs and down the hall of the third floor. More people looking at him? They stopped at Sasha's desk. Trudy looked at her cell phone, wrapped her sweater more tightly around her torso, tapped in a few things, and looked back at Scott.

"I gotta go," she said, and walked away, holding up her phone as proof.

Scott looked to Sasha for some kind of direction.

"Scott, sorry. He just got on a call."

"I can come back. Is there a Trendy?" Of course not, he thought. When did Trudy escort him to the Trendy meeting?

"Can you wait? He'll just be a minute."

Sasha was in her late twenties, and had started at the show as an intern. She was British and wore braces, the combo of which had worked its way into the show quite regularly. Dylan once interviewed a British comic who made his own mention of bad British teeth. The oxymoron of British orthodontia came up, which quite naturally led to Dylan mentioning his own assistant who had bad teeth. He'd called Sasha out to be the victim of his biting humor.

Sasha was a well-trained foil, and although she came off as put-upon and vaguely embarrassed to be on camera or the butt of Dylan's jokes, she had her own fan base of young men who wanted nothing more than to be a champion for a seemingly victimized member of the fairer sex. Their emails and tweets and texts, sometimes trotted out during a show, mostly had the tone of individuality, as if the ersatz rescuer believed he was the only one, and therefore should be invited to take care of her. What these young men didn't realize was that Sasha's appearances were never spontaneous and were in fact scheduled into the show. Scott contributed his own list of put-upon assistant jokes and supplied Dylan with a list of celebrated losers and even inanimate objects who would do a better job than Sasha, jokes which included her dental situation and eventual braces. Time was provided during the day to rehearse any Sasha bits so nothing would be a surprise to the crew. Or to Dylan. Dylan didn't like surprises, so all surprises were rehearsed ahead of time.

"Have a seat," Sasha said. "Do you want water?" Like he didn't work there or know where the water was. He shook his head. Her eyes shifted to the couch against the wall, making him wonder if he should sit. Unlike Trudy's couch, this one was free of paperwork, toys, pillows, blankets. It was free of all warmth whatsoever. It was a strange color. Not exactly neutral. Scott thought if it was in a catalog, it would be described as "Wet Khaki" or "Dried Earth," of maybe "Fired Writer." Okay, not funny but maybe true.

He took a seat. He tried to remember the last actual conversation of substance he'd had with Dylan. Most conversations were basically Dylan performing a comedic stream of consciousness with enough listening gaps for those in the room to interject some form of agreement or a supporting joke, before Dylan would continue with his riff of words. Occasionally, a writer would comment in a way that would invite ridicule, sometimes intentionally, sometimes inadvertently, and off Dylan would go on a genius-level three-minute rant. Scott appreciated how clever he was. It took a facile and informed mind to leap from topic to topic and then back to the beginning with a newly informed spin, a level of relatable self-deprecation and at times, a veiled crucifixion, as he gathered and wove together bits of factual minutiae that he somehow made into a ridiculous story.

Despite the current misunderstanding, Scott was experiencing a new sensation which had no place at work. A sense of compassion for Dylan. It was a sensation he'd had pouring the water, to love someone who was so laminated that nothing much seemed to get through. Maybe the water would in fact dissolve a bit of the hard shell Dylan had around him. Maybe it didn't matter what Dylan experienced—maybe the important thing was Scott's own heart, his own ability to see something in a different way.

It was unsettling for Scott to wonder these things, and he wished he could unring the bell and fall back into the comfort of the work schedule, the room of guys coming up with clever wordplay, solving structure problems in a joke, coming up with the best word to link to the next thought.

He did not normally enjoy emotional contemplation. Only in this new experience of his heart being more open to Dylan did he retroactively consider that maybe he hadn't been open in the past. He wondered if he'd had any effect on anything. Had he had an impact on his kids? Had he really helped to mold them? Was it all Rebecca?

Thinking of Rebecca, he felt the blood rush to his face as she, too, would no doubt be reading about Scott's arrest. But his actions had been taken in good faith, and again he remembered the phrase he'd spoken as he had poured the water.

"May you find peace with your family."

Scott thought again of the Down syndrome story, which if true or not, the PR machine had buried. Scott believed Dylan had two children, and yet he was only seen out and about with his older boy, Lipton. It was a taboo subject—no one spoke of it. According to the show website and press releases, Dylan had one child. Scott didn't even know the name of the second child. There was just the vestigial memory of the birth, an unplanned hiatus, and a week of reruns, and then it was business as usual. Scott tried to remember where this information had first leaked out and tracked it back to Dylan's assistant before Sasha, an officious young guy who wore sweater vests. He had told the mono writer's assistant, who had told Stan (the head writer at the time), who had told the other writers. All were sworn to secrecy. Which meant he had discussed it with Rebecca that night. Back when he told her everything. They had agreed that is was a likely explanation for the Flynn family secrecy.

"You can go in."

Scott forgot where he was and was jarred by Sasha's voice—wondered why he was sitting on the couch. It was low to the ground, as were a lot of the couches—a design move to make Dylan appear taller when others were sitting—and Scott put his middle-aged hands on his middle-aged thighs and propelled himself up. Despite the discomfort of new thoughts, of new ways of looking at Dylan with what seemed to be compassion, he felt a strange sense that it was all going to be okay and he'd only need to explain what he had been doing.

Dylan was alone. He sat at his desk, and his hands were folded like some energized school principal.

"Joke Monkey."

"Sir."

It was calming for Scott to hear this standard greeting as perhaps it meant "business as usual." He waited for Dylan to open the conversation, having learned long ago that Dylan liked to take the lead. Scott waited. Dylan just looked at him, which was feeling weird.

"I wasn't peeing." Not exactly the opening gambit he had been planning. On the walk up the stairs, he'd considered explaining the Ben Doss manuscript or maybe mention his agent Fred, which would introduce a friendly third party into the situation.

"Great," Dylan said. "I guess we're done here."

Scott smiled and started to back out.

"Sit down."

He sat down on the low blue couch. His knees were higher than his hips. His eyes did a quick survey of the fan art—framed drawings sent in by fans, all of Dylan. Although most of them were versions of

Dylan as a leprechaun, there was also Dylan as a Game of Thrones character, as a rock star on stage, as Abraham Lincoln, and a very random and obscure pencil drawing of him as Madame Butterfly.

"So." Dylan began. "I'm the first to admit that I love all the attention on me, on my 'brand' as Drippy would say, and my character is an attention whore, but I draw the line at my home and my family."

"I completely understand. And I'm sorry. It was never my intention—" It was as if he hadn't said anything.

"TMZ can say whatever the fuck they want about me, which is usually not much; I'm not that interesting. I mean, I'm fascinating to myself, of course, and maybe the interns here who are still gaga, but I'm not handsome or fucking around or driving erratically. So, imagine finding not only pictures of my home splashed across the stupid website, but one of my writers arrested."

"You can't believe everything you read."

"Is that the press release I should go with? 'Don't believe everything you read?'"

Dylan gave him the glare, which was usually the precursor to the verbal shit-storm that was building. Scott figured he had one chance to interject before this raged out of control.

"I can explain."

Dylan gave him a welcoming gesture with his right hand.

"By all means. You have the floor." As if they had all the time in the world, as if the sword of Damocles had nothing better to do than swing leisurely back and forth. Dylan leaned back, fingers interlaced behind his head as if he was about to hear a fun little anecdote.

But before Scott could inhale, Dylan leaned forward again and added, "Oh, and by the way, the mono is what—75 percent dick jokes, right? Do you realize what the next few weeks are going to be like? Can I even make a dick joke when one of my own writers was waving his dick all around my front porch?"

"You can't believe that—"

"Scott. I'm not saying *I* think that. Jesus. You're the most boring person I know."

"Thank you."

"But that is not the public perception at the moment. For now, a Dylan writer has been arrested for indecent exposure and urinating in public."

"Your house is not public. And I wasn't peeing!"

Dylan said nothing. He refolded his hands on his desk and looked at the floor. Scott knew the glazed look and that Dylan was in the middle of creating. In this case, probably a work-around for the whole dick joke problem. Most people knew to stay very still and not look at Dylan when he was "solving a problem." This was office speak for "coming up with a funny take on something." Scott looked at the wall. He pondered the ethereal nature of reputation and thought, "stinky for life." In his fantasy, he would hold a press conference and admonish internet readers to *not* believe everything they read. To be more discerning. To investigate. Ask questions. Gather the facts before crucifying. Come on, people!

"Okay." Dylan was in the room again. "This will blow over. No blow job reference intended. But I need to know what happened."

"Of course. It's embarrassing for an entirely different reason. But, I'll explain. You know Fred, right? My agent?"

"Wait, can you go back a little further?"

"Sure."

"Start when fish first became amphibious."

"Well, about 500 million years ago, fish started walking. And then more things happened."

"Thanks." Dylan pretended to stand, and sat back down.

"That was very *To Tell The Truth*." Scott said. They both loved old game shows and remembered how guests on this show would feign standing only to sit and let the "real" whatever stand. He said it without thinking. For a moment, it would be yet another thing he'd need to backtrack and explain.

"Right?" Dylan pretended to stand again and then Scott began to stand. Dylan sat and Scott stood. He put his hands out, like—ta-da.

Taking the role of host Robert Q. Lewis, Dylan adopted a nasal mid-Atlantic voice and said, "Kitty Carlisle, you had the most votes, and even though you have no actual skills or talents, you are a *delightful* guest and please know that any rumor of you going down on Orson Bean during the commercial break is totally unfounded. And now let's hear from our contestant, Scott Mullan, who was, in fact, arrested for urinating on the front door of a *very* famous and handsome Hollywood legend. Scott? Tell us your story." Dylan glared at Scott. There was no smile.

Scott wanted to laugh and kill himself at the same time. Dylan seemed more angry than Scott was expecting. He didn't know how to do the left turn from Dylan's feigned game show hostility into a forthcoming explanation of what really happened on his doorstep. But there was nowhere else to go except forward.

"Here's the thing. You know my agent, Fred?"

"Can we get past Fred or am I stuck in some horrible *Twilight Zone* loop? Fuck."

"He gave me a book to edit." How could he explain this? "You know Deepak Chopra?"

"The Deepak Chopra we've had on the show a million times?"

"Yes. Right."

"Deepak Chopra told you to pee on my house?"

"No."

Scott was baffled as to how to respond. Dylan was inviting a laugh from his audience (in this case an audience of one), but also knew it would be hard to chuckle and then forge ahead with his explanation.

He settled for a wan smile and continued.

"No. Fred gave me a book and I understood it to be along the lines of a Deepak Chopra book. I was asked to edit the book, which could be a big deal for me." Scott explained a bit about Benjamin Doss, his academic bona fides, people he'd worked with.

"I won't go into the whole thing, but Fred asked me to follow up on the applications, which is what they are called in the book, and one had to do with water—the healing and conductive properties of water. The hiatus was almost over, so I only had a few days left to accomplish these applications. I needed to pick someone I wanted to think good things about. With a prayer of sorts. You were out of town, I was nearby-ish, and figured I'd just swing by and give it a whirl. Cross it off the to-do list."

Scott paused, not used to having the floor for so long, and waited for Dylan to mock him in some way. But Dylan was simply listening. He gestured for Scott to continue.

"I had a bottle of water. I went up to your door and poured the water and said a prayer. That's all."

"How did the press come up with this peeing thing?"

"I believe that from the gardeners' vantage point, it may have looked—"

Dylan held up his hand. And Scott stopped talking.

"Okay. But still, the water thing—a little weird."

"I thought so too, but if you'd read that part of the book . . . at the time it made sense. In a poetic way."

"Like Body of Christ stuff. Water into wine."

"Maybe pouring wine would have been more effective."

"Then they'd think you had a urinary tract infection."

Scott laughed and felt a surge of relief. He noticed himself exhaling, and only then realized how he had been holding his breath. He inhaled and enjoyed the oxygen.

"What was the prayer?"

"What?"

"The prayer."

"May you find peace with your family."

"Hmmm."

Scott immediately panicked, worried his prayer would be mistaken for a tacit reference to Dylan's unacknowledged child.

"The thing is, it's not just a prayer book or something. It's etymological. There is a humor to the analysis of ideas. So far, it's a fun book. And yes, the ideas may seem a little foreign, and maybe I just had a week off with no crises in the news cycle. The point is, I'm done with the project."

Dylan held his hand up. He looked at the surface of his desk. Blinked a few times. He picked up a pencil and Scott expected him to go full Johnny Carson, say something glib, get a laugh, and toss to commercial. Scott was getting ready to stand. He was ready to be dismissed and get back to writing some jokes—get back to regular life. Dylan looked directly at his face.

"What time was this?"

"Around twelve thirty"

"Saturday around twelve thirty."

"Yes."

"Really." Dylan's brow furrowed as he licked his middle finger, reached for his old-fashioned desk calendar, and flipped a few pages back and forth.

"Around twelve thirty you say. And that is when you said a prayer?"

"Yes."

"This is really weird." Dylan seemed to be thinking back to that moment in time. He looked openly into Scott's face. Looked back at his calendar, his head slightly bowed as if in thought. Or prayer. And then a small smile. Was it one of confusion? Of confirmation? Of wonder?

Scott rarely experienced the frisson of new-agey woo-woo, but in that moment, there was a connection. He felt an opening, a doorway into new territory that might lead to a different kind of relationship with Dylan. This was also unsettling. And although Scott wouldn't call it in the least bit sexual or romantic, there was a feeling of potential love, like in the beginning of a love story—an intimacy that was forming. When things are fresh and alive and new and uncertain and the unspoken is spoken.

Scott risked speaking the unspoken. "Did you feel something?"

Dylan looked up at him. Was this the start of some kind of thoughtful smile, sort of like the Mona Lisa? Could it be described as beatific? Was that the word? From the beatitudes. Scott made a mental note to look it up.

Dylan seemed to struggle with his words. "You mean did I feel an intangible connection, or something like an open heart or an open channel?"

"Yes." Scott was strangely hopeful. "Subtle, but a connection. Did you feel something around that time?"

"FUCK NO, Ram Dass." Dylan stood up, signaling the meeting was over. "Listen, do what you want on your own time, blah blah blah. But not at my house. Obviously. And . . . although this is an embarrassment for the show, it will die down. But more than that, my family is none of your fucking concern."

"Understood."

"Not the end of the world."

Scott wanted to say, ". . . or the rainbow," but didn't think this was the time for an annoying leprechaun joke.

There was a light tap on the door and Scott wondered for the first time if there was some kind of button under Dylan's desk that alerted

Sasha he needed help extricating someone from his office. Whatever it was, Scott stood.

The door opened and Drippy came in, carrying his laptop. Drippy hated being called Drippy, which meant everyone called him Drippy. His name was originally George, but after an extended hiatus two years ago and a vacation in Italy, George believed he had found his people. He then asked to be called Giorgio. Along with his newfound (or adopted) identity came Italian fabrics, wines, and an expensive espresso maker, which was parked in the hallway. Drippy had seemed so keen on making himself the perfect Italian espresso, he misread the directions and misaligned the water reservoir, causing the machine to not only hiss in a scary way, but to drip on the floor. Trudy had to have the carpet cleaned. It was then Dylan started calling him Drippy. The name stuck. As did all Dylan's nicknames.

"Hey, Drippy."

"Dylan." He noticed Scott and said, "I can come back."

"No. You should be in the presence of this mystic."

"I'm not a mystic," Scott said.

"That's right. You're *opti*-mystic."

"Where's the pun jar?" Scott asked, taking a stab at lightening the mood.

"OMG," Dylan said, making a sour face and rubbing his belly. "Last night we went out for Indian food and I think I got some bad punjar."

"Where's the 'bad "bad punjar" jar'?" Scott said. He turned to Drippy. "I was just leaving."

Dylan didn't seem crazy about a meeting alone with Drippy. And in fact, liked having an audience for any interaction with Drippy. "Stay." He turned away from Scott.

"Okay, Drippy. What's up?"

Drippy sighed. This was a running routine between Dylan and Drippy, who was never actually upset by the sobriquet, but knew it was expected of him to correct Dylan. The faux argument was also part of the occasional appearances Drippy made on the show.

"It's Giorgio."

"Yeah, whatever."

"You know—the urban dictionary defines 'drippy' as 'pertaining to something cool or awesome.'"

Dylan stood and yelled out the door: "Sasha. Put 'drippy' on the Trendy."

Her voice yelled back. "Drippy?"

"Not this Drippy—the *word* drippy."

He sat down and turned back to this Drippy. "Speak."

"Are you sure?" Drippy glanced over to Scott and back to Dylan.

Dylan shot him a look. Scott didn't know how long this was going to be but remained standing.

Drippy took the few steps towards Dylan and placed the laptop on his desk.

"Okay," he said, pointing at the screen. "Do you want me to try and shut this down? Get legal involved?"

"What am I looking at?"

"My sources sent me this link. It's a prototype for a Halloween costume."

"If it involves a Dylan mask, we went through this last year. I'm fine with it. Any press as they say." He looked over at Scott. Smiled. "Well, maybe not *any* press. Continue."

Drippy whipped his head back to get the thick blond hair he claimed was due to his Northern Italian blood out of his eyes. He typed a few things and the hair fell back on his face.

"Here's a pic."

"What am I looking at? Oh my God."

"Right?"

"I thought we, as a people, hit a new low with the 'Naughty Kim

Kardashian Gagged and Bound in Paris' costume."

"The thing is, we can either get on board and not fight the use of the show logo, or we get the lawyers involved and this guy'll sell it with a lookalike. What do you want me to do?"

"Let's ask Scott." Dylan waved him over. Drippy stepped back, making way for Scott, who stepped in and looked at the screen. It was a picture of a young guy wearing a bald cap, a blue T-shirt with *The Late Enough Show* logo, white briefs, and a strap-on penis. The area of the penis was pixelated to avoid online pornography charges. The description shouted: "BE A NAUGHTY DYLAN WRITER FOR HALLOWEEN!"

"Oh my God." Scott looked at Dylan and then at Drippy.

"Yeah," Dylan said.

"To be fair, I was not in my underwear."

Dylan stood. "Okay. You know what I don't want? I don't want *any* of this crap right now—not that there's a *good* time to promote indecent exposure."

Drippy closed the computer and stepped back, as if Scott was somehow contaminated. Dylan stood up. Scott backed away and watched Dylan cross to the door where he shouted out to Sasha, "Get Morris on the phone."

This wasn't looking good considering Morris was Dylan's lawyer in all personal and show-related situations.

"Okay, Drippy, shut it down as best you can. We can't look like we're on board with public indecency."

"What about: it didn't happen?" Scott turned to Drippy. "I was *not* peeing."

"Okay." Drippy crossed to the door. Dylan told him to leave it open.

"Ciao." And he was gone.

"Fuck."

"Indeed."

Sasha yelled, "Morris is on."

"Scott, look, we'll sort this out, but for now let's take a little break. We have two weeks at Christmas and this should be sorted by then. If sooner, great. I'll talk to Morris about handling some kind of financial compensation, but this is about image. And—"

"I'm suspended?"

"Again, what are words? Let's just say it's a 'little break.'"

"There were no charges. Why the suspension?" Scott wasn't sure if he was upset about the injustice or the fear of a month at home without work.

"Why don't I just do an interview or whatever. Or I can talk to TMZ. It's completely easy to sort this out."

"How?"

"The book. *The Seven Mythic Doorways to Freedom*. It describes what I was doing. I was pouring water."

"Some guy tells you to pour water, and you pour water."

"Why do we drink the wine? Why do those of the Jewish faith leave an extra chair at the table? Why take the wafer? Why do we pray? What is baptism, if not a lot of water?"

"Oh. So this book is like the Bible? This *Seven Mythic Doorways to Freedom*. Doesn't look like it's giving *you* a lot of freedom."

"It has some things worth considering."

"Sounds more like the blind leading the blind."

"No. I'm not saying that at all. I said 'considering.' I was trying something to see if it was true." Scott was strangely pleased to see that he was open to something new. Some new way of seeing things. Despite the fact that his life was clearly turning to shit because of it.

But, Scott was now scrambling. "It's like everyone is believing what they read online and it isn't true. At least I'm trying to see what the truth is. I mean, it would be funny to turn it around by pointing out the irony. I'm being crucified because people believe anything they read. Whereas I was *questioning* what I was reading."

"So you're saying that reading *Dianetics* does not a Scientologist make?"

"Exactly. You're Catholic but you have an open mind. I mean, you have Deepak Chopra on with all his mystical stuff, but the segment still gets produced, right? You play a role with him and he goes along for the laughs. Why can't this be the same thing? Can't there be humor in this?"

"I gotta take this call. But you're on to something." Dylan picked up the phone. "Morris. One minute." He put him on hold and turned back to Scott.

"I'm thinking. Okay. This could be funny. Find the guy who wrote this fabulous opus and let's talk to him. We'll shut this down sooner or later, but hey, if we can have him on the show—do a bit, it could be even bigger. Do a segment with him like with Deepak, and then bring you out as the doofus writer. I mean we'll have to steer clear of dick jokes. But for now, you find . . ."

"Ben Doss."

"Ben Doss. We'll have him on as a 'fuck you' to all this perversion crap. Good?"

"Yep."

Dylan waved him out of his office. "There's your mythic doorway."

20

PRAY TO GOD, BUT KEEP ROWING.

Most of the staff and crew for the show parked as close to the ground floor of the parking structure as possible, but Scott parked on the roof. He liked the consistency of knowing where his car was every evening; he liked the guarantee of a small workout as he walked up the four flights of stairs. He liked walking to his car alone without any further "have a good night" yip-yap. But today, he noticed the beautiful sky as he approached his car, and despaired he was seeing it too late. If only he could go back, he would enjoy these simple things. There was a relief in knowing he could turn this around, but he also experienced a sadness or something akin to infidelity. He wasn't sure he wanted to turn Ben Doss into a joke.

His car was usually hot by late afternoon, but it wasn't even noon and the car was cool. The sun was in an unfamiliar place. He was alone on the roof. He started the car, turned on the radio, and heard the reporter going on about "perversion in Hollywood." Great. If this was being reported on his drive in, he'd missed it when he'd turned off the radio. He was retroactively embarrassed as he remembered his blithe and innocent walk across the lot to the offices just an hour earlier—before he was a pervert. It didn't help that he was still flushed with the fear of not only clearing his name, but the fear of possible unemployment. Of course, his actual name wasn't used as there was yet to be some formal accusation, but Scott thought that was more due to the fact that he was just a writer. A nobody.

He plugged his phone into the car charger and up on the screen came the photo of Rebecca and the kids when they were twelve, all covered with colored powders on their clothes, their faces, and in their hair. Rebecca had surprised them all by taking them to a local version of the Holi Festival of Colors held at a high school in Norwalk. The four of them ran the gauntlet of magenta, cobalt, and fuchsia powders, along with scores of other pigments. It had surprised Scott she suggested this, as it was a version of untidy chaos he was surprised she would embrace.

"Where did you hear about this?"

"Libby did it. There was some video piece. It looked great."

"Oh, so this is just a 'Libby Thing.'"

"I can't combine the two? Research and experience?"

"Of course you can. You are the queen of multitasking."

"I'm just trying to keep it all together. Kids. Work. Husband."

"Check." He made a little check mark motion with his hand.

She'd put her hand on his shoulder. "I didn't mean it that way. You know that."

"I know."

"You won't complain when I get a job at that not-yet-formed *Sex Show*. I'll be trying ALL kinds of new things out on you."

"Why wait? Have you applied?"

"See? You just want me for sex."

"Are you kidding? I was thinking this morning, 'it would be so nice to just linger in bed with my beautiful wife, keep the door closed, and fool around, but I'd much rather go to Covina and run down a street while people throw colored powder at me.'"

"Norwalk."

"I stand corrected."

He had a hard time saying no to her about anything, and so of course he'd said yes to the Festival of Colors, although he was a little concerned he'd need sunscreen on his head, and that the colored powders might stick to it and stain his scalp. He didn't express this to her, as she had enough things to solve on a daily basis. He could certainly be in charge of his own head.

They took the Prius, "his" car, as it was older and hence crappier. Scott looked around the car once everyone was settled. His kids were in the back with their earbuds already in.

"Aren't we forgetting something?" he asked.

"What?" Rebecca looked stricken. She rarely forgot anything.

"Handi Wipes."

"Do you think hundreds of people in India show up for this with Handi Wipes?"

"We aren't in India, and you aren't hundreds of people."

"They're in the trunk."

On the drive to Norwalk, she explained the genesis of the Holi ritual, which was an Indian welcome of spring. She gave a detailed background with her succinct sense of research, and Scott had expected there would be a similar detachment to the activity, but she had let loose, and let her children loose. He'd never seen her so exuberant. They had left their phones in the car, so she asked a fellow participant, his beard a melange of orange, green, and deep blue, if he could take a picture and email it to them. It was now the screensaver on his phone. How would he explain to Rebecca that his job could be on the line?

He thought of the deal he'd made with Dylan, which boiled down to "Find Ben, keep job." He'd sort this out. He picked up his phone and scrolled through his contacts. He had Fred's cell number but had been told it was only for emergencies, although at the time he didn't know what kind of emergency he'd face that would require a call to his agent.

Until now.

"Fred. Hey, it's Scott. I called you this morning, but ignore that. Call me back on my cell. I have to get in touch with Ben Doss. This is urgent. You probably can't give me his number, but at least let him know I have to talk to him. Or give him my number. Call me back either way when you get this message. Thanks."

He ended the call and put the phone on the seat next to him. Acknowledging his own city chauvinism, he assumed Ben Doss lived locally, as if everyone lived in Los Angeles. Did people really know where Deepak Chopra lived? Okay, *he* probably lived in Los Angeles. Maybe Ben Doss lived in Chicago. Or Edinburgh, or Dakar. But then again, the Ben Doss pages were given to Fred in a box. A box that had been found in La Jolla.

Scott closed his eyes, interlaced his fingers on his lap, and felt the AC lightly blowing across his face.

"Dear God, please help me find Ben Doss."

Scott said prayers at church but believed it was selfish to pray for specific things. He had been a good Catholic, and rarely asked for anything, his faith more of a fait accompli. Something that was just there for him, like gravity. But he figured he was owed one. He'd prayed for his children and he had recently prayed for Dylan and his family. Maybe he could ask for one small thing for himself. His face flushed with heat despite the AC. Was it all laid out and just a matter of going through the motions until all the cards were played and you died? Did prayer work? This was not a time for doubt.

"Dear God, please help me find Ben Doss." He thought of Dan, who used his "one time" when playing poker, even though as Scott had tried to argue, the cards were already in order and praying for a certain card was pointless. Scott considered now the concept of a "one time," but thought if there was such a thing, he'd save it for if the kids ever needed it. But that didn't mean he wasn't completely sincere about his prayer to find Ben Doss. Feeling invigorated, he drove home to solve this. As someone had once said, "Pray to God, but keep rowing."

He was going to row his ass off.

21

LITTLE BENNY HAS A FEVER.

Rebecca was at work and the kids were at school, so the home was quiet, except for the low tinkling of classical music coming from the radio in the kitchen. He teased Rebecca years ago, the first time they had left their new house, about why she had turned on the radio. Why they had spent hundreds of dollars on a security system, when all it took was a little classical music to deter an intruder?

"I can barely hear it. You think someone outside will put his ear to the window and hear that? 'Oops, next house; these people are home listening to classical music at like one decibel.'"

"You think that's why I leave the radio on?"

"Why do you?"

"I don't want anyone to come home and feel lonely if no one else is here."

"And is classical the common denominator of music? I have never heard the TBAGs listening to classical music. Or you, for that matter."

"But *you* do." He'd given her a hug, which had been warm and sweet.

But now, like Pavlov's dog, he had been trained to have only one reaction to the small tinkling of music. Loneliness. Music that meant no one was home.

He went into the kitchen and turned the radio off.

He couldn't figure out what this feeling was, beneath the low-grade panic. He didn't want to linger too long—better to just fix the problem now. The problem of finding Ben Doss. He went into the office and plugged in his cell. He didn't want to miss Fred's call after leaving two messages in one morning. As the screen came up, he felt immediate guilt seeing the text alerts from Rebecca. He'd ignored them, hoping to have more information before explaining it all to her.

He took the shoebox from the drawer. It was strange to be in the same room, in the same chair, with the same box of pages, but with a completely shifted relationship. He was no longer the upcoming book editor, reading the pages with an eye to continuity, syntax, and veracity. He was now a panicked detective, about to search for any clues as to where Ben Doss might live. (God, please let it be in Los Angeles. Or even California.) Fred would no doubt give him the answer, but he had to do something in the meantime. He'd marked the end of chapter two, the farthest he'd gotten before everything fell apart, but realized that any clues to Ben Doss would be found in the foreword or the acknowledgements. He'd initially set these aside, not wanting to be influenced by the usual fluff of author self-aggrandizement and subjective information, but now he flipped through to the beginning of the book, feeling the crisp paper and hearing the slight crunchy sounds the pages made as he straightened them. He appreciated Ben's attention to detail and his commitment to the sensual. Handling the paper, he was reminded again of the calm he had felt reading the words. Was it just last week? There was no denying he had begun to see things in a new way. A fresh new way. He heard people's voices more clearly and noticed smells; remembered acts of kindness and had a heightened attention to subtlety and nuance. He saw the Messiah in others.

Scott set the top of the box on his desk, face up, and noticed a page that must have vacuumed itself to the cardboard. He peeled the page away.

"Not since Joseph Campbell's The Power of Myth have I been so moved by a work of nonfiction. Seven Mythic Doorways goes one step further, however, in providing the reader with not only specific mythic tools for living in and understanding the world around us, but in offering insight into the author's own, very personal struggles."

- Rollo May

"A beautiful poem as well as a rich informative textbook, offering tangible and metaphoric tools on how to live in a world of seeming adversity. Doss is a strong crow walking in the mud."

- Robert Bly

"Keep your eye on this man. He delivers."

- The New York Times Book Review

"Picks up where Thomas Moore and Deepak Chopra leave off."

- The Chicago Sun

"His greatest, most personal book yet."

- Robert Graves

Scott realized he *wasn't* the first person to read this book. What was Fred thinking? Obviously these critics were more adept than he was in reading this type of book. This thought was followed by the realization that maybe this book had already been published. He felt petty, as if he just found out about a lover's previous paramours. Now he had two questions for Fred: Where can I find Ben Doss? And WTF?

He put this single sheet facedown on his desk and went to the foreword. From another drawer he pulled out the lined pad, flipped to a fresh page, picked up his pencil, and at the top he wrote: "Ben Doss Facts."

He began to read.

FOREWORD

"Whoever speaks in primordial images speaks with a thousand voices."

When I first read Jung's words, I was sitting in the Student Union at Cornell, eating a cheeseburger and listening to the thousand voices of the students around me, confused by Jung's words, by the sounds around me, by the many paths open before me. I was paralyzed by all the options, by the cacophony, by the vibrant chaotic choices, as Jung's words slipped into my subconscious, only to live there quietly until I was ready to resurrect them. When I would have a greater capacity to embrace the larger world around me.

Like many of you reading the book you now hold in your hands, I took the required courses in college and was plodding my way through Physics, Economics and English Lit without real excitement or direction, and it wasn't until I stumbled into "Mythology 101," that Jung's words began to glimmer inside me with the light of understanding. "The Myth is the public dream and the dream is the private myth."

A whole world opened up to me. Who can forget his first exposure to Sisyphus, Narcissus, and King Lycurgus who had been struck mad by a vengeful Dionysus. His name, his affliction, manifests in LSD (lysergic acid diethylamide), the effects of its madness I experienced firsthand during my freshman year. Although taking acid was not a conscious choice, I have come to embrace my experiences for the lessons they offer. Shit happens. Sometimes people put acid in your soda. And sometimes you gain incredible wisdom in unexpected ways. I was hospitalized but able to take so much from this experience.

I persevered in my pursuit and practice as a therapeutic analyst, and witnessed the overwhelming success of the use of specific ritualistic tools and three-dimensional steps in aiding my patients in accessing the mythic world that is available to each of us, for healing and release.

In Rollo May's analysis of Goethe's Faust, he finds "forever the active deed takes supremacy over other forms of human existence."

And indeed, the Bible tells us that "Faith without works is dead."

Admittedly, there are many paths up the mountain.

Serendipity and synchronicity prevailed one afternoon with my good friend and colleague, Sam Haxton. He and I had gone to Cornell together, and then went our separate ways. I followed this path and Sam went off to begin what would become his highly successful (and highly publicized) career as an FBI Profiler. Our paths had again crossed when he was taking some follow-up courses at La Jolla where I was teaching, which led to a renewed friendship and a shared interest in psychology and criminology.

He came to my office and I could feel his frustration, as he seemed to bemoan the fact that there was no way into the mind of a psychopath; that it was often as tricky as trying to grab onto a myth, to which I said: "Like trying to grab the ankle of Mercury as he runs past you, his sweat contemptuously flying into your eyes and stinging you blind." It was from this idea I made the leap from my "Mythic Doorway" theory to that of criminal profiling and gave him a few tools of my own trade, which he began successfully applying to some of his more difficult unsolved crimes. If we are all a microcosm of the macrocosm, we could access the mind of a criminal as a fractured rainbow in his own mind. A hologram of hell.

It wasn't until the publication of the book that was a result of our work: "Mythic Doorways in Criminal Profiling", that a larger public, albeit a public made up of psychologists, psychiatrists, and criminologists, was exposed to my theories, for it was here that I introduced more publicly, the concept of "Mythic Doorways" as a tangible way of linking ourselves to the illusive and elusive guides that are available to us through myth.

I should again like to mention the power of synchronicity in the development of this book, and explain my use of the seven deadly sins as a starting point for interpretation and guidance. Jung tells us that "in the language of initiation, 'seven' stands for the highest stage of illumination and would therefore be the coveted goal of all desire." And what better way, I thought in an ironic moment, to reach the highest stage of illumination than through the notion of "sin."

J.C. Cooper's "An Illustrated Encyclopedia of Traditional Symbols" tells us that "...seven...is the first number which contains both the spiritual and temporal." Which is the exact synthesis of elements that I use in the practice of "Mythic Doorways." Cooper's list of the symbolic power of "seven" goes on, of course, to include the mention of: "...seven cosmic stages, heavens, hells, major planets, ages of man, pillars of wisdom, lunar divisions of the rainbow, days of the week, wonders of the world, etc." Most beautiful to me, however is the image that "the seventh ray of the sun is the path by which man passes from this world to the next." It is my soul's journey and my wish for you.

I was on a roll with the number seven, and had been jotting down some notes to myself, listing all the references that came to me: the seven chakras of the mystic body, the seven steps of Buddha, Apollo's lyre has seven strings, Pan has seven pipes, Tom Thumb was the youngest of seven brothers, Snow White had her Seven Dwarfs.

I had left my work in progress for the evening, as I often do, "sevens" written over and over and over as I often do when I'm chewing on a new idea, to find the next morning that my assistant, Janice, had tidied up my desk and left me a gift that she had gotten from the Internet. (I don't work with a computer and therefore don't have access to the Internet, choosing instead to trust the information that Janice gathers for me.) I had, of course, been aware of bestsellers, such as Chopra's The Seven Spiritual Laws of Success, which had contributed to my interest in "seven," and I was astounded and amused to find that the list Janice had left included such titles as: The Seven Habits of Highly Successful People, The Seven Principles for Making Marriage Work, The Seven Stages of Money Maturity, Seven Weeks to Sobriety, and my personal favorite in this time of narcissistic obsession masked as spirituality: The Seven Secrets of Slim People. The list continued with Seven Weeks to Better Sex, Seven Secrets of Effective Fathers, and even Seven Promises of a Promise Keeper.

My ego wanted to dictate that I come up with something more special, more esoteric, as I didn't want to be just another in a long list of sevens, but this led to a wonderful self-examination as to why I would not want to be part of a long list. I am not a joiner by nature, but I am in the family of man, and so I set aside my ego needs and continued to listen to what was being said to me, and it seemed that "seven" was indeed going to be a part of the title.

This will be my most personal work to date. Some who know me might say that the children's book: Little Benny has a Fever, which I wrote as a bedtime story for children everywhere, was an intimate and personal work, knowing of the pain I suffered as the result of my fiancée Anna's miscarriage and her tragic death. But Little Benny was fiction. I went on to deal with my own loss in the confines of a therapist's office. Although I admit Little Benny may have been a love poem to the child we lost.

It is time to open up a bit more myself. To you. Little has been written about my own life, my own challenges, my own suffering, and perhaps it is in sharing these revelations that I can help others. Not to mention that suffering has its own beauty. Martin Luther King, Jr., on emerging from one of his early prison experiences, commented, "I think I received a new understanding of the meaning of suffering. I came away more convinced than ever before that unearned suffering is redemptive."

Although I have received much academic acclaim for my earlier work, for the analyses and interpretation of brain function in "Synaptic Misfirings in the Age of Reason" (Clancy Press, 1992), I find that I am at a juncture in my life where I am compelled to express, more personally, perhaps, the specific ways that I have applied to my own life, the "Theory of Mythic Doorways."

I may have science and psychology degrees, I may stand before twenty-seven eager students who want to hear my theories about myth and man, but I, too, am a student, humbled at the feet of God.

But words are not always enough.

I need to take hold of the knife.

This book is for you.

This book is for me.

I am the walrus.

And my deepest hope is that it proves as healing in its reading and application as it has been for me in its writing. If after reading this book, you can do more than just set it down and ponder, or if you are able to indeed pick up the knife, then I know I have been successful in what I have strived to do.

God bless.

Benjamin Doss
La Jolla, California

Scott looked at the notes on the pad:

Cornell

Economics

Sam Haxton—FBI Profiler—Mythic Doorways and Criminal Profiling

Now that was a title of contradictions, Scott thought. And his mind jumped to some strange couplings that could be book titles: *Children's Stories and House Paint. Infectious Diseases and Jewelry. Meditation and Lapel Pins.* He was looking out the window. He forced himself to return to his list.

Assistant Janice

He thought about Rebecca and how she'd seemed to be jealous of Janice—a woman he'd never met. Janice. Scott was curious about her as well. He circled her name on the pad and figured that would be a good place to start if he hadn't heard back from Fred.

Little Benny Has a Fever

Fiancée Anna—dead

1992 Synaptic Misfirings in the Age of Reason.

Scott made the note: *gap in writing?*

La Jolla

He was most encouraged to have the clue of La Jolla. That was less than two hours away. Maybe he wouldn't have to fly across the country to find this guy. He checked his phone. Nothing from Fred. He kept reading, although he could feel the excitement building that there were very good clues available to him. He picked up the next crinkly page.

ACKNOWLEDGMENTS

Any endeavor, no matter how small or grand (acknowledging of course that "small" and "grand" are merely subjective judgments), is not undertaken alone, although quite often in solitude. We are all, whether admittedly or not, part of the great cosmic quantum soup, and stirring it up a little in one part of the bowl affects change in all other parts. I have not stirred alone, nor have I been unaffected by the stirrings of others, and I should like to thank those who have contributed to this journey, and share a bit of the manifested light that I have witnessed emanating from those around me. A light that pours from friends, from strangers, as well as the light that shines from within me. A light that sometimes burns, sometimes blinds, but always illuminates.

As always, I must thank Dr. Andrew Schemion, who has gone before me and continues to be a sword cutting through the underbrush of the subconscious. Our work together at the La Jolla Institute of Psychology and Myth has been oftentimes enlightening and occasionally all-consuming as I cut away at my own psyche, using what I have learned from him to help guide my knife.

Love and gratitude always to my fiancée, Anna. Even after her tragic death, her heart lives on in mine. And she may live on in the hearts of those who have garnered retroactive insight, as she was the focus of my first book in the mythic series "Mortius and the Dragoness", which utilized this lesser known Greco-Gaelic reconciliation myth in the examination of the power shifts in a relationship. Anna helped me see more tangibly how Jung's Anima and Animus, when filtered through the lens of partnership, are often at odds as a result of being unreconciled within ourselves. Through her, I developed the tools of myth which can be employed to open the heart, to let the blood flow again by cutting a path through the heavy, unbending cement of stasis, opening the floodgates upon which we can ride back to wholeness. As Mortius learned, the pieces of the fractured self are not brought together by the slaying of another. It is not the other's blood that brings us wholeness. Just as the blood of the dragon was not a glue to bind together the lost and scattered parts of Mortius's own psyche. No matter how much blood is spilled. Eventually he had to open up his own heart.

To my assistant, Janice Van Vliet, who has provided endless hours of help and information, who has corrected my grammar, kept me on track for my appointments, often typed my notes into something legible, and has gently guided me, smoothing out the rough edges with her grace and femininity. ("Femininity" is not used as a derogative in this case. More on this in the chapter on Lust and Women.) She is always there. As consistent as a fine Swiss clock. "Tick tick tick." I tap my fingernails on the table, our inside joke when I'm feeling pressured by her schedule, while at the same time, needing her schedule. These words to her are merely an unsatisfying trickle of the love and gratitude that I have.

I must give a nod and a smile to the guys down at Tully's, who tacitly reminded me that I am, in fact, just "one of the guys." I have never before acknowledged them but want to say now that they made me feel welcome even when I sat silently for hours at the end of the bar with my head buried in papers as I worked out my latest theory. I was the nerd in the corner, listening to his muse as well as to the ballgame. I heard your voices, teasing me and sending me a soda when I smiled.

And to you, my reader, who plays a part in my own healing by simply picking up this book, which acknowledges that I have in fact lived. That I live. That we live. I am here. And this is my gift to you.

Scott's list was more encouraging:

Dr. Andrew Schemion

La Jolla Institute of Psychology and Myth

JANICE VAN VLIET !!!! He had a last name which he circled.

Tullys. Bar? Restaurant?

He Googled Tully's and found a Yelp listing for a Tully's in La Jolla, but it had been shuttered years before. Another Tully's had popped up further south, and it looked like the typical dusty, lots-of-crap-on-the-walls place where men didn't order girly drinks. Scott pictured Ben at the end of the bar, writing, thinking.

He made a note of the phone number but then thought it through. Calling a bar and saying, "I'm looking for Ben Doss," would probably not get him very far, especially at three in the afternoon. Maybe it would. He'd save it for later. He continued with his list.

The most promising leads, short of hearing from Fred: Sam Haxton, Dr. Andrew Schemion, Janice Van Vliet. He wasn't sure if he should start with the La Jolla Institute of Psychology and Myth or try getting through to a real person at the FBI. Maybe search Facebook for Janice Van Vliet? He was beginning to feel an unusual paralysis. Writing jokes was easy compared to this. There was a topic, all the related elements, a script jump attaching it to something unrelated. Or aligned in an irreverent way. He liked having a topic and sub-topics that branched out from the center. Like the head of an octopus was the joke and you just played with all the tentacles for a while. Now it seemed that these leads, these tentacles, would all probably lead to the head: Ben Doss. Maybe it didn't matter where he started.

He remembered something about rocking in the book. He flipped back to the applications in chapter one and found it. "If confused about what to do, rock back and forth." He closed his eyes and started rocking, first leaning forward a little, then back. It became more fluid, but he got distracted by the image of himself at the wailing wall, bald head and curly payot. He thought of Orthodox Jews. Did they use curlers? Or a curling iron? Or was electricity allowed? Or was that the Amish? He thought of his mother's pin curls she'd sometimes wear all day, the days she stayed in her robe.

He banished thoughts of his mother and pictured his body in the chair and continued his gentle rocking, emptying his mind, but still hoping to know where to go next in his search. He stopped when he heard the rumbling of the garage door opening. He listened as he looked with soft focus at the pages on his desk, waiting for the door from the garage to open. Every sound seemed heightened until his focus settled the pounding of his heart. This was not going to be pretty.

22

WHAT'S THE DEAL WITH JENNY?

"Scott?" Rebecca was calling from the kitchen.

Crap. He put his cell in his pants pocket and went into the kitchen. Rebecca was in her gym clothes, which told him she hadn't been to work. He glanced at the calendar on the refrigerator.

"You're off this week?"

"I told you, I'm taking the kids early to San Diego. But WAIT!! What is going on at work?"

"What do you mean?"

"I heard on the radio one of your writers was arrested for indecent exposure at Dylan's house. Tell me! Is the show canceled for the week? WHO WAS IT? Manny?"

He could tell she really wanted an answer as she hadn't even started taking things out of the cotton shopping bags. She was just standing there looking at him.

Buying time, he said, "So, you went to the gym?"

"COME ON. Give me the gossip!"

"The writer was detained. Not arrested. Released after a couple of hours. And it wasn't indecent exposure."

"WHO?"

"Yeah." He looked down at the floor. And then looked up, trying on his gentlest face. "That would be me."

Her mind seemed to cycle through any number of things, but she ended up saying, "That's why my brother was calling? Texts from Libby with nothing but question marks? It was you?"

Scott's cell chirped. He pulled the phone from his pocket and looked at the screen. There were several text messages and voice mail alerts. "Blowing up" as they'd discussed in a past Trendy. He'd been ignoring all the texts and calls, but this was Fred. Finally.

"I have to take this. And it isn't true. And I'm still getting paid. And I was wearing pants." He knew this wasn't exactly the big explanation demanded in this situation, but first things first. He turned away from Rebecca and went into his office.

"Hi, Jenny. It's Scott. Scott Mullan." One. Two. Three . . . He didn't have the patience for this.

"Hold, please." Fred picked up. The silver balls were already clicking.

"What the fuck?" he said.

"What the fuck what?"

"You lost your job?"

"NO." Scott realized he'd started pacing. As he turned to the doorway in his small journey around the room, he saw Rebecca standing there, holding the laptop with an incredulous look on her face and mouthing to him, "What the fuck?"

"Fred, give me Ben Doss's number."

"I don't have his number."

"You gave me the manuscript!"

"Stop coming at me, bud. I didn't write the fucking book."

"You gave it to me. Who gave it to you?"

Fred yelled something to someone—probably Jenny. "Tell him I'm on my way."

Back to Scott he said, "Lunch meeting with Reggie Watts. You know him?"

"Yes. And I don't care. Just give me a name or a number."

"Jenny gave it to me."

"Jenny? Your assistant Jenny?"

"I can only tell you what she told me. *Storage Wars* got a dud and scuttled the episode or something. Some friend gave her the book and she gave it to me, in case there was anything there."

"You didn't even read it?" Scott could feel his face was getting hot.

"I glanced at it. The guy seems smart. Maybe a little wordy. Thought you'd have fun with the to-dos."

"You thought I'd have fun with the *to-dos*? Was this all just a big joke?" The silver balls continued clicking. "It's in your best interest, Fred, to give me what you can here. I just want a name. I don't work, I don't get paid. I don't get paid, you don't get paid."

"Thanks for the lesson in entertainment economy."

"Listen, I'm hanging by a thread here. I find Ben, we're good."

He heard Fred scoot his chair back and yell out the door, "Jen, pick up and give Scott some info." There was a clicking as Jenny picked up.

"Hello, how can I help you?" He pictured slow blinking, the black eyeliner.

"Hey, Jenny. I need more info on the Ben Doss thing. On the book you gave Fred?" Waiting. Waiting.

"My friend Fatima gave me the book. Her boyfriend worked on the show and all I can tell you is that I think the storage place was in La Jolla."

"Does she know who rented the storage unit? Was it Ben himself?"

Scott sat back down at his desk, pen in hand. Hoping to get more info. Pick up pen and info will come. But nothing was being said.

"I really don't know."

"Can I call your friend? Fatima? Can you give me her number?" He waited.

"Hold on while I text her. I don't like to give out numbers without asking."

"Understood." Was he reading "frosty" into this interaction? Paranoia was setting in, and he didn't like the feeling. He liked moving around the planet anonymously, with no reason for people to look at him in any particular way. And now he was perceiving judgment and exclusion everywhere. He could hear typing and then nothing. She came back on and explained she'd get back to him as soon as she heard back.

"Thank you. Can you put me back on with Fred?"

He waited and Fred picked up.

"Get what you needed?"

"Getting there. But let me ask you something." He started whispering. "What's the deal with Jenny? Does she hate me or something?"

"I don't know. Why?"

"It's like she's taking time to decide whether to give me the time of day. Sometimes on the phone it's Christiane Amanpour on a three-second satellite delay. When I come in, it's like she's staring at me so much I'm not sure she even sees me."

"You know she's deaf, right?"

"What? No. Deaf? You mean, really deaf?"

"Yeah, didn't you notice that big fucking eyesore on her desk? One of those Caption Call things. Cost a fortune."

"Deaf." Scott tried to remember the clunky computer on her desk. "For how long?"

"Rest of her life, I'm guessing."

"Ha ha."

"See, I can be funny too. Is that it?"

"I guess."

And Fred hung up.

Scott looked out the window at the backyard. He cranked the window open and did nothing but listen. There were birds. He thought about Jenny. Jenny not hearing birds. He said a little prayer for Jenny. He looked at his pad and saw he'd nervously written a few words that were probably useless. La Jolla. Props. Fatima. Boyfriend. He checked his notes from the book and saw the name Haxton. FBI. That would be his next call while he waited to hear from Fatima. But first he'd have to explain to Rebecca.

He walked back into the kitchen. She was taking condiments out of the fridge.

"Beck."

"Yes?"

"You want to talk?"

"Nope."

She walked over to the dry erase calendar and with her index finger, she erased 'San Diego' from Wednesday and moved it to Tuesday. Tomorrow. She kept her back to him as she prepared sandwiches. He was pretty sure there wasn't going to be a sandwich for him, but when she pulled a knife from the wall mount and cut the sandwiches, he wondered if she would notice it had been sharpened. Despite wanting to take credit for yet another Ben Doss accomplishment, he knew better than to say anything.

He went back to his office. If nothing else, maybe he'd end up a famous detective. Yeah, or a fireman or a ballerina or the president of the United States.

23

THE MYTH IS GREATER THAN THE MAN?

Hunger brought him out of exile, and after eating some string cheese, he wandered into the living room. It looked as it always did. Fluffy white couch and chair (purchased after the kids had grown past the throwing up stage). Dark wood coffee table with a big art book no one looked at. The pillows were in their correct positions, and they had the little crease at the top that Rebecca had seen years before on some HGTV show. One time he'd come home early and pushed the pillows in their center, eliminating the crease. She'd come in and looked confused and then hatcheted the top of each pillow to reinstate the crease. Pretending he was sneaking around, he followed her and poofed them out behind her until she finally turned around. "Stop torturing me!" They'd laughed and he'd stopped, but Marcus had picked up the baton of messing with her pillows.

There was a smell of lavender somewhere. Rebecca and the kids were sitting at the dining room table, papers in little piles, Post-its of different colors. Laptops. Phones.

"Hey." Rebecca sounded cheery, with her usual sing-song

welcome, but he noticed she didn't look up.

"What are you doing?"

"Looking at the campus schedules."

No one said anything more until Chloe turned to look at him. She had lost some of her teenage confidence. "Are you still going with us?" Why did she sound defeated?

He looked at Rebecca for translation.

"Don't look at me."

"Okay. Dad, what's the deal with this?" Marcus was looking at his computer screen.

"With what?" Scott was encouraged to be included in some kind of problem-solving. His son turned the computer around to the TMZ link. Where there had once been a generic shot of hedges, there was now a shot of Scott, taken from his show ID.

"I'm taking care of it."

"I'm getting shit at school for having a perv for a dad."

"'Shit?'"

Rebecca chimed in before Scott could go into his speech about language and being smart and all. "Guys. You know the phrase— contempt prior to investigation? Well, that's what is happening to your dad. Someone is weaving a whole story based on very little evidence. It's a story. An entertaining story. That's it."

Marcus looked up through his hair, which was hanging in his face. "The myth is greater than the man?"

"Exactly," she said. Scott wanted to say "thanks a lot" but figured this may not be the time for joking around.

"Did you lose your job?" Chloe was sounding smaller by the minute. "Can we still afford to go to college?"

"Chloe—we're *fine*. And yes, I'll be back to work very soon."

Rebecca shot him a look. "Good to know," she said in a way that was maybe comforting to the kids, but sounded like a dig to Scott.

"And I'll be meeting up with you in San Diego."

"Okay."

"But, Dad." Marcus put his hair behind his ears. "What really happened?"

Scott remembered the books Rebecca had made him read to the kids when they were little, instructing parents to answer only the questions that were asked. She said they'd tell you how much they wanted to know. In the face of having no clue how to explain this, he thought following this suggestion would help carry him through.

"I was at Dylan's house."

"Why?"

"I was on a spiritual mission."

"What were you doing?"

"I was saying a prayer for him and his family."

Marcus didn't say anything, and Scott hoped that would be it.

"Why?" Marcus was clearly on a mission for more information.

"It was something I read in a book."

"The Bible?"

"Not the Bible."

"Why did he need you to pray for him? He's famous."

"You're right. He probably doesn't need my prayers."

"But why were you arrested?"

"I wasn't arrested. I was detained."

"Why were you detained?" Marcus said, hitting "detained" like Scott was splitting hairs.

"The gardeners called the police. And since Dylan wasn't home and I was pouring water on his front step, it may have looked like I was urinating. They were doing their job. They should have called the police. But it was a misunderstanding."

Marcus had taken in all the information he seemed to need.

"Chloe? Do you have any questions?"

She shook her head.

"Well," he said, clapping his hands. "The good news is Dylan wants to do a bit about this—I might be on the show—so I have to go to work and set that all up."

"So you *are* going to work?" Chloe asked.

"Research."

Rebecca put fresh Post-its on the brochures and paperwork, neatened them, and put them in a folder. She checked her phone and said, "Okay, kids. Time to go."

"Where are you going?"

"San Diego."

"Now? I thought you said you were going tomorrow."

"We'd rather be settled and have a fresh start in the morning."

Scott felt the sting of his obvious exclusion from the "we" category.

"You want me to go?" He didn't really mean this as he had to fix things, find Ben, work something up for Dylan, but it came out of his mouth and Rebecca assured him they'd be fine. It was important he do whatever he needed to do to sort things out.

He had been dismissed.

He went into the office and listened to them moving about, to the rolling suitcases, to the "Bye, Dads" yelled from the kitchen, to the garage door opening and then closing.

24

YEAH, LET'S BLAME FATIMA.

He'd never experienced this kind of separation from Rebecca, from his kids. Although if he still had faith, if he still trusted God, they'd be fine. Over the years there had been little misunderstandings, but they were usually just one-on-one and smoothed out over time with a conversation and humor. But now it seemed like some unspoken three-against-one, causing him an anxiety and uncertainty that could only be solved by playing detective with Ben Doss. He asked God for help, but the connection was flickering, like an electronic glitch where words rippled into nothing and then reconstituted with an even more tentative connection. He asked to find Jesus in his heart. He felt betrayed and confused, but by whom? It couldn't be God, so Fred? Ben? Dylan? Rebecca? Fatima? This last name made him laugh in spite of the situation. Like, "Yeah, let's blame Fatima." Faith was easy when things were going smoothly. He didn't know what to reach for. There was a craving, but what did he need? Water? To rock back and forth? Sex? To go outside? To be with his family? He tried to pull energy up from the floor into his feet and thought of Ben Doss. He felt no connection. No comfort.

He figured he was blocked from all that usually comforted him by the degree of anxieties he wasn't used to: work anxiety, reputation anxiety, family anxiety. He could write a joke, but could he defend himself? Could he fix this?

He looked out the window as the sun was coming up. He thought about when Rebecca had found out she was pregnant. They were living in a little apartment in Van Nuys, about twenty miles from Hollywood, with floral wallpaper and temperamental appliances. He'd come home late from a stand-up gig and Rebecca was still up, which concerned him.

"Are you okay?"

"I'm fine. Oh, Scott. I'm fine. Couldn't sleep."

Once he knew there was nothing wrong he went back to reviewing the set, words he could have changed, jokes that worked. He was looking at the floor in that glazed way, used to having quiet time when he came in late.

"How was it?" she asked.

"Sounded good from out there." This was his standard answer, harkening back to her brother Jason's standard line to the comics.

She laughed. "Hey, can you take a look at the oven? The little light isn't coming on."

"The pilot?" That would be a concern.

"No, the little light thing."

"It's one in the morning. You need to look at something?"

There was a pause, and she said, "No. It can wait until tomorrow. You're tired. I'm tired."

She knew him well. After he'd washed his face and changed into boxers and a sweatshirt, he'd said, "So the light in the oven, right?" He'd prove his father wrong. He'd show his new wife how handy he was with tools, even though he wasn't sure where the tools were, or if he should even be reaching into the oven.

He pulled on his socks and went into the small kitchen.

She joined him.

"Remember, I'm usually the guy who thinks popping the hood on a car will magically fix it."

"Take a look."

"This could take a while, in case you have better things to do."

"I like watching you work."

Crap. He pushed up his sleeves in a faux-manly way and pulled open the oven door. "This looks yummy."

"What is it?" she said, still a few steps behind him.

"There's a dinner roll in the oven."

"It's not a dinner roll."

"What is it?"

"It's a bun."

"Okay, there's a *bun* in the oven," he said.

"Oh."

"OH!"

He turned to her with wide eyes.

She'd shrugged like, "Yeah." He'd kissed her and then put his arms around her and they stood in the kitchen, both with their own thoughts, but also joined with this news. The bun had turned out to be two buns, and they made ends meet until Scott had gotten the job with Dylan.

Alone in his office, he pulled the remote from the Velcro, pushed the power button, and the talking heads filled the room with words. But when he remembered he wasn't writing jokes, he clicked off the TV. There were unread pages left in the box. He glanced at the title of the next chapter: "The Sin of Lust and the Power of Women." He reached into the box to see how much was left, figuring with his uncanny logic that if this book was about the seven deadly sins, and he'd read two, then there were five remaining. He was brilliant. He laughed out loud, even though he was alone in the room. He was tempted to continue reading, but had to be a detective now, not an editor. He had more immediate issues.

He was, however, curious how this book ended, if the last page was a summation of all that had come before, so he lifted the pages and pulled out the bottom page. He found only one word written. It was written in orange crayon, the letters about three inches high. One word: "HI." For a brief moment, he thought the "HI" was directed at him in some way. Knowing this was illogical (if not crazy), his mind jumped instead to wondering if Ben was somewhere panicking, like Hemingway. His only copy left at the train station, his opus lost forever. He slipped the last page back into the box, but then saw there was another page with an orange crayon "HI." And another. The last twenty pages were nothing but "HIs." Maybe it was an exercise he would have gotten to. Or maybe they were reminders to the reader about the application of saying "HI."

But—odd.

He gathered all the "HI" pages and paper-clipped them together. Set them aside.

He checked his phone. Nothing from *Storage Wars* Fatima.

There was no point in Googling "Ben Doss," as he'd done this when he first started working on the book. He had struck out, and assumed if this was a first book, there wouldn't be much on Ben Doss. Now he was confused.

He'd look for Sam Haxton, the profiler Ben had collaborated with.

He Googled FBI and clicked on the website. After scrolling through several menus, he typed Sam's name in the search bar. Although there were no "Sam Haxtons," he was provided with pages of entries of crimes committed by people named Sam. This was a rabbit hole he would have loved going down, but now was not the time.

He checked his notes to confirm that Sam and Ben had worked on a book together. Maybe Sam Haxton had retired to work with Ben. Scott Googled "Retired FBI Agents" and, holy grail of grails, there was an actual "Retired FBI Agents" website. He scanned the first page and then clicked around, trying to discern if the site was on the level. He found several of the links offered private investigating, protection, consultant services, etc. Scott entered "Sam Haxton" into the search box and there was the guy, looking all rugged and weathered and mustachioed and single. Lone wolf type. Scott clicked on the "contact" button and composed a short email, trying to keep his words light. He didn't want to lead with "Hi! I was arrested for indecent exposure and have to find Ben Doss." He instead mentioned he was a writer on *The Late Enough Show*, hoping Sam had heard of the show or he'd Google it and find that Scott was a real—i.e. not crazy—person. He explained he was editing *Seven Mythic Doorways*, which was written by an associate of Sam's—Ben Doss. He'd hit a snag and was having a hard time locating Mr. Doss for confirmation on some factual questions. Since Mr. Haxton had co-authored another book with Mr. Doss, could he please respond with a contact for Ben Doss? Understanding this may not be appropriate, could he pass along Scott's info and ask Mr. Doss to please get in touch with him? This was a matter of some urgency. He left his information, hit send, and put a check mark next to Sam Haxton's name.

Next up: Janice Van Vliet.

He pocketed his phone and, carrying his computer, went into the kitchen. The classical music was playing at a low level, which he took as a good sign. Even with his rift with Rebecca, some things remained. Or maybe it was just habit at this point. In the fridge was a sandwich in a baggie she had left for him. He reached for the Post-it, expecting some play on words about the ingredients, but the Post-it only contained one word: "Scott." No silly happy face. No added P.S.

He turned off the radio.

While waiting to hear from Sam, Scott took his computer and sandwich and went out into the backyard. The air was crisp. Scott was beginning to understand how native Californians were always boasting about their ability to discern the slightest weather shifts indicating the change of seasons. When he'd first moved to L.A., he and his co-workers—who had also come from the Midwest or East Coast—made fun of the natives, doing impressions of them when fall came. The day would be no different than the day before, and one of the transplanted writers would shiver and say, "Ooh, can you feel it?"

To Scott, fall meant leaves changing, and sweaters, and getting out the extra blankets. Here, it seemed, the seasons were marked by the change of beverage choices at Starbucks. Or by turning the thermostat down to offset the Duraflame logs burning in the mid-century fireplace. But now, he was happy to feel a little chill on his face and scalp.

Why didn't he and his family ever have dinner out here?

He sat down, ate his sandwich, and looked at the screen of his computer, which was still open to the "Retired FBI" site. This guy, Sam Haxton, looked old. Scott figured he must have retired not long after working with Ben on their book.

He checked his email. Nothing. From anyone. Except a group email from work, asking if anyone knew of a notary public on the lot. Someone sent out this kind of email every few months, and it always brought the same random non sequitur from Manny. "Your mother." It was stupid and silly and its repetition after any notary inquiries became its own dumb joke. Seeing Manny's response to the group email created an unfamiliar longing for when things were normal.

After eating, he went back to his office and sat down.

He Googled La Jolla Institute of Psychology, scrolled around, and eventually found his way to the various departments. He scrolled down to Psychology. He scrolled through the names but there was still no Ben Doss. He tried the "Adjunct Faculty" page, but no Ben Doss. He clicked on just about everything and eventually landed on an undergraduate faculty page where he searched for Janice Van Vliet. Nothing. He tried Facebook, entering Janice's name, but there were too many faces to choose from. He passed on the ones who looked to be younger than eighteen. He scrolled through with no idea who he was looking for, but remembered that Ben had mentioned she was pregnant. He figured what—twenties? Thirties?

He heard a ping and saw there was an email from Sam Haxton. His heart sped up. He clicked on it and read.

"Mr. Mullan. You were trying to reach Sam Haxton," it began.

Crap. Another dead end.

He continued reading. "Unfortunately, Sam died last year. I continue to monitor his email to make sure there is no outstanding business, however I am unable to give you any information about Benjamin Doss, as Sam's files are with the FBI. But I do remember Sam talking about Janice Van Vliet and I was able to find her information in his book. I'm sorry I can't be of further help. Good luck." The email was signed Dorothy Haxton. She'd included the email address: janice35@aol.com AOL? Who used AOL anymore? He said a little prayer to steady himself and sent Janice an email, explaining that he worked on *The Late Enough Show* and he wanted to talk to her about Ben Doss for a book he was editing. He didn't like dangling the show name, but at this point he'd use anything to get in the door.

He hit send and, like a child, expected his needs to be met RIGHT NOW. It had been three seconds—why hadn't she responded?

And where was Fatima?

He was frustrated with himself, with everything. He stood up. And sat down. He pulled the remaining pages out of the box.

CHAPTER THREE

The Sin of Lust and the Power of Women

"Woman draws us upward."

- Goethe

"The animus draws his sword of power and anima ejects her poison of illusion and seduction."

- Carl Jung

"Women: You can't live with them, you can't shoot them."

- Steve Wright

INTRODUCTION

Perhaps I should have begun this book with the chapter on women as they are the starting point for us all, aren't they? Everywhere you look, there they are. Women, women everywhere, and not a drop to drink. At least that is how it sometimes feels until we address the childhood longings that were caused by abandonment or abuse, until we admit that some needs will never be met and that we can only walk free among women when we realize the gifts that they offer are gifts of the present, and not entitlements from the past.

Janice came in this morning, said nothing, as if guilty about her recent absence, and I caught myself silently staring at her belly. Still flat but what was beginning to stir under the skin? What cells were duplicating at a dizzying rate, over and over and over, faster and faster?

Out of control beneath her polyester pants. The enigma that is a woman. That Janice can pad in here, so quiet, do her little duties, hardly moving the air, or so she thinks, but I can see the air move around her and I can almost hear the cells duplicating.

I won't take my vitamins.

I hate Janice for bringing them to me. Sometimes I hate her. But don't worry. This is where we can separate the sane from the insane. I know the difference. I can feel the rage, but the insane person acts on the rage, whereas I have the courage to express it here. I shall not hold my hand over her mouth to keep out the sound of the cells as they duplicate. I shall not see the blood on her pastel pantsuit, the blood on the polyester as the creature inside her gets bigger and claws its way out from the inside. Claws its way out of her belly. With the help of my knife.

Here's what I know about women.

They lie.

It is in their nature.

Let me tell you what I know about Janice. I've been told her husband works in the food services department at the University, but I happen to know that her husband works for the CIA. Janice hasn't told me this, but I've had long communications with Sam at the FBI as well as with Dr. Schemion, and although he won't confirm this, I can tell by the look in his eyes that my suppositions are correct.

And this is why I opened with my poetic visions of her pregnancy.

Of course I do not hear the cells duplicating.

I am not crazy.

But there are times, and perhaps this is what helps me be so good at my job, that I have a heightened sensitivity to things around me. Not just material things, but the subtleties, the sound of intaking breath, the mathematical patterns in certain music, the stretching sound of the time passing in certain circumstances.

And if I cast my mind back to the first sounds that I heard coming from a woman, I hear the sounds of my own mother. I won't go as far as to say that I remember the sound while I was in the womb, or that I can recreate for you here the experience of my birth. I can't. Nor would I as this is not the forum for my own analysis. But like the hypervigilance of which Alice Miller speaks, I became attuned at an early age to the subtleties of her pleasures and her displeasures.

Thinking about her now, I feel my heart race a bit, and my hand clenches. Like I'm reaching for a knife that doesn't exist.

Scott turned to the next page. This is where the typing stopped and the orange crayon writing began—the same orange crayon that had been used for all the "HIs" at the end. Maybe this is where he would find the application he was expecting, the one that brings us back to our childhoods.

I'm writing with a crayon.

This we'll discuss in later tips for accessing anger, but at the moment, I'll say that this is often a way to write the truth, to access the gods who are so much closer to us when we are young. Therefore using crayons for this work is a re-creation of a certain childhood vulnerability that enables me to access truer thoughts, feelings, reactions, guidance.

Of course I must ask Janice for paper more often, and she has to deal with the bureaucracy of work orders. "Why is Dr. Doss going through so much paper?" I imagine they ask her. I can't write that small with a crayon.

Even though I benefit from whatever research Janice does for me on the computer, there is the threat of government interference. I wonder if I'm contributing to the government tracking her. I feel she is in danger and I am to blame. Or I will be to blame if something bad happens to her. Fortunately, I have a brain and the ability to discern, as well as information as to the esoteric coding system that is employed by government agencies so that they may recognize one another electronically. Janice is not aware of this, but I see certain markings in the papers she brings me, much like watermarks, only molecularly altered so as to be recognized only by those in the know. I have developed a special way of seeing. I am trained. And they don't know it! This is where my silence manifests as a form of love, for I needn't upset her with truths that are not within the scope of her daily concerns. I am being told that the baby inside her will kill her. And I have to help. I'll find a way. I am a clever boy. I can tell when the voices are the truth and when they come from the government.

For now, I need only find a new crayon as this one is becoming dull. It is making me mad because it reminds me of the secret notes my cousins passed written in lemon juice that only they could read.

I am back. There are no secret watermarks on this paper. I have to be careful everywhere.

Breathe. I'm cold.

As I ponder the influences of women on the souls of men, I am propelled of course, finally, to the recounting of an obscure but appropriate myth that will help many of us understand. Understand the differences between men and women. Chemical differences, emotional differences. And don't get me wrong, this is not to say that there are inequities in value. But understanding the differences is the only thing that can lead to a healing between the sexes. It is not our lust that has gotten us into trouble, but everyone's fucking misinterpretation of said lust. I have to deal with the rage of patients who have come to me with both the physical and emotional wounds of having their genitalia taped down because their mothers couldn't handle the truth. Their mothers claiming that the phallus was the devil's nightstick, coming to beat you about the head and face when you weren't looking. Tape it down. See it is controlled. One patient who continues to tape down his genitalia, he's almost thirty, is trying to block—as best as he can—the sexual energy that builds up. That so threatened his mother. But not just the sexual energy builds, but the rage at having inherited a legacy of shame about something that should be so natural. This patient, we'll call him Whisper, believes that he has inherited satanic seed. But I don't want to talk about him.

In searching out a myth for this chapter on women and lust, I of course had a wealth of choices, from "Amor and Psyche" to modern-day myths as represented in contemporary entertainment, such as "Pretty Woman." But I'm sure these are all well-known to the reader and so I have chosen the little known early Greek myth: Haldolius and the Lithius Beetle. This myth was so ahead of its time in terms of the understanding of the hormonal changes that take place in adolescence, and it beautifully interprets the delicate balance between respect and rape. And that it was a woman who in fact gave Haldolius his feelings of lust.

Scott felt troubled and uncertain. This guy seemed angry. Scott's hopes of having a breezy comic healer on the show were diminishing. This was no Deepak Chopra with his faux-spiritual, quasi-psychological, light-hearted teasing about Dylan's sexual insecurities. For a moment Scott wondered if Janice was some kind of tease, or was stirring up some kind of anger in Ben Doss. Man, Rebecca would slap him for even thinking a woman had provoked this guy, that for some reason the anger was incited.

He heard a ping and jumped, as if she could see him through the electronics, that she was witnessing his thoughts about women and lust.

But it wasn't from Rebecca.

It was from Janice.

25

WAS HE WILLING TO DRIVE TO TEMECULA?

He opened her email and read her short response. She said she'd confirmed who he was with the contact number he'd provided, and that she'd be happy to meet but he'd have to come to her. Was he willing to drive to Temecula? He responded yes, and she said she was free the next day. Would that work for him? He wanted to say he could drive there now, but didn't want to seem like a nut. He said yes, but added if she wanted to connect him directly with Ben, she wouldn't have to be the middle person. She said it would be better for them to meet. Scott figured she was still protecting Ben, which he appreciated. Or maybe he'd join them. Scott thanked her for her quick response. He gave her his cell number, she gave him her address, and they ended their exchange.

He put a check mark next to *Janice Van Vliet.* Progress. He was excited. And yet still disturbed. It was getting late. The house was quiet. He wasn't tired, and there was no one to talk to and more pages to read.

THE MYTH
Haldolius and the Lithius Beetle

Haldolius was born of the gods and placed in a home with a mother and a father. He had an earth-shattering yell that the villagers used to move mountains. This vocal manifesto has been often reinterpreted, even as recently as in the character of Vavoom, from the Felix the Cat cartoons.

Haldolius was used for his voice, but after the mountains were moved, the village had no more need for his loud sounds, sounds that made the stone walls shake. But he had been born and raised to scream and continued to do so, long after the village had lost its need for him.

The villagers implored his father, Thorazcus, to silence his son. Thorazcus, who was a distant cousin of Zeus on his mother's side but had fallen from grace and no longer had tenure in the university of the gods, was willing to do anything to ensure his reinstatement. And so Thorazcus abandoned his son to the care of his mother, Natasia, who mixed up magic potions to keep him from screaming. She left candles burning in a circle around him when he slept.

Once every summer, the goddess Testicia visited the town and injected the young males with desire, and this summer it was Haldolius's turn to be injected, but his mother turned Testicia away from the door, saying that it was her job and she was going to do everything in her power to protect her son from his maleness. She had special powers and saw that Testicia was really a sidekick of Satan, and she wouldn't let her in the door. Haldolius wanted to be normal, wanted to be injected by Testicia, but his mother threatened to cut out his tongue and so he kept his mouth shut.

Testicia climbed in an open window and was able to make Haldolius a man.

Which enraged Natasia.

One dark night, Haldolius woke to find his mother pouring hot wax over his genitalia, and in a half sleep, his hands went around her throat until her tongue was as black as her widow weeds.

He bandaged his burned and misshapen genitalia and limped away from the house, finding refuge in a garbage box.

And he began to scream.

And he screamed. And screamed.

The villagers were afraid that the walls would come down and so they threw a net over him and put him on a raft made of paper, which was called Prescriptus. The more common derivation of the use of paper was the papyrus, well-known in Egyptian mythology.

And it was on this paper boat of Prescriptus that Haldolius floated so far downstream that no one could hear his cries.

He was placed with relatives but eventually landed on an island, and a beautiful woman came to him and placed her hand on his genitalia. He was spellbound and when she offered him a magic pill made of the dung of a Lithius beetle, which would ease his need to scream, he took the pill because he had never before seen such a beautiful woman. He wanted to know her name, but she said to him: "You don't need my name now, but I shall tell you and you will forget it until you need to know it. My name is Cloaepia." She sent him back up the river but his boat needed to be repapered and he stopped and met the Goat Man.

The Goat Man set about to repaper his raft and told him that this woman was one of the many wives of Thorazcus, and that she did not really care about his pain, she merely wanted to win the favor of Thorazcus by doing his bidding.

Haldolius could not speak, as the magic dung pill killed not only his screams but his words and he looked at the Goat Man for answers. The Goat Man said that the boat had taken less time to be repapered, and that he could listen for fifty-five minutes and that he would understand everything that needed to be said, even if Haldolius didn't use words. And so Haldolius sat with the Goat Man and felt a little—

Scott's phone trilled. It was a number he didn't recognize. "Hello?"

"Hey, is this Scott?" A woman's voice.

"Yes."

"Hey, it's Fatima. Jenny asked me to call you? About the book?"

"Yes. Yes. Great. What can you tell me?"

"I can't tell you much. I mean, it was my boyfriend who worked on the show."

"Did he know who rented the storage unit?"

"No. They don't get that info. I remember because I asked. I mean, sometimes he'd show me pics of the weird stuff and this one had, you know, the usual old furniture and cleaning stuff, but there were also weird paintings. And that box with the book."

"So, your boyfriend gave you the book?"

"Yes. And I gave it to Jenny."

"When was this?"

"I couldn't tell you exactly."

"Well, like weeks? Or months."

"A few months?"

"Okay." Scott hoped Ben Doss hadn't moved away or put his stuff in storage while he was on some soul-searching mission, like on a mountaintop with questionable cell service.

"I appreciate the call back."

"No worries."

Well, he was worried. He thanked her and ended the call.

He set his phone down and went into the kitchen. Walked to the slider. Back to the kitchen. He was cold, and his brain had too much information. He needed a beer. He pulled a beer from the fridge and then put it back. Although he wasn't looking forward to a night alone, he was relieved Rebecca wasn't here to see him falling apart.

26

ARE YOU HAVING AN AFFAIR?

Janice Van Vliet lived in Temecula, which was east of Camp Pendleton. He'd been driving for close to two hours, 134 to 210 to 15. If he'd been on the East Coast he would have passed through three or four states by now. He was grateful for the map app which left him free to let his mind wander as he followed the directions given by the electronic voice. He imagined Janice on maternity leave, either really pregnant or a baby on her hip. A silky golden retriever at her feet.

He wondered if he'd hear from Rebecca, although he'd have to pull over if he did. They'd instituted a no-texting-while-driving rule. At first, when they were trying to come up with a way to promote unity and conversation with their kids, they tried a no-phone-in-the-car rule. On their way to a birthday party for one of Rebecca's co-workers, they'd gathered up the family phones, and Rebecca put them in the glove box. This new system fell apart when Rebecca needed to check the directions. They'd both been waiting to hear Siri say, "In 200 feet, turn left on . . ."

She'd opened the glove box. "I'm just going to check the directions."

"No. We'll figure it out. You showed me the map and I have a rough idea where I'm going."

He looked in the rearview mirror for recognition and credit that this was a universal ban and not just another "brutal parental decision that applies only to the kids." But there was no reaction.

"Kids?"

He adjusted the mirror to find they were both holding imaginary phones, tapping their empty palms, swiping and scrolling imaginary pages. Chloe was having a hard time keeping a straight face.

Scott tapped Rebecca's thigh and nodded to the back. She turned to look over her shoulder.

"Chloe, can you get directions?"

"Whatever." She faux-sighed and flipped three quarters of her hair from one side to the other as if she was a petulant teen and the hair flip was the demarcation line between personal stuff and stuff for mom.

"It's 17899 Greenleaf," Rebecca told her.

Scott glanced in the mirror as Chloe pretended to tap something into her imaginary phone. She did a silly impression of the electronic map voice. "In 200 feet, turn right on Whitsett."

He did.

"In 200 feet, turn right on Riverside."

He did.

"You are arriving at your location on the right."

Scott pulled over at an empty lot, which was strewn with trash and enclosed by a cyclone fence tagged with a "no trespassing" sign.

"Great." He made a big show of unbuckling his seatbelt. He looked in the rearview mirror, saw Marcus looking out the window through his curtain of dark hair.

"Looks like we're early," Marcus said as he went back to his own imaginary phone.

Now he was in the car alone, his phone in the passenger seat electronically relaying directions. He'd had a twinge of guilt entering the Temecula address when in another life he would have been heading down to join his family in San Diego.

His phone rang. Rebecca.

When he'd connected with Janice, he'd sent a text to Rebecca saying that he'd found Janice, was close to finding Ben, and he'd be there Wednesday afternoon at the latest. She was calling him back.

"It's Wednesday. Where are you?"

"Are you mad?"

There was a silence, and he didn't know if he was supposed to fill in the gap or change his plan or wait for her to answer. He was expecting to feel better, anticipating that she'd tell him in her sweet and solid voice, "No, you need to work this out." But nothing came. He waited. Mostly because he had no idea what to say.

"Yes. I'm mad," she said.

"Why? I didn't plan to be suspended. I'm doing everything I can to fix this."

"That's not why I'm mad."

Again he waited.

The electronic voice interrupted the call. "Stay in the left lane and take the exit on the right. Then continue left."

"What?" he said, glancing at the phone.

"What?"

"Sorry, weird directions."

"Here's the thing," she said. Oh, good. A thing. "If you had said, 'Beck, I'm going to start a strange little project that will take me away from you and the kids. But it's important to me and I'll be back. I'll explain when I can,' I could have handled it. You've always talked to me about stuff. But I don't know what is going on with you. I can pick up the slack with the kids, but that's not it. I don't know what's going on. I don't know what you're looking for. I don't even know where you are."

"I'm on the 15 South."

"Ever clever."

"I'm sorry. I don't know. I don't know." Why did he feel this stinging around his eyes. "I've opened some door and I can't close it."

"I've fallen and I can't get up.

"So it's okay for *you* to joke?"

"I have no idea *what* to do. I don't know what's going on."

"I don't either."

"How can that be true?"

There was another long pause. A huge forty-five-wheeler or something screeched as it slowed down next to him.

"Are you having an affair?" she asked.

"What?"

"With Janice."

"Can we talk about this in person?"

"Is that a *yes*!?" She sounded panicked.

"NO!"

Scott wanted to assure her, but it would take an hour to explain this strange path that had led him to Janice. All he could do was again say, "NO!"

His phone pinged. There was a text from Manny.

"I gotta go. It's work."

"You got your job back?"

"No. It's Manny. I don't know if it's anything."

"Oh."

"So—"

Silence.

"Rebecca. There is *nothing* going on with anyone. Just Ben. And I don't even know where he is."

"Okay. So . . . Bye, I guess."

"Bye. I'll see you guys soon."

But she'd already ended the call.

27

I THOUGHT YOU'D BE YOUNGER.

Traffic had slowed to about ten miles per hour. Scott imagined a world where traffic slowed to five miles per hour then stopped, and then everyone put their cars into reverse and blindly drove backwards. Siri took him off the freeway. He glanced at the phone and was tempted to pull over to read the text, but it was from Manny and it could wait. If it was good news about work, it would be Fred calling. After a few turns and a drive down a long residential street, he parked across from the beige building where Janice lived. He rolled his head around to release some of the driving tension, tapped his phone, and read the text from Manny.

"WTF. Sasha not saying. You gone? For good? Dude. WTF?"

WTF indeed. He had nothing to report. Using his index finger, he responded, "How was your hiatus?"

"You fucker. What's going on?"

"I can't say much yet, but I'm working it out."

"You coming back?"

"God willing."

Scott looked at the apartment building across the street and experienced a surge of adrenaline. He was going to meet Janice. Finally. Based on nothing but extrapolation from Ben's book and her email address, and the fact that she was pregnant or had been recently, he pictured a woman in her late twenties, which made him oddly uncomfortable. Except for a few of the talent handlers at work and the interns, who didn't count, he was rarely around younger women, and although he had no interest in anything outside his marriage, there was something illicit and potentially dangerous about walking up the path to a young woman's apartment. A woman who had something he needed. And to be honest, a woman who intrigued him.

He walked across a small courtyard, passing a dry fountain, a few weeds sprouting around its base. At the back of the courtyard, he found apartment 105. He had a moment of picturing himself pouring water in front of her door. Would it help his mission? He stopped, a little surprised his thoughts so quickly accessed the Ben Doss book. He quickly said a prayer to God to help him accept whatever the outcome may be, and was comforted by his conscious return to the familiar. He wanted to return to his life before Ben Doss, where he didn't feel unfaithful to God, or unfaithful to Rebecca.

He knocked as nicely as he could.

A woman answered the door. She was tall and thin and maybe seventy years old. Janice's mother? Grandmother? Someone helping with the baby? Her hair was short and white and done in some style that swirled away from her face. She had bright blue eyes. She seemed wary, but not unfriendly.

"Hello." A small smile. But her eyes were still.

"Hi. I'm here to see Janice. My name's Scott Mullan."

She put out her hand. "Hi. I'm Janice. Come in."

"What? You're Janice?"

"Yes."

"I thought you'd be younger," he blurted. Crap.

"Oh?"

"Sorry." He could feel his face flush. "I just assumed . . ."

"Please. Come in."

Okay, reset. What? Clearly not in her twenties and certainly hadn't been pregnant recently. Wrong Janice? He tried to keep his face neutral and was glad she had turned her back as she led him into the living room. She was wearing grey pants and a white blouse. The room was beige and tidy, the only bright color in the room being a big vase of pink and magenta flowers. The fragrance was almost narcotic.

"What are those?" he asked, indicating the flowers. He needed to fill the air with words while his brain made sense of things.

"Stargazer lilies. My husband used to buy them for me. Every once in a while I splurge." She indicated the couch and said, "Please, have a seat. May I get you something? Water? Coffee? You drove quite a ways."

"Water, if you don't mind. Thank you." He needed time for his face to cool down. She went into the kitchen, which had an old-fashioned pass-through that opened to the living room. He was able to see her moving about, but kept his eyes on the flowers as he sorted out his questions. He heard the sound of a cabinet opening and closing. Then the refrigerator door opening and closing. Water was poured.

She returned and set a cut crystal glass on a coaster, which featured a faded photo of Niagara Falls.

"How can I help you?" She settled into the beige chair across from the couch and out of nowhere, a Siamese cat jumped up onto her lap.

"This is Sadie," she said.

"Hi Sadie." Sadie was also shades of beige, and he could feel his brain search for a new riff on all the colors of beige. He wanted to text Rebecca, "Siamese beige."

"Oh! You're not allergic are you? I should have mentioned the kitty."

"I'm fine." He didn't know where to start. "Thanks again for agreeing to meet with me."

"I have to admit I Googled you. I'm sorry, but I don't watch your show."

"It's not my show. I'm just a writer. It's on pretty late. Not that you don't stay up late. I mean, I don't know what you do. Or did. You know."

She said, "Please. Tell me how I can help you. You mentioned the book?"

"Yes. Thank you. I was given a stack of pages—they look like originals—for *Seven Mythic Doorways to Freedom*, and was hoping to edit them, but now my boss would like to do a segment on the show about Ben and the book."

Janice was listening but didn't offer anything up. Scott continued.

"Googling Ben didn't get me anywhere, and I tried finding you in the UC directories. Eventually, I emailed Sam Haxton and his wife led me to you."

"Sam Haxton. He was a good man. Kind. I never met his wife, but she and I have stayed in contact over the years when questions come up."

Scott felt like he was on a date with someone who was really making him work for information. He drank some water, then saw something pass over her face.

"Am I on a fool's errand?" he asked. "I just realized, maybe the book was already published."

"No. It was never published, I can assure you."

"Are you still working for him?"

"I'm sorry?"

"Ben mentions you in the book. Quite a bit. Are you still his assistant?"

"I wasn't his assistant."

"I didn't mean to offend you. Maybe you have a higher job title. I'm just going with what I gathered from my reading. Maybe Ben's a big ole chauvinist." This didn't seem to charm her in any way.

"What is it you *do* know?" she asked.

"Okay, from what I read, he's a professor at the La Jolla Institute, he's written a bunch of books, this was a self-help book, and you helped with the research. He seems smart. I like his use of words, but I have to admit I don't know many PhDs or professors, let alone much about mythology. That's probably why I was willing to try the applications. Did you try any of the applications?"

"Did I try the applications? No." She seemed cautious in her answer.

"I was doing them for research, due diligence, and ran into some trouble, although it's possible I wasn't doing them right."

"Can you tell me again how the book came to be in your possession? Sorry, I sound like I'm interrogating you."

Scott explained about his agent and the storage place and box of pages.

"If there's a problem, if he wants it back, of course I understand. I brought it with me, just in case."

"Would you like something stronger than water?"

"Water's fine."

"I'm going to get a little sherry."

Sadie the cat seemed in sync with her thoughts and was off her lap before Janice even started to rise. Maybe Sadie knew what the word "sherry" meant. Maybe Janice was a nutty, old, alcoholic cat lady. She stood, paused to get her balance, and went back into the kitchen. He couldn't hear anything except a loud noise in his head. Sadie jumped up on the couch, and Scott found himself petting her without even realizing it. Janice came back into the room, took a sip of sherry, sat down, and placed her glass on another Niagara Falls coaster.

She cleared her throat. "I had no idea those pages still existed. Maybe Henry had them."

"The janitor. Henry." Scott was encouraged. Another reference that sounded strangely like an old friend. Maybe Henry could be on the show as well.

"Yes. Henry." Janice focused her eyes somewhere in the middle of the room. "He had a special connection with Ben. Whenever Henry came in, Ben would write 'HI' on a piece of paper and hand it to Henry. He saved them?"

"In the bottom of the box were several sheets of paper that said 'HI.' In orange crayon."

"Yep. That was Ben. So Henry had the pages. I wondered what had happened to them." Janice was remembering something.

"Would you like to read them?" he asked.

"LORD no!" She seemed to blush as she returned her attention to Scott. "I lived it. I typed a lot of the pages for him."

"Ahh." Some pieces fell into place. "That's why the typing changes. It's like that 'footprints in the sand' thing. When he couldn't walk any more, you carried him."

"Something like that."

"Before I take up any more of your time, do you think Ben would agree to being on the show?"

"How far did you get into the book?"

"The first two chapters—well, I'd just started the third. I'll read the rest, but I need to find Ben."

"Scott. Ben's dead."

"What? What?" Scott felt the bottom drop out of any hope he was holding onto.

"I'm sorry, Scott, but you've been misled."

"My agent didn't tell me anything, he just gave me the pages. I'm sure he had no idea if Ben was alive or dead."

"I mean, you've been misled by Ben." She took a sip of her sherry. Sadie jumped off the couch and back onto Janice's lap. "He wasn't a professor. But I believe he desperately wanted to be."

"What was he? Was he at La Jolla?"

"The psychiatric hospital? Yes."

"And you? You said you weren't his assistant." Scott realized this could be Ben's mother. And he tried to roll back their conversation for facts. But facts were very slippery at the moment.

"I was his nurse."

"Nurse?"

"He called me his assistant." Janice smiled, but looked sad.

"What did he do at the hospital?"

"He was a patient."

28

THEY WEREN'T VITAMINS.

Scott tried to access anything he may have read about the crazy genius of writers. All he could come up with was Virginia Woolf walking into the water with rocks in her pockets. And Hemingway was nuts. He wondered if Ben had been committed for one of those seventy-two-hour holds or had chosen to get help. "How long was he in the hospital?"

"Ten years."

Scott looked at Sadie, but his eyes couldn't focus. He couldn't get this to fit.

"But you helped him with his book? Or is it even true that you did research for him?"

"Yes. I helped him."

"Why was he in the hospital?"

Janice seemed to cast back in her memories. "He was at a community college in La Jolla and started hearing voices and eventually there were complaints. He brought a knife to class. He claimed he could heal people. Someone died."

"I'm an idiot," Scott said. He was shaking his head.

"No. I know what he wrote. He was very smart. He could be

charming. Until the end when we realized too late that he wasn't taking his meds."

"His meds?"

"When he first came to us he was catatonic. In fact, I never did hear him speak. But I helped with his meds, and with the ECT and the cold baths."

"ECT?"

"I'm sorry. Electroconvulsive therapy. Shock therapy as it used to be called. He wrote about it, right?"

"Yes, but I thought he was administering these things. Not receiving them. I thought he was in the hospital helping with patients. God."

Scott reached for his water and centered the glass on the coaster. Moved the coaster so it was further away from the edge of the table. "Was he dangerous?"

"Not until the end. He fought to keep his demons inside."

"How did he die?"

"He killed himself."

"How?"

"With a knife."

Okay, not the funniest segment for the show. Scott took a sip of his water. He looked out the window, went over more "facts," and looked back at Janice.

"So, he didn't write a book with Sam Haxton?" Scott already knew the answer and shook his head.

"The FBI got involved when they began receiving threatening letters. This is not uncommon for paranoid schizophrenics, to accuse the authorities or demand to be heard. They often claim to hear voices, government voices, directing them through the television or through the paper. That sort of thing."

"What about his fiancée?"

"His fiancée?"

"Anna."

"Right. She was a teacher's assistant at La Jolla. According to the file, he believed she was pregnant and he needed to 'free her of the baby.' She avoided him for the most part, but according to the report, he went to her apartment and was screaming at her through her door. He had a knife. She felt she had no choice but to escape through the window. And she fell."

"Defenestrated," he blurted, thinking of the "Libby Thing" word night.

"Pardon me?"

"And she died?"

"Yes."

Scott inhaled deeply and let out a sigh. "Was he crazy? I'm sorry—that's not the right word."

"He was very damaged. He'd been dosed by some students and that most likely pushed him to a psychotic break. Although it would have happened eventually."

"Dosed?"

"LSD. Between the letters and knives and then Anna's death, the FBI became involved. That's when I met Sam Haxton. He came in to interview Ben, and then conducted follow-ups with me."

"Give me a minute here."

Scott looked down at his hands but was sorting through his own last several days. He'd taped his mouth shut. He'd stopped showering. He said Messiah things to strangers. He'd taped twigs to his head and stood shirtless in his backyard feeling energy from the earth. He'd poured water on his boss's doorstep. He could feel his face flush as his hands got colder. His brain jumped all over. The manuscript, the crayon-written pages at the end, the rocking, the small room. How had he not seen this? It was a hospital, not a university. He felt like not only a fool, but a spurned lover. How could he believe words written years ago by a delusional person who was long dead? Ben's words had opened him up to things he'd never considered.

"So, rocking isn't a way to God?" Scott said with a laugh, hoping to mask his embarrassment.

"I have no idea about God," Janice said. But her voice was kind. "Rocking can be a symptom of catatonia. Or it can be a form of self-comforting in many who are mentally agitated."

"Wait. So you didn't give him 'vitamins,' did you?"

"They weren't vitamins," Janice said.

Scott's embarrassment was quickly overshadowed by his next thought: There was no way to tell Dylan any of this.

"How did you help him with his book?" he asked.

"There was a manual typewriter in the group room. This was a good outlet for some of the patients to get their words out. While Ben was on his meds, he showed signs of improvement and used writing as a way of communicating. I wanted to help him. He became agitated after the news of the Columbine massacre and destroyed the typewriter. I took over the typing for him as it seemed to calm him and make him feel heard. Even if it was only his typed words."

"The Columbine massacre?

"Yes."

"But that was years ago—what—1999?"

"Yes."

"And when did he kill himself?"

"Later that year. 1999."

Scott's brain froze up; 1999 wasn't anything he could connect to. He had to track it back from the present to make sense of it. He did the math.

"He's been dead for almost twenty years?" Scott stood up. "May I have some more water? I can get it."

"I'll get it." Sadie jumped to the floor as Janice stood.

"What in the book was real?" he asked.

"Define 'real.'"

She took his glass and went into the kitchen. He heard the refrigerator door open and close. She returned and handed him the water. The glass was cool in his fingers.

"You can see the horrors played out in his words," she said. "But that's what mythology has always been, right? Using stories to make sense of things that either frighten, threaten, or confuse us."

"How did he find the myths to match his story? His horrors? Or did you find them for him?"

"Find them? No one found them. He wrote them."

"He wrote the myths?"

"Yes."

"So those aren't even real?"

"They're as real as you like. Remember all myths began somewhere. People have been believing stories for thousands of years. Often, they're based on nothing more than someone's words written on paper. Ben just created his own to make sense of things."

Scott was silent. He was scanning his memory for the myths as he tried to understand Ben's story when he realized Janice had stopped talking and was looking at him.

"What? I'm sorry. I'm just trying to make sense of this."

Sadie wandered back from somewhere and jumped onto the couch and took her place on the back, not far from Scott.

Janice looked at Sadie and then returned her gaze to Scott. "I'm acting like a therapist. Because I don't know how to be with you. About this. I don't have all the answers. And I'm acting as if I did. I'm sorry."

There seemed to be no more to the story, so Scott asked, "Are you still a nurse?"

Janice smiled. "I'm a psychologist." She finished her sherry. "But back then, when I was Ben's nurse, it was my daughter who was pregnant. I took some time off to help her right after the birth, but Ben heard what he heard when Dr. Schemion explained my absence to him. In his mind, I was pregnant. You have to understand. Not only was Ben predisposed physiologically to schizophrenia, but the disease can be genetic, and all indications were that his mother was also affected."

She shifted in her seat. "After Ben's death, I decided to go back to school. I guess I needed to make sense of my own story." She laughed a little. "Or maybe I just needed to distract myself with other peoples' stories and get out of La Jolla."

And Scott connected another couple of pieces. "Janice. La Jolla."

"Yes?"

"La Jolla. La Jolla was Lahoya. The tribe. The Lahoyas."

"He was clever."

"Wow."

Scott felt he should leave, that he'd outstayed his welcome. Or maybe he was just going to implode and leave a mess of black carbon on Janice's beige carpet. If he didn't get answers or understanding, if he didn't understand how he could have fallen for Ben's words, he'd walk out the door into a spongy nothingness with no clear markers of how to return to his own world. Like seeing a horror film in the afternoon, then coming out of the theater into the sunlight where you can't yet connect with the bright daylight world that was there before you went into the theater. For the first time, it seemed like this wasn't something he could sort out by using his own mind, at least not until he had all the information. He needed Janice to talk to him and tell him all she could.

"I'm sorry I'm taking so much of your time, but I'm still so . . . unclear." He was worried that if he moved, it would signal an end to their meeting and he'd lose whatever thread was still connecting him to her.

"I'm afraid to get up," he said. "That you'll be done talking to me."

"I understand that fear. We can keep talking. It helps me too."

Scott exhaled, not realizing how little oxygen he was allowing himself. He inhaled deeply and let it go, this time a little more slowly. He was still in this room, in Janice's home, and she hadn't yet asked him to leave.

"May I use the restroom?"

"Of course."

Scott stood and looked in the direction of the hall. Janice stood and indicated with a nod the direction of the bathroom. It felt like Scott hadn't been on his legs in days. He walked tentatively until he had better control over ambulation. Once in the bathroom, he washed his hands and rubbed his face with his damp hands. He ran them under the water again and then found a towel. It was beige. He missed his wife. He could feel tears welling up but didn't want to be found curled up on the floor by a woman he didn't know. Or if he was honest, by any woman—or any person, for that matter. He needed to be strong. He tried praying, but his mind couldn't settle on anything. He thought of when he was a boy, of being alone in his room, on his twin bed. He was sick and couldn't breathe easily and couldn't move, and his only comfort was the handkerchief his mother had left him. It smelled of her perfume and even now he couldn't be sure if she had orchestrated this maternal substitution, a perfumed mother manqué, or if was just something she had left behind after tending to him. He was leaning towards the former. He remembered when a school friend had been sick, and there was soup and Vicks VapoRub and blankets and popsicles and books being read. He had no such memories.

He stood up tall. He needed something but didn't know what it was, so he did the only thing he could think of: keep moving. He opened the bathroom door and almost tripped over Sadie, who was sitting right outside the door. She let out the low howl of a Siamese and followed Scott as he walked back into the living room, where he imagined he'd see actual pieces of his life scattered about the living room floor.

Scott sat.

Sadie took her place on Janice's lap.

The earth was still slowly turning, and he saw the sunny rhombus of light had moved along the carpet towards the wall. He thought of Ben's room, of Ben watching the movement of the light on a cement floor. Scott had to adjust his vision of that room. He had to readjust his vision of Ben's austere professor's office to that of a grey room in a psychiatric hospital. Of course. The windows that didn't open. The simple furniture. The single chair.

Scott was again feeling a stinging around his eyes. He pressed his palms against them, as if to force them back in.

"I feel like an idiot. Like a thread has been pulled and I can't keep it together."

He couldn't remember any grief or fear when the tooth fairy slipped away, or his reaction to learning Santa wasn't real, so why was he so afraid now? What was slipping away? Ben? Scott had believed something that wasn't true. So what? It was a strange story and maybe that could be the end of it. A story he'd tell at the next dinner party. Okay, maybe not that soon. But would the slipping away stop here? What if God was just a story? Was the comfort of a potential heaven, or even seventy-two raisins, just the next palliative in a long line of comforts from birth to death? Pulling us forward, soothing us through the pain of life? Was life indeed painful, or did he even know? He hadn't experienced anything without the undercurrent of a deeper, assumed connection to something greater than himself. That would always be there, that was taking care of him.

He looked up at Janice. "What if we're all just telling ourselves stories?"

"The mind is fascinating, Scott. The things we believe are a composite of biology, experience, trauma, inclusion, environment, nutrition. I would say it's amazing any of us find our way. But nature promotes success, and I guess I'm grateful I am not unique in this, not an anomaly."

"Is that on your business card? 'Janice Van Vliet: Not an Anomaly.'"

"I'm glad you have your sense of humor back."

"That was it. It's gone again." He looked at his hands. "What happened to Ben? Not the stories he made up in the myths, but what happened to him?"

"The truth is I'm not sure I can go back there. To that."

Scott understood. "No, listen. I appreciate all you've given me. Your time. Your experience with all this."

Janice looked away and then looked back at Scott. "I do have his file. A copy of it. It has his intake information, his history. That would probably help you."

"I'd appreciate that."

Janice stood, Sadie jumped to the floor, and together they walked down the hall. Scott waited. Her presence was like a bookend that kept him in place. When she left the room, it was like he was falling with nothing to hold him. Even the falsely comforting rhombus of sun was gone, as the sky had become cloudy. The room was now darker. His body felt weightless, and yet his heart was pounding in his chest.

29

YOU'RE DEVASTATED AND THEN YOUR TIME IS UP?

Janice returned with a few pages in her hand. Scott was relieved to have her back in the room. She handed him the pages, turned on a lamp on the side table, and retreated to the kitchen.

Scott started reading.

"Summation based on reports compiled from interviews with neighbors, relatives, and police reports. Male patient born 1969 to physics professor father. Mother became pregnant with second child at which point she began to show signs of undiagnosed schizo pathology. Ben was small. Stuttered. Was told father left because Ben was a demon child. Mother believed he was the Christ-child, baptizing him countless times in the toilet. Murky sexual boundaries with mother who taped his genitals down as he was reaching puberty. Mother also abused him by cutting him and herself. Convincing Ben that her unborn child would kill them both, she forced him to stab her. Her wounds led to her death and he was left alone until neighbors found him. Father was not found at this time, and Ben was placed with relatives in Costa Mesa, where there were suggestions of further abuse by the teenage boys in the home. Ben showed no outward signs of pathology at this point, but expressed interest in the seminary and took theology classes at La Jolla Community College, where he admitted to hearing voices. School officials provided Ben with therapy, although he was seen carrying a knife to class on several occasions. Dissociation began at this time. May have unwittingly ingested LSD at this time, which may have contributed to psychotic break. Claimed to be a Teacher's Assistant and promoted himself as a therapist in training. Offered 'therapy' to teacher's assistant named Anna. Went to her home and threatened her. She died trying to escape. FBI became involved. Interviews showed increased disconnect from reality to the point where Ben stopped talking. He was admitted to La Jolla Psychiatric Hospital. Physical exam shows anal scarring. Cigarette burns on back. Talk therapy leads to agitation. Patient given 12.5mg Clozapine upon admission which was increased over two weeks to 300mg. Aggression treated with monthly injection of Haloperidol (Haldol.) No indications of tardive dyskinesia symptoms. Although patient still agitated and using art supplies to tape down genitalia."

Scott scanned the pages, seeing various dates for ECT and other treatments. He found more of the narrative.

"Ben has formed a relationship with head nurse Janice Van Vliet and appears to communicate with her through extensive writing. His aggressive tendencies are inconsistent and, after destroying a group typewriter, he is now allowed crayons and paper. Ms. Van Vliet initially offered to type these pages for him, as that seemed to give him comfort and connection."

Scott saw an addendum.

"December 14, 1999. Patient deceased. Patient stopped accepting medication, and after trying to drown a night janitor in a bucket, he found the janitor's knife, threatened Ms. Van Vliet, and eventually stabbed himself in the throat and bled to death despite efforts by Ms. Van Vliet and other hospital personnel. Dr. Schemion claimed no misconduct by his staff or hospital personnel."

Scott set the pages on the coffee table. Sadie came back from the bedroom, looked around the room, jumped up on his lap, and when Scott didn't acknowledge her, she let out a big wail. Janice returned and picked up the pages and remained standing.

Scott knew it was time to leave. He made a slight move and Sadie took the cue, jumping from his lap to the coffee table. After sniffing the pages, she jumped to the floor.

Standing, he said, "Is this what therapy is like? You're devastated and then your time is up?" He wanted to make the obvious joke about therapy being like life, but knew that would just sound self-pitying, when actually his life *was* good, or had been. Janice gave him a smile and her blue eyes were clear and kind. They walked to the door, which Janice opened. Scott put out his hand and they shook. He experienced his own version of imposed catatonia and stood there just looking at this old woman's sweet face. He tightened his mouth to keep himself from crying. She smiled and gave him a hug. Which he was unable to return. He stepped outside. The sun was shining again, but he could hardly remember where he was. Or why.

He turned back to Janice, who was standing in the doorway.

"I don't know how to be. Everything is dissolving and I can't keep hold of anything, or even know what to keep hold of."

"Just start where you are. It's solid where you are."

"What if God goes away? Along with Ben. What do I believe in? What if there's nothing to believe in?"

"I guess you'll find out."

He turned back towards the hot, dusty courtyard. And walked away.

30
STOP THE FUCKING BALLS!

The air in the car was dry and stale. The windshield was dirty, at least in this light, and it seemed appropriate that things were blurred and diffused as he looked out. He wondered if this was what it was like to have cataracts. He wanted to start the car up and get the air blowing, but he wasn't ready to leave. The heat felt good on his thighs. He looked down and saw his pants were covered in thin, off-white hairs. He thought of the junk drawer in his kitchen. If Rebecca were here, she'd have the perfect roller for this. The "Cat Hair Roller."

He worried he had been sitting in the car too long in front of Janice's complex and that he was close to crossing the line between thoughtful man and desperate stalker. He started the car, felt the air blowing on his face. He drove forward, turned the corner, parked the car, and turned off the engine.

Where was he going? Out of habit, he asked God for guidance but felt no indication of a connection. He counted on God to guide him and tried to imagine how life would be if that door really were closed to him. His friends and family on one side, and he on the other. Or maybe there wasn't even a door. Maybe he was now a trapeze artist with no net below him. No heaven above him. He was simply in his car. How could he be in his car with nothing to believe in? Would everyone leave him?

He put his hands together and said, "Please God, don't leave me." But they were simply words. He had believed in Ben's words, but so what? People weren't always what they seemed—what was the big deal—but somehow with the dissolution of Ben's identity came a crumbling of Scott's faith in anything. Ben had used story and myth to not only make sense of his own devastating life, but to find his place in the world. Even if it was an imagined world of academia.

Scott wondered if his own pursuit of recognition was tied to some kind of story he was telling himself. Was he proving his father wrong, that he was in fact able to be a "man" and provide for his family using nothing more than his humor? What would he do if his humor left him? If God left him? Could he do this life without God? What if God was merely the hope of future solutions to current problems? He remembered John Lennon's song, *Imagine*, and laughed that he'd always thought the guy was talented but deluded. But damn if Scott himself wasn't sitting in a warm car in Temecula, imagining just this. A life without heaven.

He didn't like it. He didn't like the feeling of falling. He should start the car. Faith without works was dead, right? But what if there is no faith? He thought of the flurry of questions he'd asked Janice and laughed. He was like that woman at that start of an episode of *Sex and the City*. That would make Rebecca laugh. When she had been hugely pregnant, she had asked for only two things: 1) ketchup on everything, and 2) for him to just watch one episode of *Sex and the City* with her. He had gone to the store and bought every brand of ketchup he could find—he was a prince!—but he had dreaded the half hour watching young single women cavort and complain. He found himself drawn to the initial premise of Carrie asking herself questions, typing them out on a computer. It had turned into a Sunday night ritual until the kids were born. Watching the show that first time, Scott asked Rebecca if she wished she could have sex with other people. She just gave him a deadpan look and pointed at her belly.

"You're not going to be pregnant forever," Scott said.

"Sweetie. I look forward to having a baby with you, and then I will look forward to having sex with you. YOU! You goofball."

Except now maybe Rebecca would leave him. He was changing the rules. What could he offer her if he was no longer the man she'd married? If he had no job, no humor, no God? Would she want to stay married to a man who'd put twigs on his head? How would he explain that Ben was dead? Not only dead, but he had died in a psychiatric hospital.

His brain was clearly overheating. "Just start where you are."

He started the car. Again.

He texted Rebecca and said, "On my way."

Ping. "Only 4 hrs late."

He sat there a moment wondering what to say, when there was another text. "Sorry. Tired. Did you find Ben?"

There was no way he could explain just how far he was from finding Ben. "I'll fill you in later. I wanna get on the road."

"K. In Irvine now. Student cafeteria."

He tapped the link she'd included and started driving, having absolutely no idea how anything would work out at this point. Aside from driving to Irvine, the only other thing to do was give Dylan the news about Ben.

He put in his earpiece and made the call.

"Dylan Flynn's office."

"Sasha. Hi, it's Scott."

"Hey!"

"Has Drippy licensed the 'Pervy Writer Costume?' Is it a big hit?"

"I'm glad you can laugh about this."

"Oh yeah. I'm doubled over."

Sasha gave a little laugh, which didn't sound the least bit encouraging.

"If you want Dylan, he's not in," she said.

"That's okay. I need to make an actual appointment. Can I come in Friday?"

"Ten forty-five?"

"Great. How's the show going?"

"Fine. But we miss you." Nothing like the sound of pity.

They ended the call and he looked out the windshield. Where the hell was he? Temecula. All the shock and shame came flooding back. He made his last call.

"Hi, Jenny. Is he there?"

There was a pause that no longer annoyed him.

"Yes. I'll put you through."

Fred picked up.

"Hey. How's my favorite perv?" Scott heard the silver balls start up.

"Fred, stop the fucking balls!"

"Wow, okay. Our little Scott Mullan is all grown up." The sound of the balls stopped.

"What's so serious?" he asked.

"Fred. He's dead."

"WHO? Dylan???"

"God no. Ben."

"Who's Ben?"

"Ben Doss. The book you gave me. To edit."

There was silence and then Fred said, "Posthumous can be good. Sometimes better."

"Fred, the guy was . . ." Scott still had an allegiance to Ben, a man he'd never met—who had been dead almost twenty years. Plus, what a crap life the poor guy had had. "He was troubled."

"Those self-help guys probably are. Like shrinks. You gotta start fucked-up, right?"

"No. Troubled as in crazy. He wrote the book in a psych ward."

"Oh."

"Yeah." Scott turned on the wipers and pressed the button for the liquid. The right side had limited stream and the grime turned into more of a slimy mess.

"Well, that's too bad," Fred finally said. "Talk later?"

"That's it?"

"That's what?"

"I thought this might lead to something. Now what?"

"I don't know. I'm not your dad."

"There's some good news." Scott hung up on him.

31

THEIR MASCOT IS
THE ANTEATER.

Scott found Rebecca and the kids in The Anteatery. He'd taken four freeways he'd never been on and ended up on University Road, and eventually Mesa Road, which took him down a road lined with glass and metal buildings. He found a parking space several blocks past the cafe and tried to breathe normally as he walked down the sidewalk. The cafe had a lot of light wood and skylights and cement, the chairs were orange, and there was what he interpreted as an afternoon laziness—the lunch crowd gone, the remaining lingerers looking at various screens.

The students and servers were all about the same age, meaning way younger than he was. He scanned past them looking for his wife and kids. There was no obvious trinity of Mullans so he did another visual pass, overlooking the students until he realized he was looking at his own kids who were no longer kids.

He walked up, prepared for a chilly reception. He was steeling himself to be okay with a quiet hello as they tried on the feeling of independence or separation or tried to be cool.

"Hey, kids."

"Dad!" Chloe jumped up and threw her arms around him. Marcus waited, then put his arm around his dad's shoulder and leaned in. Sort of a modified bro-hug. For a moment, his relief was so great he forgot all that he'd lost.

"Where's your mom?"

"Bathroom." They sat down.

"How's the school?"

"Good," Chloe said, which meant it was good. She didn't say things unless she meant them.

"Dad." Marcus seemed very serious.

"What?"

"Their mascot is an anteater."

"I guess you can't have everything."

"Right? San Diego's mascot is King Triton."

Chloe said, "I'm not picking a school based on their mascot."

"Who said you have to go where I go?"

"Our DNA," she said.

This, for some reason, made Scott nostalgic for when his kids had no ideas of their own. He thought back and figured it was when they were maybe . . . eight months old? Chloe looked up and past Scott. Scott turned and saw Rebecca, who looked tired; but she smiled. Scott stood, and they exchanged a chaste hug.

"How was San Diego?" Scott asked, hoping she'd sit down and they could at least feel like a family unit.

"You can hear about it on the way home."

Rebecca decided they should split the kids up for the drive home, and the four of them walked out to the cars. The kids walked ahead, Marcus checking out girls, Chloe checking out a school pamphlet she was holding. Rebecca slowed, which was the clue she wanted to talk to Scott out of earshot of the kids. He slowed alongside her.

"Do you think they're still virgins?" she asked.

"You mean raisins?"

"Scott, I'm not in the mood for a lot of jokes."

He was trying so hard to keep things on track, but everything seemed out of his hands at this point. "They usually talk to you about that stuff. And they haven't, right?"

"No," she said.

"Although I think when they go to college—all bets are off, right?"

"Probably. Although with a metallurgy major, I don't think Chloe will be around too much partying." Rebecca made a sad face, bottom lip extended. "How can they be going to college? They're just babies."

Scott put his arm around Rebecca, which she didn't receive or reject.

"Here's my car," he said.

"It's so dirty."

"Temecula has no paved roads."

"Really?"

"I'm kidding. Sorry."

"Oh." She watched the kids walk on.

"Is she pretty?"

"Who?" He scrambled—was she asking about Chloe? That one question he could answer. His daughter was beautiful. He looked at Rebecca as if asking for more information before answering. Always the best move when asked about other women.

"Janice."

Scott laughed.

"Don't laugh at me."

"Beck, she's in her seventies or something. But yes, she's pretty."

Scott called out to Marcus. "Hey buddy. Here's my car." Marcus walked back.

"I wasn't laughing at you," Scott said to Rebecca. "Believe me, when I fill you in, you'll be laughing at me."

Scott could feel himself sinking. Right now, in her eyes, he was still the man she married, which made him feel even more like a fraud. He beeped open the locks on the car, and Marcus got into the passenger seat and shoved his back pack down by his feet. Rebecca looked down the street and held up the "one minute" finger to Chloe and turned back to Scott.

"So, was the guy there? Ben? Did you meet him?"

"Didn't meet him."

"Well, that was a waste."

"Yeah," he said and started walking around the car. "I'll tell you all about it."

"Okay." Rebecca started walking away.

"Hey," he called out. She turned back. He wanted to say, "No, the bottom dropped out. I'm a fool, I'm unemployed, I have no future. Fame is pointless and elusive and yet I was chasing it. And my thoughts about God are wavy and confusing and slipping away."

Instead he said, "Thanks for doing the whole school thing. I'm sorry I screwed it up."

He got in the car, waving a last time. He waited until she and Chloe were in their car, had buckled up, and had pulled out into traffic. He pulled out.

"Marcus, tell Siri to get us home."

"You know she's not a real person, right?"

"No. What?"

Marcus tapped a few things on his phone.

"How was the campus?"

"Cool."

Siri chimed in, "In 200 feet, take the entrance on the left to the 73 North," and then no one said anything. Scott was glad for the silence, the relative silence. There was road whoosh, an occasional Siri direction, Marcus breathing. He wasn't sure if he could drive and have the conversation he knew he would eventually have to have. He didn't even know what the conversation would be, but something was coming. He thought about The Anteatery, all cement and light and sunlight. Like the police station. Maybe the police station could use some orange chairs. Maybe he could get a job there as an interior decorator.

"Dad?"

"Hey. Questions about anteaters. Go!"

"It's not that."

"Okay, what is it?"

"Is Mom mad at you?"

Scott thought about this. "Is Mom mad at me? I think she's just worried because there's some work stuff going on."

"Because you're not funny anymore?"

"Is that what she said?"

"No. But it's either that or the arrest thing."

"I wasn't arrested. I was doing something for my boss that backfired. It'll work out. But please know—this is my problem. It's not yours. You don't have to worry."

"I'm not worried."

Marcus didn't say anything, so Scott thought he'd have to explain more. While he was thinking what to say next, Marcus said, "Okay—so when are you going to be funny again?"

That was a very good question.

* * *

That night, after they'd all gotten home, after school pamphlets were either put in the drawer or added to the "consider" pile on the counter, after Rebecca had made some work calls from the bedroom, after the kids had plugged in their phones and gone to bed, after Rebecca called to ask if he was coming to bed, after he said he'd be right there, he pulled out the last of the Ben Doss pages, the remaining pages that were written with an orange crayon.

I should be working on chapter three. The myth is wrong. I should probably rework this but for now I'll just be honest with my readers and talk about my own feelings. Women and lust. I have no lust. I am like a priest in that way. Well, a priest who has no lust. HAHAHA. Sometimes I'm very funny.

I have been given a larger mission. There are things I've been shown that have prompted action, and I can feel very strongly that I now must take said action. Janice is trying to tell me with her eyes that she is afraid. Afraid of the multiplying cells inside her. Afraid they've been implanted when she slept. I wish I could have her sleep in my room with me. I could keep her safe. I have been given a mission, and sometimes people are the action-takers and sometimes they are the action supporters. And today . . . oh my God . . . will it be today? It will be today.

Janice is asking for my help to stop the multiplying cells from taking over. From killing her or killing others— demon seed. Demon seed.

I have not told Dr. Schemion that today is the day. I was hoping to finish this book, but I am a fraud if I don't see a problem right in front of me and offer help when it is asked. I may not be a medical doctor but I learned enough in my medical rotation to know how to abort a fetus. I will save Janice and then I will save Henry. He

has asked me to baptize him. Maybe he didn't ask in
words, but I can tell.

I help so many.

Scott rubbed his head. He turned on his computer and Googled
"Promascus." Nothing. "Boy of Dirt." Nothing. He Googled
Lysergic Acid just to make sure his computer was working. There it
was. He tried "Serbian water ritual." Well, that was real. He dug into
the drawer of older pages and scanned for more "facts" as reported
by Ben Doss. "Slow Hyena." Nope. Spur Posse. Yep.

He scanned the pages and again saw, "Lahoya."

"I'm an idiot." Ben had tried to make sense of his world with
stories. And believed he'd be exalted for it.

Delusions of grandeur masked as faith.

32

YOU WERE THE
WOMAN IN WHITE.

Scott boxed up the Ben Doss stuff, his eye catching on quotes and phrases. How could the words have been real and now be so unreal? Words. Scott's life was about words, and now it seemed words were useless.

His phone trilled. He saw a number he didn't recognize and let it go to voice mail. He sat. He felt like dead weight. He couldn't imagine tomorrow, let alone the next five minutes. So he just sat.

The phone chirped, reminding him of a message. With no other apparent plan before him, he picked up the phone and focused on the picture of Rebecca and the kids covered in colored powders, exhilarated and silly.

He listened to the call and tapped to call back.

"Hi, it's Scott. Thanks so much for returning my call."

"Of course."

Her voice sounded young and open. And a little sad.

"So, Janice."

"Yes."

"It all crumbled. I mean, I reread some of the book and I was so fooled. Even the names of the mythic characters were just the names of his medications."

"We tell ourselves stories."

"Can I ask you something? There were all those positive reviews at the beginning of the book. Like Joseph Campbell, Robert Graves, Deepak Chopra. Not real, right?"

"No."

"Wow."

Scott didn't know what it was he wanted to know, so he asked the next question that occurred to him.

"Weren't you worried he was going to kill you?"

"I didn't believe he was going to kill me."

"But he could have."

"But he didn't."

"You were the Woman in White. He hoped you could save him."

"You can't save everyone, or really anyone. You just try to help. Listen where possible. Medicate if necessary. In some cases, it's just a matter of keeping the patient from harming himself or others." She sighed. "Sometimes we fail."

"I didn't mean that to sound critical."

"It didn't," she said. Scott heard a low meow and imagined Sadie had jumped up and was vying for attention, or maybe comforting Janice.

"I'm feeling crazy myself," he said. "I mean, not stabbing someone crazy."

"You're not crazy. Or no more crazy than most of us just getting through it. I'm sorry to tell you, but you're not that special."

"So my father told me."

There was a pause and she said, "Perhaps you use comedy instead of myth to make sense of things."

"Ben said to see the Messiah in others. And I did. What do I do now? How do I see the Messiah in others when there is no Messiah?"

"You can still see others in a kind way."

"How can I do that without God? What's the point? There's nothing to replace Him. I didn't have much of a father, but at least there was the church. There was a hierarchy, and I wasn't at the top of it. There was some comfort there. But now, God is gone. Ben's gone, or what I thought of Ben. And now it's just me. The next lemming. At least there *had* been a heavenly father I could look to, if not an actual father."

"And what kind of father are you?"

"I hope I'm a good father, but I have no idea what kind of father I'll be if I don't have faith."

"You still see yourself as a father, even if you're feeling uncertain about other things. That seems solid to me."

Scott was soothed by her voice. There was so little he was connected to; there was no one who had known Ben Doss, let alone read his words, except this woman. She was a lifeline of sorts. She was someone who would accept him.

"Janice, do you think I could see you, or call you from time to time?"

She didn't respond, and he felt a fraying of the last thread of connection. He could almost see the molecules disengaging, like the tiniest of explosions leading to a tiny universe of expansion and emptiness.

"Are you still there?" he asked.

"Scott, if you want the name of a therapist, I'd be happy to give you some numbers. But I'm not the Woman in White. I can't make sense of this for you. But I have faith that you'll be able to get through this."

"Faith. Ha."

"Ha. Yes. Let me restate. I'll say 'experience.' I'll leave you with this." Sadie meowed somewhere in the background, sensing perhaps that Janice was using her "wrapping it up" voice and food would soon be coming. Scott's heart sank. He wasn't ready to face the empty house. Or worse, to feel like a stranger in his own family.

"Lay it on me, sister." His attempt at light-heartedness sounded false.

"My experience is that, in nature, every death leads to a rebirth. Night becomes morning. Whatever death *you're* experiencing will lead to a rebirth. I can't say what that will look like. But, there you go." She laughed. "Wisdom from the Woman in White."

"I really appreciate the time you've taken to listen to me—to talk to me." He could feel tears starting, and he could think of nothing worse than crying on the phone, or crying at all, so he was quick to say goodbye.

"Thank you. Take care, Janice."

She said, "You too," and then there was another more demanding meow from Sadie.

He disconnected and was overcome by a heavy inertia, a weight that said, "sit in this chair until you die." A vestige of his old funny self saw the humor in the fact that if he died right then and there, the last thing he would have heard was . . . Sadie. Which wouldn't be so bad, really. He could think of nothing further, so he continued to sit. He felt the Berber carpet on the soles of his bare feet and he looked out the window. A bird flew by. He felt the chair, his thighs. He could just keep sitting there until his limbs began to atrophy.

He could stop talking, like Ben had.

"Okay."

He stood up.

Before beginning his life of faithless silence and loveless obscurity, he needed to give Dylan the news. He called Sasha to confirm he'd be in the next day, and figured if nothing else, it would get him up in the morning.

Beyond that, he had no clue.

33

I CAN'T BE EMPLOYING
CHILD MOLESTERS.

The walk to the office was familiar. For years he'd written jokes in his head on the walk through the parking lot, across the street, through security, past the bathrooms, the soundstage where they did the show, up the stairs, and into his office. Now, it was the same walk, but everything had changed. It was later in the morning, so the sunshine was subtly different. There were no topical jokes threading through his head, waiting to be written down and reworked and listed for approval. There was, however, one sentence he kept rolling over and revising: what he would say to Dylan.

Sasha was at her desk, staring at her screen, earbuds in place. As soon as she saw Scott, she pulled them out, stood up, stepped from behind her desk, and gave him a hug. She had a splint on her arm which clunked across his shoulder.

"Okay. What happened?" he asked.

"Oh, this old thing? I was moving a couch for a neighbor and slipped. It's fine. Dylan loves it."

"His clumsy assistant."

"Exactly. The timing was good, though. I just got my braces off." She gave him a big fake grin.

"What's next? An eye patch?"

She smiled. "Let me tell him you're here." She turned her head and yelled, "Dylan, Scott's here."

He heard Dylan yell back, "Joke Monkey! Send him in."

Scott went in.

Dylan came around his desk and extended his hand and they shook. He was wearing full bicycle gear. There was sweat on his forehead.

"Wow. Not douchey at all," Scott said.

"Yeah, sorry. I'm going to have to keep this short so I can shower. So, where are we? With this author. Can we bring you both on in some bit? I'm sure by now you've seen the gardeners' video. We could re-enact what you were doing, show a different angle? The Leprechaun brand needs to get past the strap-on costume nonsense."

"Not looking good."

"What's not looking good?"

"I'm an idiot."

"That's why I hired you."

"You want the truth?" Scott waited for the joke. But there didn't seem to be one coming. Banter time was over.

"Ben is no longer with us. The writer. He died almost twenty years ago."

"And this is the guy who told you to pour water on my front door?"

"There were a lot of 'applications.' I taped twigs to my head and put tape over my mouth. I'm an idiot. But yes, Ben is not available to be on the show."

Dylan sat down. "Okay, I'll tell *you* the truth. My hands are tied."

"How can your hands be tied? It's your show."

"I can't be employing child molesters."

"Yes. I would not dispute that."

Dylan turned his head in the direction of the door. "SASHA! Paper towels."

"On my way."

Dylan used his finger like a windshield wiper on his forehead to keep the sweat from falling into his eyes. Sasha came in with a roll of paper towels and set them on his desk. She left without looking at Scott. Dylan tore off a sheet and wiped his entire face. He tore off another sheet and wipe the back of his neck. He picked up the roll and held it towards Scott.

"Paper towel?"

"I'm good."

"So, what's the attraction to this cult of Ben?"

"Like I said, here is the truth." He looked at Dylan, who mimed picking up a pencil, licking its tip as if to take important notes.

"Nice space work," Scott said.

"Thanks."

Scott still remembered the basic tenets of improv: love the premise, add information, say yes, bring something to the party. And use space work—the handling of objects that didn't exist.

Scott took a breath and exhaled. "Mr. Ben Doss wrote his book with an orange crayon while he was a patient in a psych ward in La Jolla."

Dylan started laughing. Scott had the fleeting satisfaction that the phrasing he'd worked on and his flat delivery had successfully led to Dylan's laughter. The laughter trickled down into a sigh and Dylan reached for another paper towel.

"'A tale told by an idiot . . .'" He wiped his face and threw the used paper towel in the trash bin.

"And now I don't believe in anything. Like God has disappeared," Scott said.

"Hey. Don't throw the Baby Jesus out with the bathwater."

"Good one."

Neither of them said anything for several seconds.

"Scott. I'm not sure how this is going to go. My lawyers are still talking, and if it gets bounced back to me, I may have to make some kind of statement. But I'll do all I can to work it out."

"Understood. It's okay. I'll lose my job, my house, my family, and then I'll live under a bridge and I can write that stunning one-man show I've had in a fucking folder for twenty-five years. I'll rent a dumpy theater and I'll invite old friends who will come out of shame and guilt and sympathy, and I'll be hailed as a comic genius. I'll become a YouTube star and then I can be a guest on 'Libby!' which would really complete the pathetic circle, and then you'll be begging for me to come back."

"At least you don't live in your head."

Scott turned to go.

"Scott."

Scott turned back.

"What?"

"I have to ask you. Why were you praying for my family?"

"I told you."

"You know about my daughter, right?"

Scott didn't know if he should speak or wait or let on how much he knew. He had very little brain juice left and didn't think he could create some nebulous answer that would implicate no one.

So he said, "Your daughter has Down syndrome."

"Yes."

"That did not occur to me when I prayed for your family. I was praying for you, that you find peace in your family. Just as I would want with mine."

"And who says I don't have peace?" Dylan demanded.

"I was just checking something off the Ben list. Pour some water. Say a prayer. I didn't give it a lot of thought."

"Well, you know what, buddy? It's my fucking family and I don't need you to pray for me. Okay?"

"I understand. Families are a challenge, no matter what."

"'No matter what'?"

"No matter what is going on. Listen. Nothing was meant by this."

"Who else knows about my daughter?"

"It's not common conversation. But it's also not a tragedy. It's just how it is."

Dylan's face was tight. "Hey, you guys write your little jokes, but I bring them to life. It's my show. I have to protect my brand."

"Your brand? As a Leprechaun?"

"As a family man."

"A family man. Right. To two thirds of your family."

"What??"

Scott's anger had a hold of him. "This isn't about me tainting the precious show brand by peeing on the side of your house, or whatever people think. This is about me saying a prayer for your family."

"My family is none of your fucking business."

"You've made that very clear."

"I was willing to go to bat for you, but I draw the line at my family. Okay. I think we're done, Joke Monkey."

Scott turned for the door.

Dylan's voice was tight when he said, "Sure you don't want a paper towel?"

Scott said, "I'm good," and he walked out the door. The mythic doorway to nothing.

34

UP UNTIL NOW
THE POTATOES WERE FINE.

"Fuck this shit."

He put the lid on the box and dropped the box on the floor with a solid thud.

"Wow," he heard from behind him. He turned around to find Rebecca in the doorway. Her face was serious.

"At least I don't have twigs in my hair," he said.

"Just never heard you use the F-bomb."

"'Up until now the potatoes were fine.'"

"What?"

"You know that old joke. The kid who doesn't talk until he's fifteen and then he says, 'These potatoes are lumpy,' and his parents are ecstatic and say, 'But why haven't you spoken until now?'" He offered his hands to indicate that's where the punchline went, although he didn't have the enthusiasm for selling it.

Scott had returned home from his meeting with Dylan, and after a tense and quiet dinner, claimed he wasn't feeling well and went to bed early. The kids seemed to steer clear and Rebecca didn't push it.

But he didn't think he was fooling anyone.

"And what shit are we fucking?" Rebecca pulled all her hair into one hand and twisted it up in some magic way and secured it with a plastic grabber. He had seen her do this a thousand times. It was her 'getting down to business' hair. And she waited.

"I don't even know," he said.

"Were you fired?"

"Probably."

"Are we playing twenty questions?" She was pissed. "Because I'm super tired of this guessing game. Or this waiting game, or whatever it is. I'm not sure how long I can just hang out with you not telling me what is going on. If you're having an affair, or if you want to become a plumber, or if there's a health problem, or I don't know what. When I don't know, I fill in the blanks. You get that, right?"

"I'm trying to figure it out. You'll be the first to know."

"Not good enough."

Scott pulled the top off the box and riffled through, pulling out some of the pages toward the end. "You want to read this stuff?"

"No. I want you to tell me what it is."

"It's the book." He handed her a few pages which she took and looked at, but clearly did not want to read.

"Written with a crayon?" was all she said.

"Seems to be."

"It's a children's book?"

Scott laughed. Maybe it was a children's book and he was the child. The stupid, trusting child.

"You wanna hear?" he asked. "Well, this book I was editing, the book I believed in, the book I was promoting to Dylan, written by the guy I thought I'd have on the show and we could make all this perv crap go away, well—get this: he's dead. Been dead almost twenty years. And . . . he wrote the book in a psych hospital. So, I was the follower of a crazy person."

Rebecca looked at the pages in her hand.

"The twigs?" she said.

"I don't want to talk about the twigs, okay?"

Rebecca was quiet, and he worried he was shutting her out even further. But he couldn't keep himself from continuing.

"You know what else? All my faith in Ben Doss fell away in one revelation. If Ben's book was false, then all books could be false—the Bible, the Torah, the Koran, the Book of Mormon—all books written by regular knuckleheads like me. So when Ben Doss died, so did Jesus. No one is exalted. It's like I've been deprogrammed from a cult, but they went too far. Took it *all* away. I mean, what's the difference between twigs and a wafer? It's all myth. It's all fabrication. Stories to feel comforted. So here I am, with nothing. No faith. I believe in nothing. Satisfied? Glad you asked?" His fists were balled up by his sides and his mouth was firm.

"You don't believe in anything?" Rebecca's eyes were wide. "And now you're mad at *me*? I didn't go anywhere, but fine. If you don't believe in anything, I'll leave you to it."

"So, if I don't believe in God, the marriage is over?"

"I said I'd leave you *to* it. Not leave *you*."

"We built a marriage on a foundation of faith. I can't imagine you'd be too happy with me changing the tune now."

"Did I even *say* that? Thanks a lot! It's not like I'm your mother, with all her over-the-top church stuff. You think this is about God? I'm mad that you didn't trust me enough to talk about this."

She walked up to him. He was hoping maybe she'd soften and give him a hug. But she was stiff, and her eyes were drilling into him. The pages were getting crunched up in her fist.

"You know what's worse? That you sacrificed ME so YOU

wouldn't look foolish. That you made nice at the dinner party, thinking you'd gotten away with something, when you'd been ARRESTED? And I was the last to know? I hear about this on the NEWS? We had sex that night and now THAT'S a big lie. Everything from that day on has been a lie. Do you even know how embarrassed I was, not by what happened, but that I didn't know? You lied to me."

"And Ben lied to me."

"That's your reasoning? That's a stupid book. I'm a person! I'm your wife. Goddammit."

"You're right. I'm sorry. I'm sorry you were embarrassed."

"You don't have to have something figured out to talk about it. Crap. You are a big know-it-all who guess what—doesn't know it all. You think you're the only person on the planet to ever question his faith?"

"But I aligned myself with a crazy person. I believed in his seventy-two raisins. I feel completely foolish."

"Yes. Avoid feeling foolish at all costs, even if that means shutting people out."

"I'm not shutting you out. It's just that I have nothing. It's all gone."

"Wow. Thanks."

"I don't mean to hurt you. Truly."

"What can I do? Talk to me."

She was looking at him with her sweet brown eyes. He felt pathetic.

"Nothing," he said. "I'm on the outside now."

"If that's the story you need to tell yourself, fine. But just remember that I'm not the one who went away." She handed him the pages. "Except now I'm going to go do laundry, because God or no God, there's still laundry. And then I'll be at Libby's. Maybe for a few days."

His heart was breaking. He needed to say something before she left. Anything. He had had years of doing stand-up, of assessing the crowd, adjusting the pace or inserting something specific to them, or bringing up current events to pull them back if they were drifting. Or resorting to crowd work, if all else failed. "First date?" "Where you from?" "What are you drinking?" Anything to keep the ball rolling. But this was not an audience, this was Rebecca. He looked at her face. Her brown, curly hair bunched up in a clip. Her eyes were tearing up. He didn't want to make her cry. He didn't want her to leave.

"Beck."

"Hmmm?"

"I can't see my way out of this."

"Yeah, well me neither." She seemed to be going through a number of things she could say. And finally, it was this: "Don't forget you're taking the kids to IMAX tomorrow. It's on the calendar."

And she left.

35

WHAT IF MARCUS
IS A SATANIST?

"Why didn't Mom want to come?" Chloe had her head down but instead of her phone, she was reading a brochure about the space program and its history.

"I think she had some last-minute stuff for Libby's Halloween show," Scott said.

They were in line for an IMAX screening. Scott didn't think it was right to engage his children in all the facets of family life. He and Rebecca chose to make them feel secure for as long as was either possible or necessary; there were enough pressures from school and hormones and friends and the internet.

"Is that why we didn't go to church today?" Marcus asked.

Scott thought of the morning. He'd found Rebecca in the kitchen, dressed for work and moving about, doing many things quickly. She already had a cup of coffee. She'd stayed at Libby's the night before, but must have come home early to change clothes and maintain appearances. Most Sundays, at least until today, he and Rebecca had a similar pre-church morning schedule and it was a beautiful, silent, familial ballet of showering, feigned ogling, and breakfast. She'd make coffee and he'd pour the cups; she'd make the bed and he'd get the paper, which was either on the front porch, steps, curb, or grass, or in the bushes, or under the car. He'd laugh when Rebecca found the paper in some random place and she'd say, "How hard can it be?"

But this morning they were not in sync. Not in the schedule, in the day, in their clothes, in their moods, or in their relationship.

"You going in?" he asked.

"I can focus better at the office."

"Can I tell you something?"

"I don't have much time."

"Really?"

Clearly. She was in the final stages of her out-the-door prep. She'd pushed up her sleeves and made a final wipe of the counter. She'd washed her hands. Dried them. Put a dab of hand lotion in her palm and rubbed her hands together.

"If it's quick." She rubbed the excess lotion on her elbows and pulled her sleeves back down.

"You're treating me like one of the children," Scott said.

"I'm not treating you like anything."

"That too."

The sweater was next. Around the waist and tied with a yank that was probably more commentary than convenience.

Scott pushed ahead. "Remember how we'd be so worried if one of the kids wasn't home, and then we'd be so relieved, and then we'd be mad? I think you're at the 'mad at me' stage."

"Mad? Producers at work are joking that part of our Halloween parade includes a version of 'Dylan Writer with Strap-on.' I was fairly anonymous to the interns, but now I get to overhear all the speculation about 'her husband, the perv who worked on Dylan's show.' And so yeah, that's fun. Along with figuring out how to reconfigure one salary to cover the mortgage and college tuition. My head isn't spinning at all. Since you asked. Or did you ask?"

She sighed. Scott turned away.

She continued. "So, if you want to tell me some good news, I'm all ears." She had her purse on her shoulder and pulled the keys from the bowl.

"Beck, we need to talk."

"I need to get to work. Why don't you call Father McCann. I'm sure he can talk to you."

"Oh, yeah. 'Hey, Father McCann, just wanted to talk about God being dead. Is this a good time?'"

"Maybe you can talk to your friend, Janice."

And she was out the door.

He felt hands pushing him from behind.

"Dad, the line is moving." Marcus stopped his gentle push. They took a couple of steps.

"Are you and Mom getting a divorce?" he asked.

Scott made a quick look to see who was around them. He didn't want to have anything close to this conversation flanked by strangers. "Of course not."

"She's just been crying, you know, like in the bathroom."

Scott leaned in to Marcus. "They're letting us in. Let's talk inside, okay?"

Scott showed their tickets and they went inside. He herded his kids to a bench by a window.

"Marcus, it's just a bit of a stressful time with the misunderstanding at work. We'll be fine. Mom's probably just sad because you guys are growing up and going to college."

"It's not like we're leaving tomorrow. If we even go away to school. I mean, can we afford it if you lose your job?"

"Listen. The job's fine. If something actually happens that will affect the family, I'll let you know. Okay?"

"Okay."

Marcus pulled at the shoulders of his sweatshirt as if it was too tight for him. He didn't seem to be buying it.

"So how come no church today?" he persisted.

"We're at IMAX."

"Mom was on the phone and said we may be done with church."

"You know I will support whatever path you kids want to take."

"What if Marcus is a Satanist?" Chloe said, without looking up.

"What?"

"I am not. Jeez, Chloe."

Chloe had gone back to reading the brochure. Marcus stood up. He was looking out the window.

"Everything's all weird. When's this thing start, anyway?"

Scott looked at the tickets. "Why don't you go in and save seats. I'm hitting the head."

Marcus walked away from them and Chloe stood to follow.

"Chloe, wait."

She turned back. She looked so young. "What?"

"Just want to make sure you're okay."

"I'm fine."

"You aren't saying much."

"I'm reading."

"Okay." Scott stayed seated.

"Newton's Third Law of Motion. 'For every action there is always an equal and opposite reaction.' So cool."

"And objects at rest will stay at rest. Let's go find your brother."

"What about the bathroom?"

"I just wanted to see how you were doing."

Scott led Chloe into the auditorium. They found Marcus and

took their seats. The room went dark. The music started. And then a rocket was roaring and taking off from the earth and flying through the atmosphere towards the stars. He imagined himself as he had when he was young, as an astronaut who has been cut loose from the rocket and was floating away in space.

Alone.

He wanted to protect his children from ever feeling this way.

36

SETTLE EVERYONE. TAKE YOUR SEATS.

It was Tuesday, a week from Halloween. Scott had gotten a text from Sasha the day before, summoning him to the manor. It had been abrupt. "Scott. Doing the show early tomorrow. Can you be at Dylan's house at 3p? Text back to confirm."

His brain told him the days would continue, but for now he could only focus on what he was doing right now. He was standing on paper towels which he'd placed on the grimy, pee-stained tile floor of the gas station bathroom. He was wearing socks. He was not wearing pants. It was time to get into the costume. He hadn't wanted to change at home and have to explain to his kids. He was never entirely sure of their schedule, as Tuesdays could mean the afternoon off, or an AP meeting, or study group, or maybe they'd come bursting into the house all fresh and loud and backpacky. He didn't want to explain he was a little crazy, and he was meeting with Dylan for what would probably be the last time, and he'd be wearing a costume.

In a rare moment of planning ahead, he'd arranged for the costume weeks before as a surprise for Rebecca. He wanted to show her he could be silly, not just Mr. Clean. But now God was dead, and she was staying at Libby's and he was standing on paper towels in a gas station bathroom.

He folded his pants and put them on the paper towels he'd put in the sink. He pulled on the red, stripy pants which had elastic in the back, and came down mid-calf. He took off his yellow polo shirt, folded it, and put it with his Dockers. On went the little green vest with garish gold buttons. He pulled off one sock and hopped a bit as he put on the hairy, plastic monkey foot. Did the same on the other foot and felt a bit less exposed with the equivalent of plastic booties on his feet. His chest and arms were bare except for the short vest, and the chill of the bathroom was settling in on his skin. He gathered up his clothes, and with the other hand, gathered up all the paper towels and pushed them into the overflowing trash bin.

He went out to his car, which was still warm inside. On the passenger seat was the red fez hat complete with chin elastic, and the hand cymbals with elastic loops for wrists and fingers.

Joke Monkey.

He donned the fez hat and cymbals, stepped out of the car, and took a selfie. He texted the selfie to Rebecca with words: "Beck, here I am looking silly. It can be done."

He waited a few seconds for a response but needed to get going. He took off the fez and cymbals and got back in the warm car. His phone chirped.

A text from Rebecca. "Got the pic. Off with Libby."

Her commitment to text etiquette required her to respond and this felt like nothing more than that. A generic response.

He sighed, put the car in drive, and pulled out of the gas station.

He didn't need Siri to tell him how to get to Dylan's house. Scott was careful navigating the foot pedals with his awkward monkey feet, and then noticed there was cool air blowing on his nearly bare chest.

He felt a flash of embarrassment as he remembered standing in his backyard: shirtless, barefoot, twigs on his scalp. Was that the beginning of the death Janice mentioned? Was today the beginning of a rebirth? Or was today the day of death? And if so, so what? He was Dylan's Joke Monkey, and he was going to commit to it fully. If he was going to be fired, he was going to go out cymbals a-chiming.

As he neared Dylan's street, he pulled over, put the fez back on his head, and slipped the cymbals on to his wrists. He left the finger loops for later, so he could continue driving. He turned down the cul-de-sac and was relieved to see the gate was open. He didn't want to park on the street and walk up. He didn't need neighbors or gardeners reporting to the police that a crazy man was wandering the neighborhood.

He'd anticipated several scenarios: Dylan would close the door in his face. Dylan would laugh and clap him on the back and rehire him on the spot. Dylan would ignore the costume and fire him for good. Dylan would ignore the costume and apologize, then invite him in for cake and they'd get to work on new mono jokes.

What he hadn't anticipated was a televised public shaming.

As Scott turned up the drive, he noticed a media truck as well as a news truck with its transmission tower extended. He stopped the car at the bottom of the drive and wondered if he should back up, call Sasha, and just give notice over the phone.

Someone knocked on his window. He tried to press the button to roll the window down, but the cymbals clanged against the door. He used his thumb to press the toggle and the window slid down. There was a girl with a clipboard. She could have been anywhere between fourteen and thirty-seven. She had braids and a tattoo on her wrist that read YOLO. Scott knew from an old Trendy that YOLO was an acronym for "You Only Live Once." Sadly, that may now be true, he thought.

"Name?" She was smiling at him.

"Scott Mullan."

She scanned the list. "Yep. Head on up."

She waved up to someone. Scott gave her a smile and, cymbals clanging, he pressed the button to close the window and headed up the drive.

Cables streamed around the driveway and up the front walk to the doorway and snaked inside. There was a motorcycle cop watching the activity and Scott's first thought was: is this the guy who arrested him? Then he thought: why would there be news coverage of someone getting fired? Was this Celebrity CSI? He panicked as he imagined his arrest playing out live on TV. These thoughts were replaced with the slamming realization that whatever he was facing, he was facing it wearing a red fez hat with a long tassel, a snappy green vest, and hairy monkey shoes.

The cop waved him over to an open spot to the left of the house by the hydrangeas. Scott parked and wondered if he could ditch the costume. Or maybe just losing the fez and cymbals would be enough. Which would leave him looking like some barefooted Eurotrash guy. His adrenaline pumped a bit more as he anticipated the cop coming over to ask him why he was sitting in his car. He had to make a choice.

He opened the car door, clanging cymbals on the door handle and window. He put his feet on the ground, slipped his fingers into the finger loops, stood up, and closed the car door. He looked over at the cop, who gave him a wave to go inside, as if Scott was expected by everyone. He experienced the dread of walking into a surprise birthday party. It was a panic like he'd had the first time he went on stage—panic and freedom and the fear of having no idea how it was going to go. He would usually pray to keep the panic at bay, but who could he pray to now? He used to rely on God, but now there was just him. Just this moment. He experienced a strange calm that came from knowing there was no turning back. And an unfamiliar excitement that came from stepping into the unknown.

He walked to the door, taking big steps in the rubber booties, like wearing snow shoes or snorkeling flippers. He thought about the family's last trip to Cabo. Well, it had been a fun life, he thought. All bets were off now.

There was a young kid with a tablet standing by the front door. Scott knew from enough location shoots this kid would be giving the "hold" or "all clear" signal to ensure no one would walk through the door in the middle of taping. Scott walked up to him and raised his eyebrows to ask if it was okay.

In a regular voice, the kid said, "Oh yeah, you can go in." As if middle-aged men in monkey costumes were regular things. "Cool hat," he added.

"Thanks."

Scott stepped up to the large mahogany door and as he went to knock, the cymbals clanged on the wood.

"Just go in. It's open," the kid said.

Scott opened the door with more clanging and waddled through to the living room. It was still Dylan's house, but it had been transformed with lights and cables and monitors and a clothing rack and temporary tables set up for assistants and makeup people. There were two cameras and cameramen and a boom operator who was checking levels with an audio guy at a portable console. A woman in red glasses was checking things on a tablet, directing someone to pour water into the glasses on the production table. Two fancy club chairs were angled toward one another with the fireplace between them and a log blazing away. Which meant there would probably be a log wrangler somewhere nearby. The woman glanced at Scott and her brow furrowed, like "who is *this* clown." Indeed.

Standing near the chair on the right, her back to the room, was a woman with long, sunny brown hair. She was wearing a pink top that had clips in the back to make it more form fitting. It was tucked into a charcoal skirt. She was barefoot, but there were heels in front of the chair. Scott scanned the room briefly, and saw Barry standing at the production table, probably basking in his new title as head writer. Scott gave Barry a nod and an eyebrow raise and looked away.

In the corner of the room, Dylan was standing with Sasha. He was wearing jeans and a blue button-down shirt. Sasha was holding additional shirts, a bottle of water, and her cell phone. She seemed free of any obvious physical ailments: no braces, no splint, no eyepatch.

Dylan looked at Scott and said something to Sasha. She handed him the water and walked over to Scott. She was limping, and Scott noticed the boot on her foot.

"Sasha," he said.

"I hardly recognized you. Halloween came early?"

"This old thing? Is your foot okay?"

"You know the story. This week 'Sasha hurt her ankle.' *E!* was at the office getting b-roll, so I had to keep it for continuity. In case I end up on camera here."

"What's going on?"

"They're doing a profile on Dylan. Kimmi Laak. It shouldn't take long. Can you sit over here?" She led him to the makeshift off-camera area where folding chairs were set up. The seats were mostly empty except for a boy and girl pair of interns, but Scott knew that the various prep personnel would be seated near him soon enough. He sat and crossed his legs, which put one rubber monkey foot front and center. He uncrossed his legs and put his feet on the floor.

"Water?" Sasha asked.

"Just a banana."

She smiled and went back to Dylan.

It was strange to be sitting in a folding chair with all the sounds and activity of production going on around him. Usually he was part of the storm. Standing backstage with Dylan. Laughing at Dylan's little word fixes, doing the little fast-banter verbal dance that got Dylan's energy up. But now Scott was sitting in the peanut gallery. Watching. And contributing nothing. Dylan and Kimmi were getting final makeup touches and the audio guy was asking for final checks on the lapel microphones. There was a boom mic as well, in case they lost the RF signal. A big guy with worker gloves stepped around him and Scott felt the impulse to say, "I know Dylan," which was pathetic, but he said nothing and just embraced his uselessness.

The stage manager yelled out, "Settle everyone. Take your seats." A few people took seats in the folding chair area. The woman with the glasses indicated they were ready, touching Kimmi on the back and inviting Dylan to take his chair. Once seated, Kimmi and Dylan leaned forward and they both cupped their microphones with their hands and whispered to one another. Kimmi let out a laugh and they leaned back and were ready.

The stage manager said, "Rolling. And speed."

37

DEAR DIARY, I HOPE GUATEMALAN LEFTIST GUERRILLAS WILL SIGN A KEY ACCORD WITH PRESIDENT ALVARO ARZU THIS YEAR.

Kimmi began. "Dylan, first of all, thanks for inviting us into your home."

"I invited *you*. I didn't expect 150 other people. What's going on here?"

It was a silly joke, and Scott knew there were several pre-planned questions and comedic responses as there was very little Dylan did on the fly. He was very skilled at revealing information in a seemingly intimate way, but Scott knew nothing was revealed without a lot of planning ahead of time. A lot of sound and fury often signifying not very much.

Kimmi continued. "You're celebrating twenty years on television. How does that feel?"

"Twenty years? Already? Doesn't it seem like just yesterday that Alanis Morissette won the Grammy or that Guatemalan leftist guerrillas signed a key accord with the government of President Alvaro Arzu aimed at ending thirty-five years of civil war? Time flies."

Kimmi laughed.

"Oh, like you even remember. You were what, seven? Or did you have the posters on your wall, posters of Alvaro Arzu. 'Dear Diary, I hope Guatemalan leftist guerrillas will sign a key accord with President Alvaro Arzu this year.' I mean, while I was slaving away with my hopes and dreams of bringing joy and humor into the homes of billions of people, what were you doing?"

"I wasn't allowed to stay up for any late-night comedy. But my mom loved *You Oughta Know*."

"You are a cruel woman."

And on it went. Dylan had a motto: get a laugh, promote the show, reveal nothing personal. And repeat. Scott knew the writers had gone over things that had happened in the '90s in preparation for this interview, and had probably gone off on darker tangents about Ted Kaczynski or TWA Flight 800. Getting all the dark humor out of their systems before returning to the more light-hearted matter at hand.

Scott tuned out, having heard—and even written—this kind of banter, and knew they'd get into the early years of the show where Dylan started, where he saw the show going, blah blah. It would end with some more jokey stuff and a generic wrap-up, as air dates weren't always final. Once scheduled, an *E!* anchor would later promote the upcoming segment: "Tune in tomorrow for the whole interview and a look at the making of *The Late Enough Show* as it celebrates twenty years on television."

Scott looked around at the men and women in the room. Quiet. Listening. Attentive to the task at hand. Sharing a space. Breathing the same air. Doing the dance of TV production. He hadn't planned to be there long and had been waiting for his dismissal. The "let's give this some time" speech, the "better things are ahead for you" speech, the "my hands are tied" speech. He'd expected this before they started the interview, but now he found himself sitting very still, the cymbals slipped under each thigh to keep them from making noise. Loneliness was building up in him. He was alone in this room full of people. He closed his eyes, prayed to feel more charitable and less alone. He opened his eyes. Nothing. The God you are contacting is no longer in service. Could he unring this heathen bell? Could he put Darwin back in the bottle?

His pointless reverie was interrupted when the big guy with the gloves gave him a look with his eyebrows, silently asking if the empty chair next to Scott was open. There was no seeming recognition of his costume, but Scott, trying to be a gracious monkey, pulled out his hand to indicate an invitation to sit. As he did so, the cymbal clanged against the metal chair, and when he grabbed it to silence it, it clanged against the other cymbal. He brought them together with a final clang and slipped them between his thighs, but it was too late. A lot of eyes were turned his way. Kimmi hadn't moved, but Dylan was looking at him. The stage manager looked at him with a slightly punitive "we okay now?" and after a little nod, the stage manager gave Kimmi the sign to continue.

"So, Dylan . . ."

"Sorry about that," Dylan said.

She waved him off. "We'll just edit it out."

"No talk of the elephant in the room? And by elephant, I mean monkey. Scott, come over here."

Great. Here it comes.

Scott stood, stepped around the big guy in the gloves, and was deliberate with each footstep as there were cables everywhere. And he was wearing monkey feet. He held his hands away from his body as he walked, and then stood with the cymbals flat against his thighs. He smiled at Dylan.

Dylan turned to Kimmi. "Kimmi, you probably know that I require all my writers to wear costumes."

"I *didn't* know that." She smiled. But it looked like she was mentally accessing some internal entertainment Wikipedia.

"I don't really," Dylan continued. "But Scott's my head writer so he gets to do what he wants."

"*This* is your head writer?" she asked.

Scott looked at Dylan. Had he heard correctly? Dylan didn't react. Full Cheshire cat. Scott watched as Kimmi looked at her cards, scanning for some information that could get them back on track. Scott looked over to the production table where Barry was sitting. Maybe Dylan meant to say Barry was his head writer? But Barry had a look that was more confusion than anything. Scott looked back at Dylan, who smiled and nodded. Scott wanted to break into some kind of Rocky thing; he wanted to box a side of beef, run up the steps with a sweaty finale, arms raised, cymbals clapping above his head.

Dylan said, "Kimmi, this is Scott Mullan, my head writer."

Kimmi looked up from her cards. "Hello," she said as if they were at a garden party.

"I'm sure you've seen the name recently." Dylan was giving her permission to "go there."

"Scott Mullan. Yes. I've seen the costume online. Well, the other costume."

There was an odd silence in the room as Kimmi was at a loss as to how to proceed. She had no doubt been given scripted topics and questions, but had most certainly been admonished by production: No Perv Qs. No Family Qs. She seemed to want Dylan to take the lead, but Dylan wasn't saying anything, which left a vacuum Scott knew was his job to fill.

He smiled and said, "It wasn't a strap-on."

"Okay," Kimmi said, looking at Scott, then at Dylan for permission to continue. He gave her the "be my guest" hand gesture.

"Can you explain the incident here a few weeks go?" She went from gracious hello to ruthless fact hunter.

Scott didn't know what to say, how far to take this, how much truth to reveal.

Dylan jumped in. "Scott is considered family and was invited to the house. I had the date wrong. Well, Sasha had the date wrong. Damn British Mail-Order Assistants. Anyhoo. Scott and I were supposed to go over some ideas for a Halloween show which required his coming over in costume. This was all at my request."

Dylan lifted his hand. "So, tell us Scott, what costume was it exactly you were wearing that afternoon?" Scott wanted to laugh at this improvisation trick of setting up an improbable premise only to dump it on someone else to explain. ("I hear you've developed a new theory connecting tectonics plates to celebrity divorce. Can you explain that a bit more?") Dylan kept a straight face.

"I was . . ." Scott paused as he found the words. "I was 'Naughty Lead Singer Guy from that band Disturbed.'"

Dylan laughed, even if no one else did.

"Obviously," he said. "All right Scott, go sit down. We have things that are more important to talk about. Like me. We'll talk later."

Then added, "But just so Kimmi is clear," and in unison, they said, "It wasn't a strap-on."

Kimmi said, "Got it." And she knew the topic was closed.

Scott realized Dylan would keep the truth a secret, even if it was rich with comedic gold. Dylan could have done five minutes on New Age woo-woo and burning sage and color therapy and sound therapy and water therapy and dream boards and mazes and mandalas. And water pouring. He could have painted Scott as the quirky Deepak Chopra of writers, but for some reason kept it quiet.

Scott waddled back to his seat. The big guy with the gloves leaned over and whispered, "It *was* a strap-on, right?" Scott gave him his best

Mona Lisa. He knew this was now a thing of myth, and would be promoted by Drippy in some way, as part of the "edgier" Dylan brand. A boost to Dylan's subtle shift from goofball to a sexier late-night persona.

Kimmi continued, and Scott sensed a different tone.

"Talking about family . . ." Kimmi stopped and she shifted her body, looking over to the production table. She covered her microphone as she called out, "Jess. Mark that if we need it, but I'll do another version if we edit out the, uh . . ."

"Monkey business?" The woman with the glasses made a note.

"Exactly." She turned back to get settled.

"Jess, can you adjust the clips again?" Jess came over and fiddled with the clips that kept the shirt hugging Kimmi's torso.

"Thanks." She waited for Jess to step back to the production table, then glanced down at her cards and counted herself in. "Three, two . . ."

Her smile returned. "Dylan. Let's talk about family."

"Let's," Dylan said. "You have two boys, right?"

"I do. Have you been stalking me?" She gave a flirty laugh that had no actual flirtiness, but was more of a space filler as they moved into the new topic. Scott wondered how far Dylan could go, deflecting the interest in his own family and making it about Kimmi.

Kimmi continued. "You and your beautiful wife Pinky moved out here from the East Coast. How has it been for you and your family to adapt to a West Coast lifestyle?"

"It's been fantastic. I mean for me, what do I know? I go to work and I come back. That happened back east. But I like to call Pinky an adaptive warrior. She keeps the kids happy and educated and fed and entertained and I'm amazed every day by her abilities."

And there it was. "The kids." A slip? But Dylan never slipped. Had Kimmi been pre-briefed on the Flynn Family party line? Wife:

Pinky. Son: Garrett. Dog: Jefferson. Full stop. Half the room seemed to perk up, and Scott imagined that the other half had better things to wonder about, like their ailing parents, a failed smog check, or knee surgery.

Kimmi, rolling with it, asked, "And how old are the kids?"

"Garrett's ten and Isabel is seven. And our dog, Jefferson, is four. Isabel decided we needed a dog."

"Kids seem to know those things, right?"

"Yes, Jefferson has been a godsend. A delight. A corgi like the queen has. Because yes, I'm royalty," he said. "Plus, he makes me look taller."

"Do the kids know their dad is famous?" Was there a slight emphasis on 'kids'?

"My wife doesn't even know. She has better things to think about." Dylan turned to look over his right shoulder at his wife.

"Pinky?" He turned back to Kimmi. "She hates being on camera."

Pinky came out from the dining room. She was wearing a plain black skirt and a crew neck sweater, her black hair was cut short in a pixie style and—she was wearing TV makeup. Hmmm. Dylan reached out to embrace her waist. And finally half-stood to kiss her on the cheek.

Pinky smiled at Kimmi. "Hi. Pinky Flynn." She reached out her hand and they shook.

"Your husband speaks very highly of you."

"I hope so. Especially on your show." She smiled.

"But it's all true," Dylan said. He had dropped the comedic pretension. "Really."

"Okay," Pinky said. "Back to the Tollhouse cookies." As she started out, Dylan added in a stage whisper, "She used to make cookies. Now she makes us eat kale flan. It's hell, I tell you."

Pinky called out from the dining room, "I heard that." And then she added, "Oh, here comes Isabel. She wants to say hi."

Out came a seven-year-old girl, her eyes a little more almond shaped than usual, her face a little more square. Familiar Down syndrome with her own dazzle.

"Hi, I'm Isabel." And she came up to Kimmi and hugged her. Then she hugged Jess and then the audio guy. "I will hug all of you."

"Honey, come here." Isabel went to her father and sat on his lap. "How are you?"

"I'm smart and I'm patient and I'm kind." She took her father's face in both her hands and kissed him.

Scott recognized the phrase from the YouTube link Rebecca had shown him. It was a video of Sofia Sanchez, a seven-year-old girl talking about what it was like to have Down syndrome. The girl and her mother had been on "Libby!" and Rebecca fell in love with her. In the video, Sofia made a hand gesture that Scott now recognized as something Dylan did when he was feigning enthusiasm. His magical Disney move.

Dylan held his daughter. "Yes you are." Dylan wasn't feigning anything.

"Who can I hug?" she asked. There was nervous mumbling, no one wanting to cross the line. No one sure what to say. But then the guy next to Scott raised his gloved hand. Isabel spotted him and scampered over and gave him a hug. Her shoes twinkled with each footfall. On her way back, she saw Kimmi's shoes.

"Do your shoes twinkle?"

"I wish they did," Kimmi said.

"You can have mine." And Isabel kneeled down to untie her shoes.

Dylan went to his daughter and swung her up into the air and carried her back to his chair. "We'll send Kimmi some twinkly shoes and then you'll both have them. Okay?"

Isabel nodded. And she was off his lap and hugged Kimmi again and skipped into the dining room. Scott knew that a week later, Kimmi would receive a form of twinkly shoes with a note from Isabel. Written by Sasha.

"Tell us more about Jefferson."

Dylan started telling stories about Jefferson and the corgi's need to sleep on Pinky's head and how the dog liked to eat rocks and . . . that was that. Scott thought it was beautiful. The "yeah, so what?" feel of the interview. Scott bounced back and forth between the amazing news that he was head writer and the fact that Dylan shared his true family. It all amazed Scott and he couldn't stop smiling.

Kimmi and Dylan yip-yapped about the special, who were some of the upcoming guests, what was it like having Bono try and flip water bottles, and was Dylan going to do an Alexa challenge. Scott remembered when "Alexa challenge" had come up in a Trendy meeting. "Didn't I just do a mannequin challenge? I mean, bucket challenge, deodorant challenge. Isn't *life* enough of a fucking challenge?" Dylan had asked. Now, Scott half-listened to the response, which was smooth and seamless, and he wanted to tell Drippy that the Trendy meetings were paying off.

Eventually, he could hear the tone change and the interview wrapped up. Kimmi was standing. Kimmi and Dylan were hugging. Jess with the glasses was joining in. Sasha limped in with a bottle of water. Crew people were starting to move. PAs were typing. Audio people were removing microphones. And Scott stood. Although he had no actual function, he had no problem standing there as part of the employed staff. Head writer.

Dylan waved him over. Scott played up the comedy of his awkward monkey-feet steps as if this was normal. He shook hands with Kimmi as Dylan hit him on the shoulder. He turned and gave a little bow to Dylan, indicating gratitude and that he was leaving.

"Wait a few minutes," Dylan said.

Scott stepped over to Barry, who had extended his hand in congratulations. But they both saw the cymbals would be an impediment. Barry gave him a thumbs up.

"Hey, good going! Head writer. Long time coming."

"Thanks. Unfortunately, Dylan has asked me to wear this every day."

"Cross to bear. See you tomorrow, dude."

Scott stood by the production table and overheard the PAs and Jess as they discussed editing. "We'll move the family stuff later. Dylan went a little early with the Down syndrome stuff, but it will work wherever we put it. Kimmi wanted to end with family, but I like wrapping it up with the celeb stuff." And it confirmed for Scott that there was still nothing Dylan hadn't planned for.

One of the PAs asked, "Should we keep the shoe stuff?"

"Let's see where we are with time and what Kimmi wants. Could be too cute. Or maybe fine." Jess looked at her pad of notes. "We'll see how much Dylan wants to use. But the Isabel reveal is big enough. We don't want to pull focus."

Scott noticed Dylan waving him over and he began the little waddling journey back to Dylan. General chatter continued, but the room was closing down. Crew members moved in and around one another like they'd done hundreds of times. Second nature.

Dylan said, "So how was it? Sound good? Enough funny?"

"It was great. Good riff on the Alexa challenge."

"Barry gave me some good stuff. But I talked too much."

"Never. It was just what they wanted."

Pinky popped out and said something to Dylan. Her eyes lit up when she saw Scott.

Dylan said, "You know Scott."

"Yes. So good to see you." She smiled. She gave Dylan's forearm a little squeeze and left. Dylan looked off into the room and Scott could tell by the set of his mouth that he was formulating an idea, a thought. It was better to stand silently by and wait. A few moments later, Dylan inhaled and looked back at Scott.

"I told Pinky what you said." Scott waited, but there wasn't more coming.

"What did I say?"

"At our door. The prayer. That you'd said for our family."

And it made sense to Scott, what had happened today. He was putting it together when Dylan continued, making light of it all. "On your day of public perversion."

"Yes," Scott said.

"And the beating you gave me in the office."

"I didn't . . ."

"Stop while you're ahead."

"Good idea."

Dylan smiled. "So. See you tomorrow."

"Great."

"And see Drippy. He's got paperwork for you."

38

I'll be home soon.

Scott stepped around the people who were working, waved to the big guy with the gloves, went out the front door, and waddled to his car. The sun was setting, the air felt cooler. He wanted to leap up and down with head writer joy and satisfaction and vindication and relief. His heart was pounding and he could feel the smile on his face. The motorcycle cop looked over and nodded and Scott assumed the position and clanged his cymbals together, which made the cop laugh. Scott thought: maybe there was no God, no Ben Doss, no quantum physics, no grand plan, no dung beetle pushing the sun across the sky. But there was this moment.

After leaving Dylan's house, Scott pulled onto another street, changed from the vest back into his shirt, and replaced the monkey shoes with his own. He'd thought of changing at Dylan's, but knew the visual joke was better if taken all the way out the door.

It was getting dark. He picked up his phone to text Rebecca. But how to phrase it? "Your husband is again gainfully employed." But what if "husband" was arrogant and presumptive when there was still some kind of argument to be had. Things hadn't been resolved, but this was big enough news he had to send her something, and he settled on just the facts. "Got job back. Head writer. I'll be home soon."

He pictured her in the kitchen checking her phone, then realized she may not even be at home. Maybe this was the end of "home."

He adjusted the AC and glanced at the phone, waiting for the usual immediate response. So far, nothing. It had been—what—five seconds? He told himself he'd wait one minute. He looked at the time on the phone and waited. A minute went by. Nothing.

He put the car in gear and as he drove, he replayed the tangibles of the afternoon. He smiled when he thought of Isabel. He liked the big guy with the worker gloves. The laughing cop.

Eventually, he settled into the drive. Once he got over the hill, he turned right on Ventura and headed east. It was a much-used, familiar stretch of the boulevard, and his mind wandered.

So now he was an atheist? The word was foreign to him. Maybe it was too soon to sum it up with a label, which in a sense was its own mythology. But if his faith was gone, what would take its place? The thought seemed like a whoosh of emptying, of his whole life shifting. The loss seemed retroactive as he looked back fifty years.

"Atheist." The word itself was anathema to his life up until now, and he almost expected the car to spontaneously combust from this psychic shift. But nothing happened. He wondered if a veil had been lifted, opening him up to a whole big world he'd never considered. Or if a curtain had been drawn, closing him off from all that he loved.

He felt empty and uncertain, but no longer afraid.

People were on the planet moving about, believing, not believing, solving problems, losing their car keys, falling in love, getting root canals, camping, getting tattoos, buying baby clothes, trimming rose bushes. He was pretty sure they weren't wondering if there was a guy on the planet somewhere losing his religion. He didn't have to alert the presses. Nothing would be trending.

Accompanying the loss of his own importance was an openness, a freedom.

He turned on the radio and life was going on. Traffic was still being reported regardless of whether he was an atheist or a believer. He laughed at himself and turned off the radio. Would he be able to write? Were atheists funny? He had no way to really reconcile any of this, and was surprised by the thought that he was glad his mother wasn't alive to witness this abandonment by her son. His mother who had abandoned him for the church. Or maybe the church had simply been an easy excuse to abandon the chore of mothering. He thought of his own family. Would they feel he was abandoning them along with his faith? He was running out of strength to anticipate the future, or to anticipate anyone's reaction to anything. He was too tired to do anything except drive home.

He turned onto his street. The house was dark. He pulled into the garage next to Rebecca's SUV and felt the familiar vehicular coupling. If anyone was home, there'd be at least one light on. Libby had probably picked them up for dinner. A sadness washed over him.

He grabbed the hat and vest from the passenger seat, got out of the car, and put the costume in the trunk for a later drop-off at the dry cleaners. He'd be going to the dry cleaners . . . as an atheist. His self-absorption with these ideas made him sigh. Was he going to analyze every aspect of his life wearing these new atheist glasses? The idea was so unwieldy he was forced to abandon it.

He let himself into the house and closed the door behind him. It was dark inside. No food smells. No kid smells. What else was missing? There was no classical music. Was that her goodbye? No more classical music? He'd survived the day, but where was his family? Was there a parallel loss coming to balance the seeming gains of the day? Head writer but alone? Is that how it was going to work? Was he being punished with this new emptiness? But, who would be doing the punishing if he was just a man standing there?

He listened to the silence, which wasn't silent at all. There was the usual dog barking in the distance; there was the creaking of the house as the wood cooled; there were voices from another house—an outdoor party with little bursts of muted laughter. People were having fun somewhere. He waited to hear a cat in an alley, but that was just in the movies.

He flipped on the light in the kitchen. On the counter were more school pamphlets, the top one being from UCLA. Was this the discard pile? UCLA had never been a consideration. He went to the fridge. There was a Post-it note on the handle.

"Scott. We're out back. It's 'Eat Outside' night."

He looked past the counter to the sliding doors and realized the sounds of laughter he had heard, the familiar sounds he was wistfully envying, were the sounds of Rebecca and the kids. He saw the glow of the twinkly lights in the trees. He walked through the dark living room feeling like an outsider, a different person who wouldn't be welcomed, and that the best he could hope for was a quiet acceptance. A chilly peace. He hoped things would slowly warm up, but imagined they would never be the same. And just like that, exhaustion flooded through him and he was too tired to anticipate more, or even figure out what he should say.

He slid the door open and went outside.

It was chilly, but the lights in the trees warmed the area across the grass, and there were hurricane candles glowing on the table where Rebecca and the kids were sitting. He walked over. There were several red and white cartons of Chinese food spread out on the Halloween tablecloth.

"Hey, Dad!" Marcus said. He turned to his mom. "Can we eat now?"

Marcus had something in his hair. Was this the new iteration of a man bun? Scott looked, trying to make sense of something that wasn't initially familiar. Marcus's hair was hanging down, but around his forehead, like an eighties headband, was a circle of silver duct tape. Wedged on each side of his head, held by the tape, were twigs. It still didn't register until he looked at his daughter, who was wearing a similar crown of twigs pointed upward into the night air. He shifted his gaze and looked at Rebecca—perhaps for an explanation—but she too was wearing a silver headband of twigs. She was reaching for one of the cartons.

"Yes! Let's eat!" she said.

Scott stepped to his place at the table and sat down. On his plate was a most beautiful thing. His own crown of twigs. He could hardly breathe. He lifted the crown and placed it on his head.

Marcus and Rebecca were busying themselves with the business of eating. Chloe sneaked a peek at her father, smiled, and went back to her food.

Scott felt the cool air on his face. He looked down and tried to keep it together as he listened to the sounds of his family, the chopsticks clicking on their plates. He looked up. His eyes began to sting and the twinkly lights in the trees blurred and silhouetted the twigs of their crowns.

Made in the USA
San Bernardino, CA
03 October 2018